By Richard S. Wheeler
from Tom Doherty Associates

Aftershocks
Badlands
The Buffalo Commons
Cashbox
Eclipse
The Exile
The Fields of Eden
Fool's Coach
Goldfield
Masterson
Montana Hitch
An Obituary for Major Reno
The Richest Hill on Earth
Second Lives
Sierra
Snowbound
Sun Mountain:
   A Comstock Novel
Where the River Runs

SKYE'S WEST
Sun River
Bannack
The Far Tribes
Yellowstone
Bitterroot
Sundance
Wind River
Santa Fe
Rendezvous
Dark Passage
Going Home
Downriver
The Deliverance
The Fire Arrow
The Canyon of Bones
Virgin River
North Star
The Owl Hunt
The First Dance

SAM FLINT
Flint's Gift
Flint's Truth
Flint's Honor

The First Dance

A Barnaby Skye Novel

RICHARD S. WHEELER

A TOM DOHERTY ASSOCIATES BOOK
NEW YORK

This is a work of fiction. All of the characters, organizations, and events portrayed in this novel are either products of the author's imagination or are used fictitiously.

THE FIRST DANCE: A BARNABY SKYE NOVEL

Copyright © 2011 by Richard S. Wheeler

All rights reserved.

A Forge Book
Published by Tom Doherty Associates, LLC
175 Fifth Avenue
New York, NY 10010

www.tor-forge.com

Forge® is a registered trademark of Tom Doherty Associates, LLC.

ISBN 978-0-7653-6174-5

First Edition: July 2011
First Mass Market Edition: May 2012

Printed in the United States of America

0 9 8 7 6 5 4 3 2 1

Acknowledgments

The Métis Culture & Heritage Resource Centre, Inc., in Winnipeg, Manitoba, supplied much of the social and cultural material about the Métis that I have employed in this novel. Its website offers valuable information about Métis traders, history, languages, food, dress, and biography.

The First Dance

one

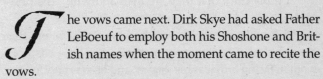he vows came next. Dirk Skye had asked Father LeBoeuf to employ both his Shoshone and British names when the moment came to recite the vows.

"North Star, wilt thou have this woman to thy wedded wife? Wilt thou love her, comfort her, honor and keep her in sickness and in health, and forsaking all others keep thee only unto her as long as ye both shall live?"

"I will," the young man said.

"Therese, wilt thou have this man to thy wedded husband? Wilt thou obey him and serve him, love, honor and keep him in sickness and in health, and forsaking all others, keep thee only unto him for as long as ye both shall live?"

"*Oui,*" Therese said.

Dirk gazed happily toward her. She was small, glowing, and dark, and her eyes were only for him. A bit of moisture on her brow caught a few strands of her chestnut hair. She stood across from him, lit by the lamps of the saloon, wearing a simple gown of white muslin, which had cost her family all the cash it possessed, and it possessed very little indeed.

She was a refugee from Canada, where her people had been dispossessed in the great Red River upheaval of the 1860s. Like Dirk, she carried two bloods, hers French and Cree, his British and Shoshone.

The Red River Métis had flooded into the States in the 1870s, but they remained dispossessed, often unable to take up land and renew their farming life. Therese was very thin.

Father LeBoeuf hurried on.

"I pronounce that they are man and wife," the priest said.

Dirk had not caught what had been said before that. He only knew he was now married. And this wisp of a woman facing him was his forever, and he was hers forever. And they would live together, rear a family together, and someday die in the midst of love.

He gazed at her through the consecration of their marriage and the benediction. She gazed back at him, something wild flaring in her eyes, as though this marriage would burn itself out on this altar, leaving only a pile of ash.

They held hands. Her left-hand ring finger now was encased by a small band of silver which shone brightly, reflecting the lamps of the saloon. There was no church in Miles City, and no meeting hall, and only an itinerant priest drifting through the Yellowstone Valley, offering the sacraments to whoever sought them. A priest with a French name was good enough for her people. Nothing else would do.

"Amen," the priest said, and smiled at them. Dirk remembered to smile back. All his smiles were for Therese. She was not smiling, and seemed to stare at the saloon lanterns above.

Dirk was alone. She had a dozen relatives there, and fifty more Métis friends. He lacked so much as a brother to stand with him; she had sisters and aunts and nieces and childhood friends to stand with her. His family was dead.

He wanted to kiss her, but didn't know if that was proper. She smiled slightly, as if to say yes, kiss me now. But somehow he didn't. There were parents and grandparents and siblings and nephews and brothers watching. He took both her hands in his own, and she squeezed his, and then the Métis swarmed them, shaking hands, hugging both, laughter lighting their faces.

There were so many of them, some with liquid brown eyes, others as pale as Europeans, others burnt chestnut, most of them the color of gold. One thing about the Métis: they didn't breed true to any form or color. Their clothing was as diverse as their flesh. The women wore neck-to-ankle velvet in subdued colors, with moccasins underneath. The men mostly wore brown corduroy pants, gaudy beaded moccasins, and Hudson's Bay Company wool shirts. And many wore the florid red and blue and white sashes of their people, two or three yards of bright-colored webbing that held their pants up and wrapped around their necks and served as a badge.

Now they crowded close, a babble of oddly guttural French laced with Cree words, filling the gloomy tavern with its smoking lamps. He slid an arm about her thin shoulder and shook the hands of her people as they

clustered close. Her father, Montclair Trouville, offered
Dirk a bear hug; his wife, Helene, offered a soft brown
hand. Her brother, Francois, shook hands heartily and
combed his black beard with his fingers. Her cousins—
the Desportes—were lined up to embrace the bride and
groom. Their friends, the Lesages, were waiting patiently, and so were others Dirk didn't know. Ah! They
were a bubbling lot. Their lovely Therese had taken the
vow of matrimony, and with a fine fellow, himself two-
blooded, even if one blood was Anglo. But some things
could be forgiven, if just barely.

The gloomy tavern absorbed the joy, which seemed to
cast light into its bleak corners. It was one of many thrown
up in the settlement to cater to the rough blue-clad soldiers at Fort Keogh just to the west, along the Yellowstone
River.

"*Marie fait la soupe.*"

"*Voici le pain.*"

Dirk Skye listened to the Métis version of French. The
saloon's proprietor, Billy Stiles, hovered behind the bar,
disapproving of everything about the goddamned foreigners except the occasional brandy he poured. Therese's
people had stocked the bar with *les baigne*, or fried bread;
la rubaboo, or soup; *les boulettes*, meatballs; *soupe au pois*,
bean soup; and *le flaon*, custard, and some cracked bowls
and wooden spoons for all this.

There were no English-speaking people other than
Stiles, the priest, and himself, but the Métis knew a little
of it, and Dirk knew enough French and some Cree. He
had needed it to win the heart of Therese, whose English
was small and tentative. None of the soldiers from the fort
were present, and by design, because there were walls of

silence and moats of trouble between the soldiers and the French-Cree people who called themselves Métis.

Dirk Skye was employed by the United States Army as a civilian translator, and in fact he was an intermediary between the officers and the various tribes around the post, including the Crows, the Sioux, and the Cheyenne. It was not the best of jobs, but it was employment, and many a day he could operate on his own, far from the stern command. He knew half a dozen Indian tongues, as well as French and some Spanish he'd picked up. Enough to make him valuable to the army.

It had been his bleak task to inform the French-Crees who were drifting into the United States in the wake of the troubles in Canada, which drove them from their ancestral holdings, that they had no status here, were not citizens, could not take up land, and had to move on.

It had never been a pleasant task. They were hungry, these people. They wanted only a little land for their farms, or a corner or two in towns to set up shops. They wanted only to practice their faith. They wanted only to settle peaceably, speak their odd tongue, and offer their devotions to the Virgin. And that was how he had met Therese, thin to gauntness, with eyes bitter-bright and alive with both joy and bleakness—and beautiful beyond anything Dirk had ever known.

She had delft-blue French eyes and strong Cree cheeks. She had a voice with an edge, a voice that carried, so that if she said she loved him, everyone in the country heard it. If he had been smitten in one blow, so had she. He had come, actually, to inform her parents that they could not settle in the Yellowstone Valley above the fort, on land claimed by a rancher who wanted the good hay land for himself. He had come to tell them that they must move on, orders of Major Bullfinch, and they must abandon their gardens, pile their goods into their creaking Red River carts, and be on their way.

And had fallen in love.

Father LeBoeuf devoured *la véyant*, meat; *la gallet*, bannock; *aeñ paták*, potatoes; and a little brandy. Stiles eyed the Métis through hooded eyes. Dirk knew what the man was thinking, and it didn't matter. Let him think what he would. Dirk had paid him out of his small wage and spent the rest on a silver ring.

He heard the fiddles. This time there would be two, one played by Pierre Duplessis and the other by Jacques Langlois. The Métis had migrated far from the Red River, but the fiddles came with them. They were homemade, wrought from maple and birch. He heard the fiddlers tighten the strings, until they were more or less in tune, and then there was a sudden burst of scraping fiddle music, a lively jig, almost without rhythm as the crowd quieted and sipped and waited to dance with the bride, which they all would. Every male Métis would jig her once, twice, thrice, and kiss her for good measure, and secretly ache inside.

It was an ideal place for a dance. Plank floors worn smooth by army boots stretched across the room. A few homemade tables, hewn from local wood, mostly miserable cottonwoods, lined the walls. A wagon wheel chandelier, with three smoky lamps, tossed wan light into the evening shadows. Stiles propped the front door open, letting in a welcome evening breeze.

And then they waited.

Dirk finally realized they were waiting for him. The

first dance. He slid a hand into Therese's and guided her
to the floor and the fiddles exploded, almost a screech of
noise scraped out of catgut. Dirk didn't know a waltz
from a quadrille, but he swept Therese around, and the
Métis howled.

She smiled up at him.

"You are beautiful," he said.

"You are plain," she replied. "And *non,* you can't dance."

There was absolute truth in it. He had broken mirrors
simply by staring into them. Babies howled when they
saw him. He could no more do the jig, or the step dance
these people performed, than he could bay at the moon.

The close air drew moisture to her face until it glowed
in the yellow lamplight, and her hair clung to her forehead.

"You will be even more beautiful later," he said.

"Mon Dieu! A barbarian," she replied. "Do you think I
will surrender?"

"No," he said, "you'll resist to the last."

She dug her fingernails into his arms. "The better to
annoy you."

He rattled her around the plank floor, and she bore it
for a while.

"Métis, they can jig," she said. "But you are British."

"Shoshone," he said.

"My papa, he is drunk," she said. "It's your sin, getting
married in a saloon."

She forgave him his British heritage, or at least she
endured it.

The fiddles whined and chattered, and one of her
brothers, Pierre, cut in. Dirk knew he'd not hold his bride
close again until every Métis male in the smoky saloon had
stomped away the eve with her. The raw spirits parleyed

by Billy Stiles were inflaming the evening. He was selling the Métis his absolute worst. It didn't matter whether it lit lamps or went down throats. The fiddles sawed away, the messieurs and mesdames whirled, a fine aura of lust and piety settled over the celebrants, the priest vanished, and the evening settled into merriment.

Now Francois was dancing with her, then Pierre again, then Boniface, then Alexandre, then a stranger. Moisture rose on their faces, making them glow in the lamplight. The fiddlers never stopped. While one rested, the other sawed out new melodies, more and more of them sad or sorrowful. It was as if the fiddler were directing the evening, setting its mood, and now the mood was that the Métis had lost their jewel to an outsider, and the wedding was sung as loss and the breaking of a dozen hearts.

But of that Dirk Skye had only the faintest understanding. He watched them whirl his bride. He watched their big male hands slide up and down her shoulders, their fingers yearning. He watched the Métis women in velvet watch the men in corduroy. He sipped Billy Stiles's rotgut and waited. At some future moment he would cut in, reclaim Therese, and hustle her into the night, and the celebration would swiftly wind down.

He would take her to the flatboat at the riverbank, pole her across the lazy Yellowstone, and walk with her a mile or so up Sunday Creek to a comfortable cabin with a fine fireplace and a great mound of buffalo robes and bearskins, which would be their heaven for a few days until his leave from the post came to an end.

When he judged that the time was right, and the Métis celebration was withering, he went to claim his bride. But she wasn't there. Well, then she was changing her clothes somewhere. But he didn't know where. No doubt in a room nearby. But she didn't appear. He headed toward the foul outhouse behind the saloon and knocked. But she wasn't there. He looked for her among the departing Métis, but she was not among them. He tried the raw streets of Miles City, but she was not there. He called to her in the shadows, but she didn't respond. He stopped knots of Métis, but she was not among them. He returned to the saloon to await her return, but she didn't return. Billy Stiles was blowing out lamps and eyeing him without curiosity.

He walked the rutted streets of Miles City, calling to her. "Therese, Therese," but she did not answer him. He tried the riverbank; she might be waiting for him there. But she was not there. Her lovely white muslin gown did not catch the moonlight. He hiked this way and that, in ever wider circles, but she was gone.

two

*N*ight fog formed over the river and soon
hid the solemn moon. Dirk Skye stood at
water's edge, lost. Until this moment, he
had thought of all this as a missed connection. She was
somewhere, expecting him. He was here, expecting her.
Would they not take the flatboat across the moon-silvered
water, and hike up to that sturdy log cabin that would
be their paradise for a while?

Now, though, his thoughts grew darker. There were
three hundred sixty degrees of night about him, and
Therese might be separated from him by any degree. She
might have fled the marriage. She might be at her parents'
smallholding downriver, unwilling to begin a life with
him. She might have been kidnapped by some Métis rival,
and unable to reach Dirk. Something might have happened. A fall, a blow to the head, the kick of a horse, con-
fusion, a bride adrift.

This is where she would come. Here beside the river

where there were some flatboats to take them across the dark waters. But she hadn't come.

The Métis had gone back to their farms. Some had walked. A few had ridden horses. Some of the older ones had come on the beds of the groaning ox-drawn Red River carts that those people employed to carry most anything. By now, they were all in their homes, lamps out. And Therese had probably gone with them.

He thought to go to her parents' place and wake them up. She was there. She had fled the marriage. He would learn from the Trouville family what had happened and where he stood. But to think it was to reject it.

There was one thing left to do. He dragged a flatboat off the bank, added a pole and oars, and pushed into the stream. The current was taking him east. He poled across, caught in swirls of fog, sometimes seeing the opposing shore, sometimes caught in a lonely universe. He touched land perhaps a hundred yards below and beached the flatboat. He followed the shore until he found the turnoff, and then hiked up the broad gulch, and located the forlorn cabin. It was dark and silent.

"Therese?" he said.

He pushed open the plank door and confronted the cold dark.

"Therese?"

By instinct, he found the kerosene lantern and the metal box with matches beside it. He lifted its chimney, struck a match, and touched the wick, which flared tentatively and then glowed yellow. He replaced the glass chimney. She was not there. Nothing of hers was there. She had not been there. His last hope vanished. He carried the lamp into the night, circled the somber cabin, and returned the lamp to its table. He cranked the wick down until the flame blued out and darkness descended.

"I've lost you, Therese," he said.

He felt the whirr of a night bird.

He would not stay in that place of dead dreams. He could not bear the thought of a night in hell. So he made his way down the dewy slope, struck the river, found the flatboat, towed it upstream, and then poled his way back to Miles City.

Some wedding, some wedding night, some marriage, he thought. Did he love her? Could he love her tomorrow? Yes, he thought. But did that silver ring on her finger mean anything at all to her?

He looked about the town, wanting to tell someone, anyone, what had happened and where he might be found. But the storefronts were black. No light slid from any saloon. The red lanterns at the bordellos were snuffed. None of the rickety boomtown houses leaked light. Miles City slumbered.

Ah, God. At first light he would pursue the mystery. She was somewhere, and he would find her, and he would discover whether his dreams were shattered or whether this was just some odd setback, some fluke, something that would pass. He would not surrender to despair. It was not in him to do that. He could whistle a little, no matter how deep the dark.

He had a small cubicle at Fort Keogh in quarters for civilian employees. The post was built on a broad quadrangle a mile west of the town, with civilian quarters close to the stables. The newly married man walked the worn road westward, over the Tongue River bottoms,

and reached the post at some small hour. Here was the
might of the army, little used now except to stabilize country that had been Sioux turf not many years earlier. Now
it was merely a duty post, its ongoing task to pacify the
countryside as settlers filled it up.

Dirk had always felt malaise around the post. It was
a white man's place. Its purpose was to subdue the tribes,
including his Crow mother's people. Yet it was also a post
that would keep the tribes from warring on one another,
and it would help to turn the various peoples toward
stock growing and farming, and to ensure they would
have a reserve that would be off-limits to white settlers.
The post was also there to protect the tribes from white
predators, land-grabbers, and crooked traders, and perhaps
that was why Dirk could reconcile himself to working
there. It was also a wage, a rare paid vocation for mixed-
blood people like himself.

Dirk let himself into the row house, four small rooms
in a line. It would not be a good place for a bride, especially a Métis one, but it would have to do. There were no
affordable places in town, especially for people of mixed
blood.

He lit a lamp. She was not there, not lying on his bed,
not awaiting him. She was nowhere, a name on a marriage
register, a memory in white muslin. Here in his own bleak
quarters sorrow fell upon him, and he sat on the bed, rubbing a hand over the gray army blanket, rubbing the blanket as if his hand were tracing her lithe figure.

He pulled off his boots and stretched out on the bed,
still in the suit that had seen a wedding and a loss in the
space of a few hours. He tried to think what he would do
in the morning. He would head for her parents. And if

they hadn't seen Therese, then . . . he didn't want to think about that. She was there with them. Surely she was. Things would get better.

He had friends there at the fort, and for a moment he thought to awaken them and share his misery with them. His aloneness was overpowering. But he pushed the impulse aside. No one in the post thought much of the Métis, and he had not invited anyone from the post to his wedding. The presence of blue-clad soldiers would have stirred bitterness in the breasts of the Métis.

It was not far to dawn. He settled on his bunk and lay desolately through the small hours, making sense of nothing. At dawn he arose, washed, and headed into the morning. It would be an hour's walk to the Trouville farm, an hour's walk to Therese. He hiked the silent trail into town and continued downriver and then turned up a broad valley out of the north.

The cottage was silent. A milch cow stood in a pen. Some chickens scurried away at the sight of him. A Red River cart, with its two six-foot wheels, stood empty. He knew he wasn't presentable. He hadn't scraped the darkness off his face. His wedding suit was rumpled, his shirt stained. It didn't matter. There was only one thing in him: to find Therese, discover all the whys, and if humanly possible, claim her still.

"Ah, you arrive," said the voice.

Dirk turned to discover Montclair Trouville standing in shadows.

"I—Therese, is she here?"

"*Oui*, she was here. She dishonored us, coming here after she was given to you. Helene, she was filled with sorrow."

"Is Therese—is she safe?"

"Ah, monsieur, we must speak no more of her. We have turned our faces against her. She came here and shamed us."

"But is she safe?"

"We will not speak of her."

"Where is she? I need to find her, sir."

"All honor is lost. She did not heed her vows for an hour. We will not welcome her, monsieur. We have lost a daughter."

"But I want to find her, talk with her."

Therese's father stared into the dawn, stubborn and silent.

"I need to talk with her, sir. Is she there, in the house?"

"Again in my house, never."

"Please tell me what happened. I don't know. She vanished. I spent much of the night trying to find her."

"The daughter I have disowned—I will not speak her name—came here, and sent her away I did."

"Did she say why?"

"You are not Métis."

"Not Métis? But why does that matter so much?"

"Ask her those things. Ask them, I will not."

Now he saw Therese's mother in the doorway, smoothing her apron.

"Ah, seigneur, I know nothing but shame," she said. "To think that this has befallen you. Ah, I cannot look at you."

The farmyard was coming to life in the morning mists. A rooster flapped to a fence rail and crowed.

"Madam, I am lost. I would like to find my bride. I'd like to hold her hand. I'd like to tell her that love . . ." That love abides, and love endures setbacks, and love transcends hurts.

"Monsieur, I think maybe she went to the Desportes," she said.

Cousins, then. "I will go there," he said.

Now the household was awake. Francois hovered behind his mother. The sun topped the eastern horizon.

"Wish me good fortune," Dirk said.

But Madame Trouville was dabbing her eyes.

The Desportes were farther downriver. Therese had stumbled there through the darkest of nights. But now, at least, he knew where she was. He tried to frame some thoughts, some tenderness, but he could think of little to say. He hadn't any idea why she had fled only a few hours after she had repeated her vows. Had he done something terrible? Was she afraid? Was the giving of herself to love something she could not imagine? Had she suddenly decided she didn't love him? That marriage was a terrible mistake? That she must run? Was there suddenly another, a Métis youth? The very thought tore him to pieces.

He had no answers, not even a clue or two. She was a mystery now; only hours before, she had been a friend with eyes that lit up whenever they stole a kiss. He set himself upon the path downriver, and found it oddly difficult to walk toward the next Métis homestead. There was in him a deepening thread of bitterness. He had been rejected by a fickle woman. Maybe he was better off. These were strange people. Maybe it was doomed, this marriage. Maybe they'd have it annulled. Maybe no one cared. Maybe it was a very bad joke. Some Métis peacocks who would tell the tale of the rejected Dirk Skye over many an evening's brandy.

He pushed bitter thoughts out of his head and continued his lonely walk along the bank of the great river, a walk that lifted him into the morning. He passed red-winged blackbirds in the marshes, and turtles sunning themselves on flat rocks.

He had never been to the farmstead of the Desportes, though he had ridden past on the river road often enough. Their place lay back of a cottonwood forest, well hidden from river traffic. The less people saw of the Métis, the safer they felt, and their simple homesteads reflected their ever-present fear. He felt a certain empathy. He was alone. They were alone and without citizenship and at the mercy of any American who wanted their land.

He turned up the two-rut trail and walked a half mile up a modest gulch, with a spring-fed trickle running toward the river. Ahead lay a low ranch house, part sod, part cottonwood log, and the usual barnyard, extensive gardens, and animals.

She must have known he was coming, because she was standing on the porch.

three

herese clung to the door, ready to bolt inside, but she held her ground, watching him.

"Therese," he said.

She didn't respond at first. She simply stood there, still in the white muslin dress, soiled now.

"I am glad you are safe," he said.

She eyed him softly. He saw the stain of tears on her cheeks.

"I am glad your cousins have welcomed you," he said.

He stopped, a few feet away, sensing that if he stepped closer she would vanish into the gloomy interior.

"Would you like to go sit under the tree and talk?" he asked.

There was a towering cottonwood nearby, with thick sheltering limbs and giant roots. She glanced swiftly at it and shook her head. *"Non,"* she said.

"I worried that you might be sick. Or wounded by some creature in the night." He included human creatures in that, but didn't wish to say it.

"Monsieur, it is no good," she said.

He didn't know how to respond at first. He didn't know what was no good. "Therese, I hope someday it will be good," he said.

"I know," she said. "It is sad."

"Would you come with me? Are we strangers? May we become friends?"

"*Non*," she said. "We are not strangers, not friends, not anything."

"Are we married?"

She peered at him through doe's eyes, liquid and brown, and didn't respond.

"What can I do?" he asked.

"There is nothing you can do, monsieur."

"Am I monsieur now, and not Dirk?"

She stared softly, quiet as a hare.

"Have I done something to hurt you?" he asked.

"It is who you are," she said.

"Who I am?"

"I will go in now," she said.

"Therese—please don't. Please talk with me."

"It is who you are," she said.

He sensed she was done; she was on the brink of vanishing into that little cottage. There was no one else in sight.

"Therese, may I come see you tomorrow?"

"*Non*," she said.

"May I come after a little while?"

"It will not be good," she said. "This marriage. It will not be."

"Would you come see me? In Miles City?"

She slowly shook her head. "Now I have told you," she said.

"May I hold your hand, for just one moment?"

She took pity on him, and held out a brown right hand with small and thin fingers. He took it and held it quietly, sensing the flare of feeling in her, feeling he could not identify. The thin silver ring still encased the ring finger of her left hand. She had not removed it.

"I will come tomorrow," he said.

She slowly shook her head. "*Non, non,*" she said. "Do not torment me."

"I will come," he said. "If only for a moment. Just to see you standing there."

She turned away, and slipped into the house. He stood staring at the doorway she had occupied only moments before, his bride, still in her marital gown, still wearing his ring on her finger, but now a thousand miles distant.

He peered about. There was no sign of anyone. It was as if the Desportes had seen him, and fled somewhere to give Therese utmost privacy. He wished they were present; he wished they were beside her, smiling, welcoming him. But he grew aware of the silence, broken only by the cawing of crows, and the breezes toying with the large kitchen garden the Métis had planted even before they had built their house.

It would be a long walk to Miles City. He started out, aware of a weariness that was new to him, a weariness rising out of his very bones. He hadn't slept, but that was not new to him. This was new. He couldn't put a name to it, but he knew it was sadness and it had invaded every particle of him. She had not found him worthy.

He wasn't angry. Maybe that would come later. But not now. He reached the riverbank trail and headed upstream while the anonymous Yellowstone flowed past.

He kept on going, each step taking him farther from her, and after a while he reached town and the landing where the flatboats were beached.

He had two more days of leave, days he had intended to spend in the sweetness and mystery of love. He didn't want to return to Fort Keogh. Even less did he want to linger in town, where by now his wedding fiasco would be the gossip at all the saloons. He eyed the silent river, and chose to pole across it. He would head for the borrowed cabin where he intended to spend his first hours with Therese, and there he would sleep until it was time to report to the post once again.

He dragged the flatboat into the water, along with the pole, pushed off, felt the current tug him downriver, and then he poled hard, feeling the long shaft strike bottom. Then he pushed powerfully, letting the pole's purchase on the riverbed propel him. He reached the far shore, beached the flatboat, turned it over, and slid the pole under it. Then he hiked the obscure pathway up a long gulch that took him to the honeymoon cabin, and found it silent and welcoming in the midday warmth.

Within, he instantly sensed something different. Then he saw the bouquets. There were few flowers in bloom this late in the year, but someone had gathered asters and daisies and chokecherry branches and cattails and a dozen other things, arranged them in vases made from whiskey bottles, and filled the small, sorrowful cabin with sweetness.

He couldn't imagine who. There on the hearth were two stately bouquets. And over in the kitchen area, where there was a rough counter, stood a smaller, humbler bouquet, a spray of brown cattails, and beside the bunk, with its buffalo robes, were small bright bouquets of daisies and asters, mixed with something blue. Someone had come here; someone had sought to lift his heavy heart.

He couldn't imagine who had come, or why. But what he saw was love, spread everywhere in that small place. He was overwhelmed with the weariness, and tumbled into the bunk, falling on top of the soft robes, and that was the last he knew.

It was dark when he awoke. He hadn't the faintest idea of the hour. Time had stopped. He arose, found a gibbous moon casting silver over the lonely valley. Whatever the hour, he was washed in silence. The moon seemed cold and distant this night, as if to rebuke him. He lacked a timepiece and didn't know whether the night was young or old. But it didn't much matter.

The cabin was a place of broken dreams. It had been erected of cottonwood logs two years earlier by Jack Hopkins, who was attempting to build a small ranch there, little by little, and sell his beef in town. But it was doomed before it was started, by alkali, sagebrush, and thin forage. Then Hopkins vanished after a late-night poker session in Stiles's saloon, and it was widely assumed his body had drifted down the silent river and the young cowboy would never be seen again. The cattle had vanished and the cabin stood empty. No one wanted a spread that could hardly support a dozen beeves. Dirk had cleaned out the cabin and turned it into a honeymoon haven, but the cabin that had jinxed Hopkins had now jinxed Dirk Skye. Or so he thought. He didn't much believe in hoodoo, but there he was, on Sunday Creek, as luckless as the previous occupant.

Dirk settled on the stoop and let the night breezes

caress him. He wouldn't give up on Therese, but now he was wondering whether he had really known her, and why he hadn't seen this coming. How could he have missed it? He found himself less troubled by her sudden change of heart as he was by his own blindness. Somehow, the woman he had proposed marriage to was utterly different from the one he had married, and he had yet to fathom what was different. It wasn't that he was a boy, inexperienced and full of heat. He'd been around. He was pushing thirty. He'd had two remarkable women in his life, his own mother Mary, or Blue Dawn, of the Shoshones, and his older Crow mother Victoria, or Many Quill Woman, both made of steel.

But here he was, sitting alone on the stoop of an abandoned cabin in the middle of a late summer's night, blindsided by a Métis girl who—he could admit it now—he didn't know. He'd always been haunted by beauty, and she was that, all right, the magical combination of France and Cree melding into a spiced woman.

He pushed away a momentary bitterness. There was no very happy place in the world for two-blooded people like her, like her family and Métis relatives, and like himself. He had found something of himself in her; a mind juggling two ways, the way of the Cree and the way of the French. The way of gods, and the way of one god. A house divided cannot stand, he thought, puzzling at the source of that wisdom. Was it the Bible? Or Lincoln? But it was true. People like himself, pulled hard by differing beliefs, could not stand. She had fled. He, alone in this doomed cabin, had fled too.

He would try to pull his house together for a while, and then if he failed, let Therese go. He knew that he had lost her and that any effort to reclaim her was doomed but he needed to try. He didn't relish the foreknowledge that he would not see her, he would not kiss her, and he would eventually forget her, and she would drift away with her people only to marry a Métis someday, if the church would annul the marriage that never was consummated.

As for himself, he didn't care whether the marriage was annulled or not. His Indian side didn't give a damn. He'd find a woman or two or three and live with one or another. It was only Europeans who nurtured the nonsense called love. He could never be like his English father, Barnaby Skye. Dirk had loved and admired his sire, but he was different.

He felt a stone in his heart. His mind was leading him where he did not want to go. He wanted to be gladdened by the brightness of her smile, the caress of her hands, and a whispered promise in his ear, that she would never leave him, not ever, ever, ever.

He studied the night sky, gradually realizing from the position of the Big Dipper as it arced around the north star that it was early evening. He had slept through the bitter afternoon and dusk. He decided to abandon this house of broken dreams, this alkaline place that had ruined a young cowboy, and this salt-ruined place that mocked Dirk now. There were nothing but busted dreams here. He stood, stretched, felt hardened and strong, and ready to face the world again.

He collected the bedroll and the groceries and sundry other things and divided them into two packs. It would require two trips down to the Yellowstone to take out all the stuff he had hauled up to the cabin of his dreams only a couple days earlier. Now he hefted one heavy roll and started down the gulch that carried the waters of Sunday Creek now and then, when it was running. He left the roll at his flatboat, went back for the other, carried it to the water, loaded his flatboat, collected the pole, and set sail. Over on the Miles City side of the river, he cached his stuff in brush where it was well hidden, and hiked through the evening toward Fort Keogh. It took another couple of hours to collect his mount, load up his stuff, and return it all to his quarters.

The marriage was over. Heartbreak cabin, as he now named it, would swiftly be forgotten. He had a job, he had a paycheck, he had a future right there.

And after he had settled in his own bed, once again not long before dawn, he kept seeing in his mind's eye Therese's brown hand with the thin silver ring still on the ring finger.

four

M ajor Bullfinch was quick to put Dirk back
to work.

"I hear she quit you at the altar," he said.

"No, sir, we were married."

"But she ditched you. Some wedding that was."

"You wanted me, sir?"

"That's what you get, marrying a half-breed. You get
two bloods flowing in someone, and they can't figure out
who they are."

"I do rather well, sir."

"Well, you're English. Mix French and Cree, Skye, and
you've got a lit fuse poked into powder. You're better off,
you know."

"I am hoping for the best, sir."

Bullfinch arched a brow. He was massive, as wide
across the shoulders as any two recruits, and ruddy as—
an Indian. "Best! Best! That's a corker," he said. "Here's
what you're about to do. You're about to chase some Canadian redskins back to Saskatchewan. That's where they

came from and that's where they're going, courtesy of the United States Army."

"The ones here, sir?"

"Not at the moment. The others, flooding in, the ones that just got whipped by the Royal Canadian Mounted Police and a few brigades up there."

Bullfinch lit up a Havana cigar, sucked and exhaled. "We're going to chase them right back over the line."

"They have no place to go, sir."

He smiled. "Exactly."

"This country usually welcomes refugees, Major."

"White refugees. Not native trash. White refugees will settle the land. That's fine with me."

"The Canadians aren't exactly natives, sir."

"Well, it's this way. If you've got Indian blood in you, you're Indian. If you got colored blood in you, you're colored. If you got Chinese blood in you, you're an alien around here." He eyed Dirk again, with an assessing gaze. "I'm sending a company up to Fort Maginnis. The Judith Basin; that's where these breeds are taking up land. You're going along to tell them to get their red asses out, just as fast as they can git. And head north. You can say it in Cree, say it in French, say it in hoodoo, say it in sign language, but you'll say it, and Captain Brewer's orders are to enforce it. And right now. His orders are to burn shelters, tear up crops, kick their sorry butts north."

Bullfinch exhaled a fine blue cloud of smoke, and smiled. "And if you don't feel like telling them that, you can join them."

That was the major, Dirk thought. "You are inspiring, sir."

They both laughed.

Captain Brewer was painful news. He was descended from *Mayflower* Puritans and never let anyone forget it. He was perfectly straightforward about his beliefs: the country had filled up with undesirables and was going from bad to worse. He couldn't do anything about the Germans and Dutch and Italians and Norwegians and Danes and Poles and Russians and Greeks, but he could certainly do something about Indians and breeds and he could try to keep colored people out of the north. Lock them up in Alabama. Brewer was likely to start a shooting war, but that didn't deter Major Bullfinch. Maybe the major relished a shooting war.

And Brewer would harass Dirk Skye the whole trip.

Fort Maginnis was a small post east of Lewistown, largely devoted to helping ranchers in the area curb rustling and livestock theft by wandering Indians. It served simply to enforce the whims of local settlers, its purpose political in nature. The U.S. Army was at the service of cattle barons there. But now, with a migration of Métis flooding into the area, the post wanted some reinforcements.

The Judith Basin was famed for its lush grass, good and abundant water, and bright vistas with mountains in most directions. It was probably the best ranching country in the Territory of Montana. And that's where the Métis refugees from Saskatchewan were settling. No wonder the cattlemen were howling for help. They were grazing public land and had no legal right to evict settlers. But the army could.

Dirk saw some good in the trip. He knew the Métis and more or less talked their tongue. He could dissuade the Métis from settling there and risking serious trouble with the government. Better that the Métis heard the news from him rather than Captain Brewer. If he failed, there might be bloodshed.

It would take him a long way from Therese, though. Therese was always present in his mind, but there was nothing he could do at the moment except wait. Some marriage, he thought. Maybe it was good that he would be a couple hundred miles from her for a while. That's what he told himself, anyway.

He packed his kit carefully that evening. As a civilian translator, he was responsible for his own outfit, but he would share the mess with the troops. Brewer would be taking mounted infantry with him, veterans of the Sioux campaigns, and even that understrength company would be more than a match for the Métis refugees.

The soldiers ran their mounts into Northern Pacific boxcars the next morning and then crowded into two others, one for officers, the other for the men. As a civilian, Dirk got to ride with the two officers, which included Brewer and Lieutenant Collins, fresh out of West Point. The diamond-stacked Baldwin huffed to life and dragged the train off the Fort Keogh siding and onto the main line. They were headed for the railroad division point, Laurel, which offered an easy route north to the Judith Basin. Coal smoke drifted in through the half-open doors, and Dirk could see the river valley and sometimes the river as the huffing train churned west.

Brewer lay on a pile of loose hay, swaying gently with the car.

"I can't even fill a pipe in here," he said. "They should have given me a coach."

Dirk kept quiet. A boxcar loaded with sweet-smelling hay was a luxury.

"This the first action for those men, sir?" Collins asked.

"There's a few salty dogs, but most of them are right off the immigrant boats," Brewer said. "Be at ease, Lieutenant. Between officers, there's no need to follow form. And you too, Mr. Skye. We're all one happy family in here."

That struck Dirk as piquant.

"Say, fella, I've heard a bit about you. Your father was a great scout, eh?"

"A fur trade man and guide, sir. Barnaby Skye."

"A bred-to-the-bone Englishman."

"Yes, he was, Captain."

"Among us, my young friend, I'm Willard. Now, how did he arrive in the New World? An explorer?"

"No, Major, a pressed seaman. A press gang snatched him off the streets of East London."

"Ah, a rough start on life, but he made good."

"He escaped at Fort Vancouver and made his way into the interior."

"Escaped? Are you telling me he deserted?"

"He was pressed; he escaped."

"Oh, that puts a different light on him. Cockney, maybe?"

"The son of an export merchant, Major, and destined for Cambridge."

"Well, something's not right about all that." He eyed Dirk. "One never knows," he said.

The boxcar thumped steadily, probably because of a

flattened wheel. The rattle blotted out conversation, and Dirk was grateful. He didn't like being cooped up with a man like Brewer.

The train squealed to a halt at Forsyth to take on water and coal, which was available in abundance in the area. Brewer jumped down and lit a pipe. Blue-shirted soldiers dropped off the neighboring car and began to piss. Dirk slipped down to the ground and hiked into town a hundred yards or so. There wasn't much there; a store and saloon and blacksmith serving the neighboring ranches. If he had tried to buy a drink at the saloon, he probably would have been refused. He was surprised at his own loneliness. This was the white man's world, rising at every stop on the Northern Pacific, and he was kept out of it.

A moan of the steam whistle summoned the army, and moments later the rattling train huffed west. The captain and lieutenant had ceased to converse with him, not because he was a mixed-blood, but because his famous father had deserted a Royal Navy ship. In fact, the boxcar had an invisible line through it: the officers bedded in the hay at one end, and Dirk at the other.

He was amused. They were the ones who got dosed with coal ash and smoke.

The diamond-stacked Baldwin eight-wheeler rattled ever westward into the twilight, and finally scraped to a halt at Laurel in evening dark, having made good time with speeds up to thirty miles in a single hour. The Laurel yards had a ramped platform that made unloading easy. Dirk unloaded his personal mounts, tied down his gear, and waited for the United States Army. It was hard to wait. The hardest part of being an employee of the army was the waiting, which seemed endless. As a free man he might ride off at will; as an army employee he was at the beck of everyone from a corporal to a general.

Still, the army got things done, and eventually the company of forty-two mounted infantry formed up and rode two abreast north through moonlight, where gentle grades would take the party out of the Yellowstone Basin and into rolling high plains.

He noticed that the lieutenant, new to the area, was riding by compass rather than letting the contours of the land dictate the passage. He was heading north, without the slightest deviation. But maybe that was good. In a couple of hours, the company hit Canyon Creek, and Lieutenant Collins called a halt. It wasn't a bad choice for a late-night halt, Dirk thought. Water, grass, and far from mosquitoes. He wondered if Collins had consulted some army maps, or was simply reflecting the orders of Captain Brewer, who rode along quietly.

The men settled in, subsisting on hardtack for the night. There were only half a dozen packhorses, so this outfit was traveling light. Dirk nibbled on the hard biscuit and was content. He'd eaten worse. Collins didn't post a watch; that was okay too. This was settled country, and there were no wars afoot.

Dirk pulled his bedroll over him, knowing it would be plenty cold later, and lay quietly. They were still three days away from Fort Maginnis. This was big country, this Territory of Montana, with room enough to absorb hundreds of thousands of people, including the Métis. It was hard to understand why the government, the army, and the settlers were so opposed to them. The Métis were good farmers, living quietly on their homesteads, doing nothing provocative or harmful until the Canadians of British descent decided to oust them from their seigneurial holdings, derived from French tradition. The first great upheaval was on the Red River in 1869 and 1870. And now, in 1885, the French-speaking mixed-bloods struggled against further evictions, finally warring against the Canadian Mounties and army at little places in Saskatchewan, such as Frog Lake, Fish Creek, Cut Knife, Batoche, Frenchman's Butte, and Loon Lake. The result was a rout. Their leader, a thoughtful Métis named Riel who did his best to negotiate a settlement, was hanged. And now a flood of these miserable refugees was pouring into Montana Territory.

There was plenty of room for them here, Dirk thought. And they'd make good citizens of this republic. But their race and tongue were against them.

Dirk struggled with that for a while, and fell asleep, glad to have something to divert his mind from Therese, who seemed to be present in his every waking moment. He wasn't escaping her. She occupied a hearth-spot in his mind, the place where home would be, with the pair of them creating a family, a life, a foothold of joy.

But maybe it was good that he was daily slipping farther and farther away from her. Maybe someday soon she would take the silver ring off her slim brown finger. He couldn't make up his mind about any of that.

Captain Brewer's company traveled north the next day, braving a mean wind with a hint of fall in it. They traveled forty more miles the next day, subsisting on beans. They traveled a like amount the next day, passing close to the

Little Snowies, gorgeous pine-clad peaks that gushed small creeks into the surrounding prairie.

That's when they encountered a caravan of half a dozen squeaking Red River carts, drawn by bony oxen, and a crowd of swart and worn people.

five

Captain Brewer's mounted infantry soon engulfed the immigrant caravan, and the fearful breeds stared uneasily at the soldiers.

Dirk looked the group over. They were Canadian Métis, gaunt and weary, the women almost in rags, the men wearing patchwork corduroy britches and ancient leather tunics over Hudson's Bay Company woolen shirts. The oxen stood motionless, their great heads lowered.

"That's them," Brewer said. "The Canadians. Looks like we'll have a little practice even before we get to the fort."

"They're harmless, sir. They're simply a few families trying to find a place to settle," Dirk said.

"Well, tell them they're going to turn right around and get themselves north of the border, just as fast as they can move their red butts. They're Queen Victoria's problem, not ours."

Dirk hated to do that. On the other hand he was being paid to do it. He studied the weary families, seeing thin children and some elderly Métis sitting on the backs of the rickety Red River carts. The carts themselves were burdened with the entire possessions of these people. There was no iron in the carts. They had been assembled without a nail or a bolt holding them together, and even the huge wheel rims were made of *shaganappi,* or green buffalo hide dried to hardness.

He directed his attention to a stocky man who seemed to be in charge, copper-colored, but with green eyes and a heavy wooden crucifix at his chest.

"Parlez-vous français?" he asked.

The man stared and slowly shook his head.

"Are you Cree?" Dirk asked, in that Algonquian tongue.

The man shook his head again. He looked like a lynx ready to run.

Dirk tried a Blackfoot word or two, which was also an Algonquian tongue. And then Cheyenne. And Assiniboine. He tried Spanish, for good measure, but these people just stared.

"Captain, the Métis speak several languages, depending on the group. These are not speaking French or Cree or any Indian dialect I can come up with. I'm not sure who they are. I'm not even sure they're from Canada. We have some of our own in the Dakotas."

"Well, tell them to head north. They know the hand language. Wiggle your fingers, Skye. Don't just stand there."

Dirk attempted to converse with the hand signs of the plains tribes, but these people just stared. The men stared fearfully at the soldiers, who mostly sat in their saddles, staring back.

"Michif," the headman finally said.

"Captain, they speak a dialect called Michif, which is a mixture of French and Cree, but follows no known rule, or so I'm told. I've never heard it spoken."

"Well, get on with it, Skye. Tell them to turn around and move, or they'll be eating lead instead of buffalo."

Dirk tried desperately, employing French nouns, Cree verbs, and a lot of hand signals. The Métis simply stared.

"I'm not having any luck, Captain."

"Well, I'll tell them myself. Some translator you are, Skye."

He withdrew his saber, swirled it about violently, and then pointed north with it.

"And don't come back," he shouted.

They stared.

Dirk dismounted, headed toward one of the oldest of the elders, a toothless man in purple velvet who slumped on the back of a Red River cart. An old one might remember.

"Hello, honored old one, I am North Star, and I translate for the army," he said in Cree.

The old one watched and nodded.

"I bring the captain's words to you. He says you must return to British possessions; that you are not a citizen here, and must go back."

Dirk knew the old one understood.

"That is the command of the army, and it must be obeyed," he said.

The ancient one nodded slightly. "We will all die, then," he said in some tongue that had many Cree words but was difficult to grasp.

"I wish it could be otherwise, old one. Start back or

the army will force you back. That is what the captain says."

The old one slid off the cart and padded to the head-man, and talked in Michif to the leader. Then he approached Dirk.

"You have killed us all," he said.

"What did he say, Skye?" Brewer asked.

"He said we have killed them all."

"Well, it's their own fault for crossing the border. Tell them that."

Dirk summoned his courage. "The captain says the blame is yours for coming to this country."

The old one sighed. "We will go bury ourselves, then."

"What'd he say, Skye?"

"They will leave—and will bury themselves."

Brewer grinned. "That was easy. And we're not even at Fort Maginnis yet."

Even as the soldiers watched, the headman, his gaze sulphurous, led his mottled ox in a wide loop, dragging the howling Red River cart, and the collection of families slowly turned around and groaned their way toward Box Elder Creek, northeast.

"We'll get all these buggers out of our hair in a month," Brewer said.

"Or bury them, sir."

"No help from you, Skye. You hired on as a translator and now I learn you can't even talk their tongue."

"It's the first Michif I've ever heard, sir."

Brewer nodded curtly. The command watched the Métis families slowly hike northeast, their carts creaking and groaning.

"We should follow along behind, just in case," the lieutenant said. "Like a whip ready to strike."

"Nah, my boy, they're on their way. Those red buggers took a long look at our repeaters and got religion," Brewer said.

"Yes, sir, you're right, sir," the lieutenant said.

"You sure can hear those carts squeal," Captain Brewer said. "You'd think they'd know enough to apply a little tallow."

"The axles and hubs are wood, Captain," Dirk said. "You apply grease and they soon pick up grit and wear down the axles and the hubs. Grease ruins them."

"Well, they're too dumb to use iron," Brewer said.

"They would if they could, Captain."

"What makes you such an expert, Skye? Did I hear you conversing with that bunch?"

Thus dismissed, Dirk sat in his saddle and watched the weary immigrants whip their oxen north, back to nowhere. He doubted the old ones would make it, but the younger ones might. Then again, this bunch might break apart and drift in various directions, none of them north. That's why the commander at Fort Maginnis had asked for reinforcements. There were thousands of square miles to hide the immigrants, and bands could slip into any gulch and stay more or less invisible.

The captain formed his company into twos and headed westerly, toward Ford's Creek and the nearby fort. This was handsome country, well watered by creeks springing from the Snowies and the Judith Mountains. Every watershed had a lush bottomland, with red willow brush, cottonwoods, chokecherries, and buffalo berries lining the creek. It would be a good place to settle down, raise some crops and a few animals, and add a little game for the dining table.

The forty-seven mounted infantrymen relaxed in their McClellan saddles. They had seen how easy it was to turn these half-breeds away. The whole operation was going to be easy, and no one would get hurt, at least if the other bands were as easily cowed as this one. And tonight they'd be in barracks or tents, well fed and resting up. Easy duty! Even with Captain Brewer in command, this would be a lark.

Dirk wasn't so sure. He thought the Métis might scatter, and not even their squealing carts would betray them. He also suspected the only way to drive them back would be to gather them by the hundreds and then escort them to the Canadian line. The thought sent a bleakness through him. Those people wanted nothing but the means to survive.

Not ten miles from the fort, a man in a black buggy, drawn by two trotters, blocked the two-rut road. He didn't move and didn't rein the trotters to one side. Brewer halted the column and eyed the man, who was plainly a rancher.

"You took long enough," the man said.

"Who are you, sir?" Brewer asked.

"Harley Bain," the man said. He waved a languid hand. "My land. In fact, the military reservation was my land too."

"Your land, sir? Not public land?"

"Prior rights," Bain said. "Here first."

"Well, that's fine, sir, but if you have no further business with us, we will proceed," Brewer said.

"Oh, but I do," Bain said. "I'm requiring the army to fulfill its mission. The United States is intended for the use of its citizens. Keep it that way."

"Oh, that's what the army is here for, Mr. Bain."

"No, you've failed miserably, and your little command won't help much. The Department of War has failed me. Failed my friends. Failed the settlers. We were here first, you know. I have a herd here, another in the Judith Basin, and a third in the Fort Benton area, all on range that I claimed first. The army's delinquent. That's the word. It's done nothing to protect me from these worms and grubs crawling in."

"I assure you, Mr. Bain, that will change swiftly," Brewer said.

"No, it won't. You need a thousand men for this job, and you don't have two hundred."

"Let us show you what the army can do for you," Brewer said.

"You already have. These gents are off the immigrant boats and haven't fired ten rounds. And you call them mounted infantry."

Brewer reddened.

"Actually," Bain said, "I'll do most of the job for you. I have riders."

"Thank you, Mr. Bain, but this is a task for the army, not your riders."

Bain grinned. "But we've already begun," he said. "I was hoping we might finish the job before you arrived."

"Doing what?" Brewer asked.

"Riding through the night, surprising trespassers in their beds, and persuading them to leave. It's quite successful. An exodus, you might say. There is nothing like a band of armed men waving torches to convince people to go away while they can."

"Mr. Bain, I will tell you just once: that is army business, not yours, and you will desist."

Bain smiled. "That's not what the command at Fort Maginnis says, Captain. They want all the help they can get. And I'm able to field about fifty men. I'd say my fifty are worth about three companies of regular army."

Brewer ignored the insult. "We won't have night riders here," Brewer said. "I'll say that right now. And I am certain that Major Brevoort is in full agreement."

Dirk listened intently. As much as he disliked the captain, he had to agree that Brewer was taking a stand against something very dark.

"It's army business," Brewer added.

Bain smiled and nodded gently. Dirk thought that the man's politeness simply concealed what he was really about.

"I'll be discussing the entire matter with the major this evening, sir," Brewer said. "I should add that we appreciate your offer to help with this operation. Most kind of you."

Bain nodded. "Perhaps I've underestimated the army. Or perhaps I'm more aware of the size of this migration than the army is. Of course, if the army is able to drive these people out, my services won't be needed."

"Mr. Bain, there are lawful and honorable ways of dealing with these migrants. The army intends to pursue them."

This was a side of Brewer that was new to Dirk. And not a bad side, either. Dirk had no use for this descendant of *Mayflower* Puritans, but he had less use for Bain. For once, Dirk was on the army's side.

Bain smiled again and reined his open carriage to one side, letting the command pass by. Dirk watched him, trying to get the measure of the man, and decided Bain was a rattlesnake. A very polite one.

There was some good in it, Dirk thought. The cards were all faceup on the table.

SIX

ort Maginnis's white frame buildings were the only thing of interest in the valley of Ford's Creek. Dirk knew instantly why the army had chosen this obscure place: it was superb hay meadow country. Indeed, for miles up the grassy valley, hay rose in stacks, ready for winter feed for the mounts at the post.

Beyond that, it had nothing to recommend it. It wasn't located on any strategic route to anywhere. The Judith Mountains were distantly visible, and so were the Little Snowies, but the soldiers at Maginnis would find nothing but grass to feast upon.

Now the company of mounted infantry was riding into the quadrangle, and bored soldiers swarmed out of the buildings to see the new contingent. There would be action soon: a concerted effort to sweep the Canadian breeds back to where they came from.

Sergeants soon directed the new troops to their tents, located in a long row behind the wooden barracks, while the officers vanished into the headquarters building, and the stable crews began to unsaddle, brush, inspect, water, and feed the weary mounts, which had borne troopers for three days.

Dirk, a civilian at loose ends, was free to wander. This was a horse soldier post if ever there was one. The fort's mission was to prevent the theft of stock and remove wandering Indians to their reservations. A political post, Dirk thought. It served no strategic purpose. Some powerful ranchers, probably led by Bain, had talked the War Department into it. And now the soldiers here would fight the ranchers' fight once more: drive away the breeds so the white men could get rich running cattle on public land.

Dirk had no idea where he would be quartered. He led his buckskin and his reserve horse to the stables and began his own grooming and watering.

"We'll do that, sir," said a ferrier sergeant.

"I'm a civilian employee, so it's up to me to care for my stock," Dirk said.

"We'll do it, sir. Nice nags you have there."

"I wouldn't know a fine horse from a bonehead," Dirk said. "But I had a good trader pick these out for me. I told him I wanted sound mounts and left the rest to him."

"Well, the bloke did just fine, I'd say." The sergeant was running a hand over pasterns looking for heat, and nodding. "You've got good saddlers here."

"No thanks to me," Dirk said. "I'm a translator."

"You can speak this Métis?"

"Some. The groups have their own dialects. We ran into some whose tongue I'd never heard. Called Michif. I didn't understand a word."

"Well, every bloody tribe's got its own ways, and them Canucks are just the same," the sergeant said, loosening the girth strap. "Our tribe too. I got officers talking to me with a mouth full of marbles and I don't know a thing they tell me."

"I found an old gent who could still talk Cree. Finally got word to the bunch to turn around."

"We'll get these beasts well cared for, good and proper," the stableman said.

"I'll be riding them hard over the next days," Dirk said. "So anything you do to keep them fit would help."

"Count on the army, sir."

Dirk collected his kit from the second horse and drifted to the quadrangle. He'd have to find the Officer of the Day and get instructions.

He hiked toward the headquarters, marked by gaudy regimental colors.

The commanding officer, Major Brevoort, was hosting Captain Brewer and other officers in deck chairs on the shady verandah, and it was plain that their debate was vigorous. They were working out the operation that would probably begin in the morning. Dirk steered clear. If they wanted him, they would summon him.

And they did. A Maginnis lieutenant corralled him later and led him to the half-dozen bearded officers lounging on the verandah.

"Skye, this is Major Brevoort, commanding here," Brewer said.

"Skye, heard of you," the major said. "Mountain man, guide in the old days."

"I've never been in the fur trade, sir."

"Well, whatever. You know the savage tongues. Or a few, anyway, Brewer said you didn't fathom the tongue of a bunch of breeds."

"Correct, sir. They were talking Michif, which I'd never heard."

"We're sending out patrols tomorrow, platoon strength, seven in all because we have a hundred forty able-bodied men. You're the sole translator, and not much good it seems. We've got to tell them to turn their carts around and get across the border fast, or they'll be in big trouble. How do we do that?"

"Their grandfathers or fathers were French, sir. Try French on the oldest ones."

"You think they understand it?"

"Some might."

Brevoort fingered his walrus mustache and pondered it. He turned to his aide. "Who speaks French?"

A lieutenant lifted a hand. "A little, sir."

"Who else?"

No one volunteered.

"What about the noncoms?"

"Irish, sir."

"Same as the enlisted men."

"You don't need translators," said Brewer. "They can be told where to go and how fast with a sword. I did it myself, just hours ago. The message was not lost on them." He gestured toward Dirk. "Fact is, we don't need him or anyone with those skills. Just ride down the immigrants and point north. And if they resist, the cocking of a few revolvers will suffice."

"What if they protest? What if they've something to say? What if there are difficulties? Misunderstandings?" Brevoort asked.

"There won't be. They will get the message in a pointed saber and the bore of a barrel aimed their way."

"Yes, but what if they've someone sick, or need to rest their oxen, or whatever?" the major asked.

"They came here illegally and can leave the way they came," Brewer said.

"I don't like it, Captain," Brevoort said. "This is not war, and these people are not criminals and their exodus is hardly an invasion. They're people in trouble."

"Foreigners, sir."

The debate depressed Dirk. The need for a translator with each patrol seemed so plain to him it was beyond argument. A translator could prevent violence. A translator could make sure the people being sent away were not American citizens. A translator could help negotiate issues, deal with illness or other emergencies, obtain agreements, achieve peaceful emigration.

"What do you think, Skye?" Major Brevoort asked suddenly.

"I think that translators should be with every patrol, sir. To prevent misunderstandings and trouble."

"He's just protecting his civilian job," Brewer said.

The rest nodded. It was as if the views of a civilian counted for nothing. As if a group of West Pointers would not listen to anyone without their credentials.

"They have a right to know why they are being ejected from the country, and a right to reply. Maybe some are citizens," Dirk said. "Maybe some have broken carts that need repair."

"Enough, Skye. We know all that," Brewer said. "We're done with you."

Brevoort nodded. Skye stared a moment at that bunch and drifted away, filled with foreboding about the morrow.

It would all be so easy. Send out strong patrols, locate the immigrants, and start them north. What could go wrong?

Dirk found himself eating at the enlisted men's mess. Beef and beans, not bad fare for an isolated post, far from any depot. The soldiers eyed his bronze flesh and said little. He ate his beef and beans and retreated into the quiet parade ground. It was an odd moment. His abilities were deemed unnecessary; his mixed bloods withered friendship. He found himself alone once again, which had become the story of his life. He didn't fit anywhere and his skills weren't needed.

He watched the fatigue details tote buckets and firewood to the barracks and officers' quarters, while others of the troops were on kitchen duty, and still more were hoeing and watering the vast vegetable garden adjacent to the post. Most frontier duty was little more than farming, he thought. Herding horses, herding slaughter cattle, herding sheep, planting, hoeing, weeding, harvesting. For eleven dollars a month.

No one showed up to offer him quarters, and he imagined the Officer of the Day may have been reluctant to billet a breed on the post. It didn't matter. Dirk headed for the stables, where some of the post's mounts were collected for service in the morning. Most of the horses would be pastured under guard on the surrounding grass.

He liked stables. There would be plenty of places to bunk down. He liked the acrid smell of horses, and even the acrid smell of the horse apples. But this night, with any luck, he'd spread his bedroll in the hay barn, out of weather and with a mountain of hay under him for a mattress.

"Thought you might show up here," said the sergeant who'd cared for Dirk's two horses.

"Good place to bunk, if you've no objections."

"I do it myself. Can't stand the noncom barracks, and no one objects if I spread out here."

"I'm Dirk Skye, sir."

"August Mack, laddie. A son of Ireland, and pining for it too."

"Where's a good place to settle in?"

"Anywhere the horse apples don't land on you."

"Hay barn?"

"Too warm for me, but maybe right for you."

Dirk headed for some tall double doors and found a mountain of hay kept under roof there. The sweet smell of dried grasses caught in his nostrils. It would do.

The sergeant was sitting on a split-log bench, eyeing the evening sky. "You going out tomorrow?" he asked.

"They don't want a translator. And there aren't enough anyway. Seven patrols, all on extended duty."

The sergeant spat. "They'll ruin most of my horses. Cavalrymen off the boats can't ride, and the mounted infantry shouldn't even try. How come you ain't going?"

"I'm in the way. If they don't have to palaver with the Métis, they can just send them packing and look for the next bunch."

"They're just gonna point and wave a few revolvers?"

"I offered to translate."

"Skye, them Canucks are half-settled. They've been drifting in all summer. They got their farms staked out. They got sod houses up, and gardens going, and potato patches, and spring houses and root cellars built. And likely some hanging meat, and it ain't all game, either."

"That's what I was afraid of. This is a rancher deal, right?"

"There's a lot of Métis in the territory, they tell me. Not enough game left to feed a crowd like that. There's bloody few deer or antelope around. So the patrols, they'll find some beef hanging from the cottonwood limbs. And then there'll be trouble, and no one can talk to the other."

"What'll they do?"

"The ranchers got night riders, they tell me. There'll be a few necktie parties, and the army, it'll look away and see not a damned thing. Actually, the army's kept the lid on so far, but the ranchers are getting itchy and are primed to stretch some rope."

"Where are these Canadians?"

"To hell and gone, up every draw, up in the hills, most hidden from sight. And the whole Canuck lot are trying to get fixed for winter. Stowing away the cabbages and potatoes, stowing the huckleberries, catching trout, jerking meat, hanging up onions, finishing up their cabins, putting roofs on, sewing up leather coats, cutting firewood, or scratching a little coal out of all them seams around here."

"And the army's going to shove them out."

"Yep, and likely won't give them time to load up the Red River carts, either. It's like a death sentence, if you ask me," the sergeant said.

"Who can I talk to about this?" Dirk asked. "I need to be the voice of these people."

"This is the army, boy, and they're gonna do it the army way."

seven

They summoned Dirk Skye at dawn.

"You'll ride with Brewer," said a lieutenant he'd never met. "Take a kit. You'll be out three or four days."

That wasn't surprising; he would report to the Fort Keogh mounted infantry he came with.

The parade ground teemed with horses and riders, forming into patrols. Dirk loaded his kit onto his reserve horse and mounted the buckskin, feeling the familiar pleasure of a good horse under him.

He mostly kept out of the way, watching the army begin its campaign against the Canadians. The horse soldiers assembled in lines for review and then formed by twos into columns. There plainly weren't enough officers on hand to lead all the patrols, so sergeants were commanding three of them. By some process not explained to Skye, a territory had been meted out to each patrol. A half a dozen pack mules were going with each patrol, which meant they would be out only two or three days and weren't taking shelters. Maybe the army expected to send the Métis packing in that brief time. This would be a lark.

There was no sendoff this fall morning. No regimental band, no colors, no war talk. This was just a patrol operation, and hardly worth trumpets and guidons. Dirk watched Major Brevoort review the patrols. It was plain the post commander wasn't going out. There were plenty of soldiers not going, including the entire stable crew.

Dirk steered his nag and spare over to Brewer's patrol and settled in beside a sergeant he knew. Captain Brewer eyed Dirk sourly, as if to announce that it wasn't his decision or his desire to have a translator along. Dirk simply nodded.

The captain, in the van, simply pointed, and the patrol spurred the mounts into a brisk walk, while Major Brevoort watched silently. This wasn't the spit-and-polish army; this was the everyday army, trotting off to eject some half-breeds.

That was all right with Dirk. If they had started off as if for battle, with the band playing "The Girl I Left Behind Me" and colors flying, that would have worried him. The one thing that did surprise him was that Brewer was doing field duty. The pasty-faced captain had been well known for his prowess commanding a desk.

Dirk hadn't the faintest idea where the patrol was headed this fine autumnal day. He saw other patrols turn north and east and south, but Brewer's platoon kept up a brisk walk westward, along a well-traveled trail that cut between the Little Snowies and the Judith Mountains, and into the lush Judith Basin.

Dirk turned to the sergeant. "I'm Skye, translator," he said.

"O'Hara," said the sergeant. "Ten years out of steerage and all of it serving Uncle Sam."

"You know where we're headed?"

"The captain, sah, is not inclined to share his plans."

"You know what he'll do when we find some Métis?"

"Jabber awhile, string 'em up, bury them, make a lot of noise, who knows, sah?"

"I mean, how does a platoon drive Canadians back to Canada?"

"In a pine box, sah. That's how to do it fast."

"Those Red River carts are slow and break down. It'd take a month to drive those people out of this country."

"I think the army doesn't plan to wait a month, sah. I'd guess them Canucks are fated to start hiking and go until they drop. You have to understand, sah, that this republican army is humane, unlike the Brits, which means we'll drive the herd at sword point instead of just shooting the whole lot."

"I don't think Brewer would do that, Sergeant."

"Well, sah, if I may say so, he's got his priorities. One Yank cow is more valuable than one Frenchy half-breed. So the trick is to be kind to cows and herd up the breeds and send them to the slaughterhouse."

Dirk smiled. This sergeant would color the trip like an artist.

The column snaked over a winding road that skirted pine-clad foothills, paused to water at a cold creek, and continued onward toward a hazy vastness far ahead.

The captain lifted the troop into a trot, and the patrol clattered westward, harness jangling, shod hooves clack-

ing on rock. The farther they rode, the worse the tension
that was building in Dirk. He didn't like this, and worse,
the commander didn't like him.

They topped a small divide separating drainages and
started down a long grade, through rocky foothill country marked by glades of yellowing aspen and black pine
forest. And then, on a distant flat to the south, the captain
spotted a camp. And some carts. And some people moving about.

He halted the column.

"There's some of the devils," he said. "All right. We'll
ride in. Spread wide, keep your carbines sheathed. This
isn't a war. There will be women and children, I imagine.
I'll do the talking." He eyed Dirk. "You. Come in beside
me."

Dirk steered the buckskin forward.

"I'll talk, you translate," he said. "And tell me exactly
what they say. Exactly, you understand, Skye? Or is that
beyond you?"

Dirk smiled.

The encampment looked to embrace several families. There were five Red River carts parked here and
there, akimbo. Three cook fires burned. This was not a
permanent settlement, but simply a resting place, probably rich with game. Dirk spotted seven adult males,
nine adult women, and assorted children. The women
were stirring whatever was in the pots hanging over the
cook fires. Soup, he thought. The Métis lived on soups
and stews.

It was a peaceable scene.

The patrol was discovered now, and people stared. A
few children retreated toward their mothers and hid

themselves in the gray and black skirts that seemed to be the only colors these women wore. The black-bearded men, who had been caring for the oxen or cutting wood or cleaning a carcass of a buck mule deer, paused and stared uneasily.

The captain didn't slow, but rode in close on his well-groomed bay horse, and behind him the patrol spread wide, in essence cutting off escape in most directions. The Métis, wary but not afraid, mostly stopped whatever they were doing and stared. One burly one with a full beard carefully lowered his axe and straightened, his gaze finally settling on the captain. Several of the women straightened up, their hands finding and comforting the children.

"Well, I see you're Canadians," Brewer said.

No response.

"You're Canadians, and here illegally, and we're sending you back. You've got to pack up and go, and right now."

Several of the men frowned. If they understood English, they didn't reveal it.

Brewer singled one out. "You, there. Tell them the United States Army says they must leave."

The man shrugged, spread out his hands, and addressed Brewer in a tongue Dirk thought might be an odd form of French.

"What's he saying?" Brewer asked his translator.

"I can only get the gist of it. He's saying he doesn't know what you're saying. He's from Manitoba and they're settling in the area."

"Tell him to speak English, or French, or Cree if he can, or the sign language if that's the only way."

Dirk had trouble with that, using Cree first, and then

some French. But at least the burly man nodded and plunged in.

"He's welcoming you. He's inviting the soldiers to have some soup. There's not much for so many, but he will share it with the blueshirts. Tonight they will roast that haunch of venison and make a feast with the army."

"Tell him no. The army of the United States requires that they head back to Canada immediately. No delays. Put out the cook fires and go."

Dirk descended from his horse. He never liked to translate from horseback. He hoped his example would encourage Captain Brewer to do the same.

"Messieurs," he began, even as other of the bronzed, jet-haired Métis men collected around him, "the *capitaine* says that you are not citizens and must return to Canada at once. Right now. He says put out your fires and go."

"*Non!*" said the one who seemed to lead. "*Non!* We cannot return. It is not safe. *Hiver* arrives. We are hunted like deer."

Dirk turned to Brewer. "He says they can't. It's not safe. Winter is coming. The Canadian authorities are hunting them."

"Tell the fellow I'm sorry. They can't stay here. That's final. They must leave at once. If not, we'll start them on their way by whatever means."

The man seemed to understand, even without translation.

"Give us time," he said. "Let us rest the oxen and find some game."

Oddly, Brewer seemed to grasp the gist of that. "No time. We have hundreds of Métis camps to visit and can't abide the slightest delay."

Dirk saw an old muzzle-loading long rifle resting against one of the carts. One or two of the Métis men were eyeing it.

Brewer was growing irritable. These people weren't hopping about, throwing things into their carts, harnessing the oxen. He leaned over his saddle. "Now! Immediately!" he said.

The burly one eyed the soldiers. "We wish to finish our meal. The soup, it boils soon. We wish to feed the little ones. They will be unhappy. They want a little soup in their bellies. And then when they are fed, American soldiers, then we will go."

Dirk had trouble extracting meaning from this jumble of French and Cree, and he had to make a few assumptions. He turned to the captain.

"He's asking to stay long enough to feed the children. The soup will soon boil. Let them feed the children, and then they will go."

Brewer was plainly getting testy. He sat irritably, eyeing the black iron kettle that was not yet steaming. The children peered up at him, solemn and shy. One boy, dressed like the older men, had a buffalo-skin cap.

"Serve them the soup now, hot or not, while the rest of you pack up and harness the oxen," Brewer said. "You're wasting our time."

"Messieurs," Dirk began. "*Le capitaine,* he says to feed the children now, warm soup or not, while the rest of you pack up."

"And where will we go?" asked the man who had taken charge here.

"Where will they go?" Dirk asked.

"North to Canada. The way you came," the captain

said. "We're going to make sure you go. There are other patrols making sure you head for Canada, and without delay."

Dirk managed to convey that. The men swiftly ordered the women to fill the bowls, no matter whether the soup was ready. He saw the women burst into action, ladling the cold soup into wooden bowls. The men, concealing whatever was boiling in them, wearily backed the oxen into the wagon trees, and buckled them in place. One pregnant woman comforted a small girl, who had begun to weep.

The burly one tried another question: would the *capitaine* permit them to rest this night and leave in the morning, if he promised on his honor to go?

"He offers to leave, on his honor, in the morning if he may rest his people tonight, sir."

"What honor? They are subversives in Canada, fomenting rebellion. And now they bring that rebellion here. No, Skye. Tell him plain and clear. They will go now, or be driven out at the point of a bayonet."

Dirk tried to recast that in this odd semi-French dialect. "Go at once or face the bayonet, says the *capitaine*."

"I will stand and face the bayonet if that is my fate," the man said. "I am Georges Piccard. Tell him Piccard will face the bayonet so the others may rest."

The captain absorbed that. Dirk hoped he had translated correctly. He could barely fathom the Métis dialect, which scrambled sentences.

Brewer mulled that for a while, and Dirk could almost see the options pass through the captain's mind. The mounted infantry waited, not liking any of it.

"Sergeant," he said. "Dismount the men and confiscate

those ox carts and start them north, one drover to each ox. If these breeds want to keep their stuff, they'd better run. The rest of you draw your sidearms and protect the drovers."

Sergeant O'Hara dourly did as he was required. And soon there were soldiers leading the howling ox carts away from that glade. And then came a rush of Métis, desperate to catch up with everything they possessed.

After a mile or so, Brewer halted the procession.

"Tell them to keep on and tell them not to return," he said.

Dirk Skye did and watched the funeral procession wend its way north.

"That's the way to do it," Captain Brewer said. "No lives lost."

eight

Captain Brewer was in a fine mood. He was pushing through the Judith Basin, scattering Métis wherever he went. It wasn't hard. The whole business of commandeering their Red River carts or wagons worked just fine. Wherever the Métis resisted, Brewer ordered his men to harness the oxen and start the carts rolling. And then the Métis would hastily break camp, catch up to the creaking carts, and start their exodus to Canada.

Then they came to a Métis farm, snugged into the northern foothills of the Snowy Mountains. There was a sturdy log house, a vegetable garden, most of it harvested; a log barn, a fenced paddock, a spring house, and livestock scattered up tan fields bordered by dark pines.

An entire family rushed out of the house to greet the column, a fine strapping papa, with mustachios, two lads pushing into their teens, a younger girl, and a stout mama, carrying a rolling pin.

They watched without consternation as the column halted in the yard.

"Ah, friends, welcome," the patriarch said in English. "What brings the army to my door?"

"You're Robicheaux, right?"

"Indeed, my friend. Pierre Robicheaux, and my sons Jacques and Remi, and my wife Francine, and my dear child Marie. Do step down and refresh yourselves, eh?"

"You're Métis, right?" the captain asked.

"Yes, indeed, sir. We were farming in the Red River country of Manitoba, and removed ourselves to the States seven years past."

"But you're Canadians, right?"

"Why, my frien', maybe we are Yankees now, eh? We settled, learned English. See, even my boys speak English. We sell produce to the good people in Lewistown, eh? We've filed homestead claims here. My wife and I, we each claim a hundred sixty acres, eh? It is registered."

"But you're not citizens. Our mission is to return Canadians who are here illegally to Canada."

"But we are here seven years! We have filed on this land!"

"Well, show me your citizenship papers," Brewer said.

Robicheaux stared. "But, sir, that will come when we can. There are no officials here."

"That's right, and you're here without the permission of the government. So it is my duty to send you back to your own country."

"Ah, Captain, forgive me. But we are settled here now. This land, see how we have subdued it. Those are our cattle and goats, eh? See the house. I barked and smoothed every log, and split off every shake for the roof, eh?"

"You should have gotten your papers in order. I'm here to move you."

"But, Captain, I will get these papers. I will go to the place where I can get them. Is it Helena? I am on my way to Helena. I will produce these papers just as fast as they can be issued, eh?"

Brewer slowly shook his head. "Robicheaux, you are not in the country legally. We're here to move you out. Now fetch your personal things, get that wagon loaded, and we'll escort you."

The command hung there in the sweet morning of an autumnal day. The dark-haired girl, Marie, slipped to her mother and hung on her mother's gray skirts. Robicheaux lifted his sweat-stained felt hat, ran a bony hand through his gray-streaked hair, and stared somberly at the officer who was about to tear his life apart.

"I wish to appeal to the authorities," he said. "I will go with you to the marshal. We will ask him."

Brewer shook his head stonily.

Remi clenched and unclenched his fists. The infantrymen, who had heard and understood the entire exchange, spat their chews. Robicheaux stared at them, at his family, and his cattle grazing peacefully on the autumn-tanned meadows.

Dirk sat on his buckskin, a quiet fury spreading through him. This wasn't sending Métis back to Canada. This family's home was right here, and had been for as long as this area had been settled. Seven years here made it 1877. This was different. This was Brewer's passion to eject anyone, everyone, whose pedigree didn't go straight back to the *Mayflower* and Plymouth Colony. This had nothing to do with legal or illegal entry, and everything to do with *us* and *them*.

He eased his buckskin forward.

"Wouldn't you say, Captain, that this is a different case?"

Brewer glared.

"These are settled people. They've put down roots. They've been here long enough to be granted citizenship."

Brewer turned slowly, until he was staring directly at Dirk.

"What is your rank, sir?" he asked.

"I'm a civilian, Captain."

"And what is your office here?"

"Translator."

"And what empowers you to address me in this fashion?"

"The need to consider this matter, Captain."

"Is that part of your duties as a translator? These people speak plain English, do they not? So what gives you the office to address me, eh?"

"Removing these settlers isn't part of your mission, Captain."

Brewer was getting hot. "I asked you what empowers you to address an officer of the army? Does being a translator turn you into a colonel?"

"I speak as a civilian, Captain."

"Then don't speak at all!"

But Dirk would not be put off. "This needs thinking out. This man's request is valid. He has every right to go to the authorities. He has every right to be left alone."

"Corporal," Brewer yelled. "Put this man in irons."

A corporal pushed his horse forward. "Captain, sir, we have no irons."

"What am I accused of?" Dirk asked.

"Disobeying me."

"I believe I am a civilian under contract."

"Disobeying me, Skye."

"Asking you to reconsider."

"In this army, Skye, you don't ask an officer to do anything. You sound like a jailhouse lawyer. Let's call it insubordination. Every time you open your mouth, you make it worse. Since I haven't any manacles, here's what's going to happen. You are discharged from service here and now. You will leave this patrol and report to Major Brevoort. You will tell him I have terminated your service. You will leave here immediately. If you aren't out of sight in five minutes, I will instruct my command to hasten your flight by whatever means they have at hand. Am I clear?"

Dirk registered that and nodded. "Very clear, Captain. And when he asks what happened, I will tell the major exactly what happened here, and what you are doing to this family."

"Out!" Brewer roared. He waved violently.

All this was absorbed by the Métis family as well as every man in the command.

Dirk turned to Robicheaux. "Don't despair. Your case will be known, and you'll soon be secure here."

The Métis barely nodded, not wishing to inflame the situation.

Dirk slowly rode his buckskin to the rest of the family. "Take heart," he said.

"Skye!" Brewer yelled.

"Take heart," Dirk said to Robicheaux.

He collected his spare horse that was carrying his pack and rode swiftly east, down into the magnificent Judith Basin, aching with golden grass, icy creeks, and warm skies. He didn't look back. In the allotted five minutes he had rounded a bend and vanished from the view of the patrol.

His work for the army had come to an abrupt end and yet he rejoiced. This had been the most harrowing mission he had been on. Maybe it was time to do something else, but he didn't know what. The army was the enemy for the time being. The army was pushing and shoving, and it was getting ugly.

Dirk debated whether to return to Fort Maginnis at all. He was out, and what difference did it make? He would never again receive a brown pay envelope from the War Department. Or any government agency, for that matter. He knew he was not done with this. The Métis were good people. Different, friendly, peaceful, and very hard workers. They should be welcomed, not booted out. He itched to talk to someone in authority.

But he didn't know what he might do. He was facing the might of the army, of the government in Washington, of the territorial government in Helena, and all official-dom. Even if he wanted to help these Canadians, he didn't know how.

He rode his lonely way east, his packhorse following along behind him as he traversed a vast country girt by dark and distant mountains in most directions. He thought of Therese, wondering what she was doing that very moment; wondering whether she still wore his ring, and whether the torments of her heart had somehow quieted. His own feelings hadn't changed. Therese was still a dream and a horizon.

Far ahead, he saw some riders, and even at a great distance he knew they were drovers, and they would be wearing their great felt sombreros and would have lariats tied to their high-backed saddles, and would have spurs on their boots and six-guns strapped to their belts.

He liked cowboys; always delighted to share a camp with them.

This bunch closed fast, so Dirk halted his buckskin, settled in for some palaver. The riders swept in and swiftly settled round him, as if to block his movements.

There was one old drover who was tanned to the color of a chestnut, and seamed by a life in the sun and wind. But he had bright hard black eyes, and for a moment Dirk felt uneasy.

"Howdy," Dirk said.

"What've we got here, boys?" the old boy said.

"Looks like we got us a breed, if'n I read him right," said a young ferret-faced one.

"And he's got him some fancy nags too," slurred another, with a wad of tobacco in his cheek.

"I'm Dirk Skye. And you?"

"Well, this here breed speaka da Engleesh a leetle," said the black-eyed one.

"All my life," Dirk said. He was not liking the way this was going, but there wasn't much he could do about it.

"You speak a leetle Frenchie too, you bet?" asked the ferret.

"I speak English, Crow, Shoshone, the Algonquian tongues such as Blackfoot and Cree, and yes, I had three years of French when I was in school in St. Louis."

"A bunch of them tongues in redskin," said tobacco-wad.

"That's my living. Army translator. I came up here with the Fort Keogh company."

"That sure is a tall tale, Canuck. If you was with the army, then that's where you'd be, stead of parading along with a couple of extry good horses."

Dirk saw where this was leading, and didn't like it. "Care to ride back to my unit? About two hours that way?"

"We don't cotton to the army, breed. It's just messing up our business."

"Which is?"

"Cleaning out the country—of breeds."

"You working for Bain?" Dirk asked.

"It's *Mister* Bain to you."

"My father, Barnaby Skye, always called himself Mister. He said in the New World, everyone should be addressed as Mister. So, sure, he's Mister Bain, and I'm Mister Skye, and you are Mister—?"

"You sure are full of palaver," said tobacco-cheek.

"I'm on my way to Fort Maginnis to report to Major Brevoort. Care to ride along with me?"

"Where'd you get them nags, breed?"

"Miles City."

"You got papers?"

"At my home."

"But not here, eh?"

"The bills of sale for these horses are in my quarters at Fort Keogh."

Black-eyes ignored him. "Maybe we should just haul this here breed to Bain and let him look over them horses."

"He might recognize me. He met the column on the road near the fort. Sure, let's go."

"No, let's not go. You get off that nag, breed. We're going to return these here horses to their rightful owners."

Dirk felt the heat boil up in him. He also checked it, knowing suddenly that he would be lucky to escape with his life. He was unarmed, except for the revolver he carried in his pack on the other horse. He slid off, touching ground lightly.

No one had drawn a gun, which was a good sign. Maybe his connection with the army was slowing down these hard-riders a little.

Black-eyes grabbed the reins of the buckskin.

"Thanks, breed," he said.

They rode off, leading Dirk's two horses, and then he was alone on the trail, with nothing, no one, at his side, and miles to go on the road to nowhere.

nine

Therese walked up a grassy gulch that rose to prairie, where scarcely a tree intruded and nothing slowed the wind. She wore her white apron, for in it she would collect buffalo berries, or chokecherries, and bring them to her cousins. She drove her feet hard, pushing through the thickness of her gray skirts, but no matter now fiercely she walked, she could not escape her past or her fate. She had shamed her family by fleeing her new husband; her cousins barely tolerated her and permitted her to stay only because she worked hard.

Her feet could not take her far enough or fast enough to spare her, and she always returned, sometimes with a few berries to offer the Desportes as propitiation for her foolish conduct. This day was no different. She was aching for something, she knew not what.

The people had gravely asked her why she ran away from Skye at the celebration, especially after she had made her vows before the priest, and she had the simplest of answers for them all: she suddenly realized she didn't like

Dirk Skye. Not one bit. He had no steel in his heart and was betraying himself and others, doing what he did. He wasn't worth the time of day, and that was that.

At the head of the gulch was a small amphitheater with dense brush lying at its heart, and here she paused because it was the home of red-winged blackbirds, which she loved. The males had bright red shoulders with a yellow band, while the females were nondescript and freckled, just like the Métis people. They were kinfolk of the Métis. The men were gaudy; the women retiring. Now, the males were hopping from twig to twig, and the sky was transparent, and she could see beyond the world and beyond the heavens, to the place of beauty.

She was not religious but this place was always filled with the mysteries. Theology and the church were for men, and there was nothing for her in them. But here, just below the lip of the grasslands, was a holy place where she sometimes came to make things right in her soul.

And here she rested, amid a sweetness that lifted her heart to the sky.

And here, this hour, she beheld a woman in white linen descending ivory stairs from blue heaven, a woman she knew at once to be her name saint. This homely lumbering saint was smiling at Therese, and finally stood just apart, glowing in her robes, while all the world stood sweetly quiet.

"Therese, we give you a mission," said Saint Therese. "We rejoice to find you here, your heart opened up to us. We rejoice that you are ready and willing to help your people. For your mission is very like mine. It was given to me to found many Carmelite convents and reform our order. And so it is given to you, my sister. Gather your people together and build a church. Raise the church where your people are gathering. Then you and your Métis can live on the very land that the Blessed One gives to you for all eternity."

Saint Therese smiled, and her voice was sweeter than any that Therese had ever heard, and she marveled, and wondered whether this vision was true.

"Lead the Métis to their new home. Let them gather around the church you shall build, for that is to be their true home. Go, Therese. There is a place called Lewistown where you will build your church. You will find your people gathering there. They will hear you. They will help you. You will leave here, leave your family, go to where your people are gathered, waiting for you to be their shepherdess. Gather your sheep. Do this and you will never be alone."

Then the saint was gone. The ivory stairs vanished. Therese saw the red-winged blackbirds again, and there was a red-tipped feather in her lap. She drew the perfumed air into her lungs. She smelled roses, sweet and thick, though no roses grew anywhere near.

She sat very still, unable to absorb all the miracles that had pierced her at that moment. There was no wind, nothing but aching silence. The air caressed her lungs. But she was not the young woman who had climbed the gully moments before. She was new, and strange to herself, and she marveled. She felt weightless, as if she had been lifted free of her mortal flesh, and could soar at will through the empyrean light. She felt that she could touch a plant or a tree or a bee or a butterfly and make it grow.

She sat quietly. How could it be? Why had it been visited upon her and not someone else? Saint Therese had wrestled with the church hierarchy, worked tirelessly to restore the faith. The young woman who had just fled a marriage was bewildered, but it didn't matter. She barely knew the story of Therese Sanchez de Cepeda y Ahumada, a few things learned in homilies about saints. But she knew this much: the nun had changed Spain. And now Therese must change Montana.

The Métis were poor, scattered people, with only a few tools among them. There would be no army of stonemasons and carpenters and joiners among them to erect a great church, if indeed that was to be her mission. In truth, she hadn't the faintest idea what it all meant, and she could do nothing until more was revealed to her. She finally stood, aware that the world had been restored to the only one she knew. But the bright red-winged blackbirds were there, a cordon of honor awaiting her steps down the long gulch.

She walked, but couldn't feel herself walking. It was as if she was being transported softly, on air, her feet never touching the earth. She marveled at this. She was living outside of her body.

When she reached the farmstead, she found her aunt Celeste bustling about the kitchen.

"Where are the berries? Don't say there were none!"

"Madame, it was not for me to pick berries this day, for something beyond telling has happened to me."

Celeste Desportes stopped in her tracks, a big spoon in one hand and an onion in the other.

"Ah! Not for you to tell me, eh? You've found a new way to be lazy."

"It was a vision. That's what I saw. It came to me at the top of the gulch."

"A vision, was it? First you run away from your husband after making the vow; now you are chasing visions!" She smiled. "I suppose you saw Dirk Skye up in the clouds."

"It was a saint, madame. And the air was filled with the scent of roses, and there were red-winged blackbirds watching me."

"A saint! After what you did to the honor of the Métis, you talk with saints! The potatoes need scrubbing."

Therese saw how it would go. "I'll make the stew," she said.

"No you won't! You'll tell me about the saint that came down from heaven to have a little talk with you."

"It was Saint Therese, my name saint."

"Saint Therese! Now I know you are fevered. What did she say?"

"She was dressed in white linen, head to foot, and light shown around her, and the skies were so clear I could see up the stairway of ivory to the heavenly world."

Aunt Celeste marched over, slapped a warm hand on Therese's forehead, and held it there. "Just as I thought! You'll climb into bed and hope the Lord above forgives you, telling such tales."

"I am not sick, madame. I saw what I saw."

"What did she say, Saint Therese?"

Therese wasn't at all sure she should say anything. But there was her aunt, waving a big spoon at her, ready to beat the truth out of her.

"Madame, she said I had been chosen to raise a church."

"Ah! Now I know you are fevered. You must make a full confession for this sin."

"She said she reformed an order called the Carmelites in Spain, and I must build a church."

"Therese Trouville—or should I say Skye? Where is the money for this?"

Therese had no reply, so she washed potatoes.

"Where are your builders, eh?"

"Madame, I should have said nothing. I will make the stew now; your husband, he'll be ready for supper before we are."

"Trouble, that's what this is! Too bad there's no priest around to hear you. Build a church! This story is so lunatic it would require a bishop! And he'd likely send you into the forests to feed the bears. No wonder our dear cousins Montclair and Helene sent you out of their house! What else did she say?"

"She said the Blessed One wants me to build this church in the village of Lewistown, where the Métis are settling."

"Ah, trying to get us into trouble, is she? Saint Therese faced the Inquisition, she did."

"Madame, she told me to lead our people. That is all I know. The church will be at their new home."

"Wait until Monsieur hears this! He will banish you from the house! He will put you out. It all started when you walked away from your husband, and now this! *Mon Dieu!* That was the beginning of trouble, and now the trouble is ten times worse! What did she look like?"

"White linen, madame, and she was filled with light. There was strange light everywhere."

"Whoever heard of a saint in linen? And strange light. It's all nonsense. The sun goes up and the sun goes down, and there is only one kind of light. You are making this up."

Therese was tired of this. She sliced the potatoes and dropped them into the stew, which was heating up in a kettle hung in the hearth, where flames licked its blackened belly. This was a good time for stews, with the root cellar bursting with garden produce. She found a fat cabbage and sliced it into big chunks and added those to the stew. There was still a haunch of antelope Monsieur had shot, and now Therese began to saw it into stew-sized chunks, and added them to the pot.

Madame kept eyeing her, as if something alien had settled in the Desportes homestead. But Therese ignored all that. She had seen what she had seen and had told her aunt, and what else was there to say?

Ambrose Desportes showed up at sundown. He had been cutting wood against the brutal winter, a task that consumed his every waking hour. There was nothing worse than plunging into a bitter cold day in February with no wood to heat with or to boil a stew.

Monsieur pulled off his leather gloves and vest and eyed the women, who silently served up large bowls of the stew.

They ate in deep silence, interrupted only by Monsieur's questioning gaze at the women. This meal was unlike the other, affectionate ones at the Desportes table.

"So, what passes?" he asked.

"Therese has something to tell you," Madame said.

Therese started in boldly. She had no fear. She was telling the truth, and that was all that mattered. She was even enjoying it. No such thing had ever happened to her, and she intended to milk it for all it was worth.

Monsieur ate slowly, and sometimes his jaw stopped the mastication, especially when Therese was talking about transparent heavens and the scent of roses, all of which raised the bushy black eyebrows of the master of this farmstead.

He asked no questions. He didn't interrupt. He listened quietly, nodded, stared at the rafters, pushed his bowl toward Madame, indicating he wanted another serving, and finally simply stared at Therese.

"How will you build a church?" he asked. "Can you dress stones and cut beams?"

"I will do what was asked of me, monsieur."

"Of course. You will inspire carpenters and stonemasons and build the church. And where will this be?"

"In the village of Lewistown."

"That is a good place. That is where the Métis are collecting. This saint of yours, she knows a thing or two. Why did she choose you?"

"That is not anything I can say, monsieur. She came to me in brightness and asked me to do this thing."

"I suppose you'll be leaving us, then. How will you survive, eh?"

"I have not given it a thought, monsieur."

"How do you know this is a true vision?"

"Madame felt my forehead and there was no fever, monsieur."

"The devil leads people into folly."

"The Saint was very tender, monsieur. As if she knew what would be placed before me. And how hard it would be."

"And you intend to do this?"

"*Oui*, monsieur."

"It comes from God," he said. "The Métis need a place to gather. We were driven out of our homes, and our blood lies upon the fields of Manitoba and Saskatchewan, and we are scattered to the winds, family torn from family, friend from friend, and now we are like chaff in the wind. And now this vision comes to this young woman who sits at my table, and it is a good vision. Erect a church, and the Métis will collect around it and make this place their home. It is the gift of God, and he has sent his messenger."

Therese stared. She had been expecting derision, or skepticism, or worse, and now her uncle was finding miracles in it, and hope in it.

"I will help you," he said.

He was struggling with himself, even as his hands clasped and unclasped at the thick rough homemade table.

"Take the donkey," he said.

"But, sir, you need the donkey for the plow and—many things."

"Take him. What I need more is the knowledge that the people have a destiny, and that God has chosen a place for us to go, and that you, my own niece, has been given this task. Tomorrow we will make a pack for the mule, and we will fill it with the things you need, clothing, moccasins, grain, flour, a thing or two to cook with, and your blankets. If this is what is ordained, my *chérie*, let it be said that Desportes offered his hand."

ten

Therese Trouville—for so she called herself now that her marriage was dead—left at dawn, leading a grouchy donkey that refused to submit to the will of a woman. But a resounding slap from Desportes improved the donkey's attitude and Therese walked quietly away, even as her aunt and uncle watched, adding their blessings to her. She turned to look back and saw them standing rock solid, unmoving, as she led the donkey along the worn trail that would take her to the great valley of the Yellowstone River.

So much had happened in the space of a few hours. Now she was on her way, obedient to the mission that was visited upon her, scarcely knowing why she had been chosen. Why her? Why not someone more qualified? Someone with a deep faith, unlike herself. She had hardly bothered with her religion; it mostly got in her way. But here she was, leading a donkey to a muddy little crossroads called Lewistown, where a few stores and saloons huddled, far from anywhere she knew anything about. It was somewhere near where her husband Dirk Skye might be, and she fervently hoped she would not see him at all.

The Desportes vanished behind her, and now she was alone, treading the north bank of the river, along a familiar trail that connected smallholdings to the town of Miles City. The village basked in the morning sun, mostly invisible across the solemn river. She hurried on, passing Fort Keogh, white rectangles surrounding a sleepy parade. It didn't look at all sinister, and yet its soldiers were away on a mission to drive her own people across the Canadian line—just in time for winter. And her husband was assisting them.

She would seek an annulment. But first she had to build a church.

The chuffing of a steam train caught her attention. She peered into the hazy valley, and discovered an eastbound Northern Pacific freight, drawing a few boxcars and a caboose. She watched it pass, and then started along the path again. There would be no trains to Lewistown, which was a long way from anywhere. The donkey rebelled for a moment, but she gave the line a hard yank, and the beast settled in. Then it decided to trot past her, and she was barely able to yank it to a halt as it sailed by.

"The saint has told me to build a church," she said, "so behave yourself."

It yawned and settled into a shuffle that matched her stride.

She settled that night in a berry patch. She found herself in a damp draw, surrounded by hackberries, chokecherries, buffalo berries, huckleberries, all in thick brush. She wouldn't need anything else for a supper, and soon was feasting on her bonanza. She picketed the donkey, unrolled her blankets, and settled down for the night, up-hill from the moist gulch to avoid mosquitoes.

The next evening, after a day of lonely travel, she reached Forsyth, a railroad coal stop and little more. From an ancient bachelor who tended the coal and water chutes for the railroad, she learned that from this place a trail swung away from the river and would take her where she wished to go. The old droopy-eyed rogue didn't look like anyone she wished to be around, so she started off at twilight and hiked until full dark, when she no longer could see, and then she bedded off a way, behind a mound. It was a good choice. She heard traffic pass in the night.

The next day she traversed open country so vast she could see into tomorrow; she could see so far ahead that she was looking at country she was still two or three days away from. The great plains were endless but never boring; there were cutbanks and springs and hidden valleys choked with cottonwoods. The land had been grazed, but she saw no livestock, and the buffalo had all been shot away. She felt lonely at times; what if she were in peril? There would be no help for her. So she took great care not to disturb rattlers or make her presence known. Only a few years earlier the tribes roamed freely, and there was still a remnant of those people hidden away in obscure canyons or uplands.

Why would mortals fight over land, when there was so much? There was more here than any reasonable person could use or want, but still it was fought over, and blood had been spilled. The whole of the Métis people could live here without disturbing others. It wasn't a pretty land, but it would do, and it would support cattle, just as it had supported buffalo. So why was this land so coveted? And why were there wars? She could not answer these things.

For days on end she saw no one. Sometimes she dipped deeply into the cornmeal and wheat she carried; other times, she feasted on lush berries and all the fruits of late summer which had not yet succumbed to the antelope and deer and foxes and elk and eagles and hawks.

Her shoes wore out; these had been cobbled, but now she would resort to moccasins, which she could repair as needed. She gained strength as she walked, and the donkey did too. She made sure the beast had ample to graze upon each evening. Once or twice they were stranded without water, but the road did supply most wants and seemed to steer itself toward every spring and seep, and so the miles passed by, and the weather held, with cool evenings and mild days.

And still she saw not a soul. Off to the south a railroad had been forged across this great land, but here it was as if civilization had never arrived. One afternoon she reached a valley with an oxbow river wending through it, and knew it was the Musselshell. Here she discovered deer and antelope and some wild horses, and the prints of shod hooves that suggested traffic. She settled in a grove of red willow brush and quietly bathed herself in the warm, sluggish water, and thought that it was heaven. She kept a sharp eye for visitors, because she felt vulnerable and without defense. She had no weapon other than a butcher knife. She stayed in that gentle haven a day, mending moccasins, sewing rents in her skirts, letting the donkey feast. It was a good place, and she was on a good mission, and somehow she would fulfill the task given to her by her name saint.

Soon after that, she found herself drawing ever closer to the Little Snowies, as well as the Judith Mountains, and she knew she was not far from where she would begin to find her people, the ones who fled after several pitched battles fought with the Northwest Mounted Police, or other armies of the ruling English people. The closer she came to those forested slopes, the more signs she saw of human activity: wagon ruts, horse droppings, the cold black ash of campfires, sometimes bones and kitchen waste. But still she saw no one. For two weeks or more she had seen no one. But quite possibly, there were those who were watching her, and sooner or later she would find herself face-to-face with—someone. Soldiers? Renegades? Rough and dangerous men, with assessing gazes?

She muttered swift prayers, often to her name saint asking her protector to intercede and help her complete this strange mission.

The moment came when she was not far from the foothills. She rounded a bend in the trail and confronted a man. He was simply standing ahead of her, unsurprised and waiting. She knew at once he was one of the people. His bright red and white and blue sash told her all she needed to know.

"Bonjour," he said.

So he knew her to be one of the people too.

"You know me, then," she said.

"Only by your blood. You are very foolish to walk this road."

"I'm Therese Trouville," she said. "And, Monsieur?"

"I am simply Pierre. That is all for you to know, for now."

"It is so bad, then?"

"You do not know? Are you new here?"

"I've come a long way. My papa, we have a farm far to the east. Do you know Miles City?"

"Ah, your people fled the Manitoba troubles in the sixties; we here are from Saskatchewan. Come. It is not good for us to stand in this road. We will go there."

He pointed to a gulch along the foot of a ridge. She followed, leading her donkey into the serrated countryside, which could hold a thousand secrets. He led her to a shaded area, where alders, just starting to turn gold, crowded the banks of an intermittent stream, now dry. It was a sweet place, sheltered and peaceful.

"Now then, you walk alone, madame, going from somewhere to somewhere." It was actually a question.

"Monsieur, I blush to tell you, for you will not believe a word of it."

"Then don't tell me," he said.

That startled her. And yet it was all of a piece with his secrecy. "Then tell me what is here, that I should be wary of," she said.

He stared at her, assessing. "Where is your husband, Trouville?"

"Monsieur, I am barely married and will obtain an annulment. I was wed to a man who is against us, and fled. He is no good anyway."

"And his name?"

"Dirk Skye, or North Star in his mother's Shoshone tongue."

"Against us?"

"A translator for the army."

Pierre stared at the blue sky. "Then I can tell you nothing."

This was so shocking to her. A Métis, like herself, saying these things to her. Very well, then.

"I will tell you my story," she said. "Even if you will not hear it." She waited and received only his steadfast gaze, which never left her face. "I live in dishonor among my people. I walked away from a holy wedding. My parents would not have me; I lived with an aunt and uncle. Then I received the vision that brought me here."

She saw not the slightest change in him, or evidence of curiosity, or anything that might be taken for warmth.

She told him of her daily berry hunt, and the redwinged blackbirds, and the heavens so blue and clear that she could see into a different world, and the saint who walked down the ivory stairs, and who was her name saint Therese of Avila, and how this glowing woman in white linen charged her with an impossible and strange task, which was to build a church in the village of Lewistown, where her people were gathering.

"And you see, sir, I am doing that. I know nothing about building churches. But I will find land and men who can carve beams and dress stone and make windows and big doors. And I will find a way because I would not be asked to do this if I could not."

"Who will build your church?" he asked.

"I will find the men."

"Where will you get the land?"

"I will ask for it."

"And who will come to worship if we are all driven away, eh?"

"Maybe no one, monsieur."

"This is a great sign," he said. "I will tell the people about your vision. We have been waiting, and now the waiting is over."

A sign? Of what? But even as she wondered, she knew. It was not just a church of stone and wood she would be building, but a congregation, and that congregation would be her Métis, and the commission she had received was really a promise to her people: build a church and this will be your home. She felt her heart soar.

"What did you say your name is, monsieur?"

"Pierre, and that is my name saint you know."

She stared at this man, wondering how he spotted her, or knew of her coming, and whether it had happened by design, or whether he would help her.

"It is like this," he said. "Our people were defeated by the Mounties this summer, and there were hundreds of families that walked or rode the carts here, because it was known among us that the Judith Basin here would be a good place. There are families living here who came in the seventies. It was because of them that we knew to come here.

"But the Yankee ranchers never liked it; they grazed their cattle on public land and thought it was theirs to keep, and they have made it hard for us to settle. There have been whippings and burnings and destruction of crops and many terrible things. But our people kept coming, and the Yankee ranchers appealed to the army, and got Fort Maginnis, so the army is doing their dirty work now, driving us out of our homes and farms."

"I have heard a little of this, Monsieur Pierre."

"They don't have enough soldiers and this is a very big

land. They thought they could evict us and send us on their way to Canada with a warning not to return, and that is what they did, simply driving us from our homes, or stopping new settlers and turning them north. But, madame, there are not enough soldiers to do it. Our people, forced to leave our farms, start north until we're well away from the blue-shirted army, and then we hide. The Métis won't leave. We have fled to the hills, and moved into mountain canyons, and settled like me on remote creeks for the time being, but none have returned to Canada. We have runners, and we know where the others of us hide, and whenever the army raids another farm, we help the people. We will stay here, madame, but winter is coming and the times will be very hard. There are not enough soldiers in the entire Yankee army to drive the people back to Canada."

"They're hiding?"

"Even as I hide, madame. And you are the sign sent to us. We will help you build your church. For this is what every man and woman of the people have ached to see. You are the messenger we have prayed for, the promise that this will be our home forever. The church will rise, and the people will gather."

"How did you know to expect me?"

"A woman among us had a dream: salvation would come with a Métis woman leading a donkey."

"She dreamed that? She dreamed of me?"

"She is my mother. Every day I have waited here for you to come. I will tell her of this thing, and our messengers will fan out across this territory, and whisper these things. The dream was a true dream, and your vision is a true vision, and we will make this Territory of Montana our home."

Therese was frightened. Everything seemed a thousand times larger now.

"I do not know what to do now," she whispered.

"Do what you were asked to do," Pierre said. "Go to Lewistown. It's a miserable place, with a few stores and a few saloons, and a lot of dangerous cowboys wearing revolvers. But it is set in a handsome valley, and it has ice-cold creeks and plenty of firewood from the nearby forests, and it lies in the heart of the home that is given to us."

"I will go, then," she said.

"And then we will build our church," he said.

eleven

That *homme* Pierre, he seemed to know everything, and he shared all that he knew with her.

"Two Métis families live in Lewistown," he said. "The soldiers don't trouble them. It's only the Métis out on the range who are driven away. Poule Blanc and his wife Cherie live in town. He is a miller and makes flour for the ranches. The other is a widower, Armand Trouffant, who is a firewood dealer. He and his sons harvest the forests and supply the needs of the town. They cut down trees, saw logs, cart wood, and do what lazy Yankees won't do. Go to them. There is no safe place for a Métis woman. You would be fair game for any cowboy or soldier who takes a fancy to you. Poule Blanc lives on the west side of the village, and he and Cherie would find a way for you to subsist safely. Trouffant lives just east of the village."

"I have not one centime," she said.

"Tell them of your vision, and they would be pleased

to take you in," Pierre said. "Tell them you have come to build a church."

"*Merci*, this is helpful. I didn't know what I would find there."

"There's more, madame. There are gangs of young men roaming about, making life hard for our people. They are what's called cowboys, herders of cattle, but the ranchers have set them loose upon us. If you encounter such a gang, you would be in great peril. You understand?"

"How might I protect myself, then?"

"I know of no way other than to invoke the protection of God."

"It is my fate to do what has been given to me, monsieur. And so I will go to meet my fate."

The man she knew only as Pierre gazed sadly. "Adieu, then. Be with God."

She tugged the line and started her donkey along the road once again, knowing that Pierre was still there, watching her walk toward her destiny. She had gotten from him some valuable information. Names of families that might offer safety. A warning about what to fear.

Her donkey trotted along easily, having enjoyed a swift meal while she and Pierre talked. There wasn't much cornmeal left and she was out of most everything else. She still was three long days from this village called Lewistown, where the Métis had collected. But now she was in the country being scoured by soldiers, roamed by hard young men without scruples, but still populated by the Métis, who lived like ghosts in distant valleys and hidden plateaus.

With each hour, the mountains ahead grew larger, and the forests on their slopes grew blacker. She had thought that pines were green, but by some trick of light, the pines that covered these slopes seemed to lay a blanket of blackness only to be checked by outcrops of towering rock.

Somewhere off to the north would be Fort Maginnis. Somewhere ahead would be a low pass that would take a traveler from this high plains country into the Judith Basin, where it was said that grasses grew up to the belly of a cow, year after year. But she saw no soldiers, nor any gangs of armed cowboys. She had expected to see the signs of trouble everywhere; Métis families, leading their oxen north, soldiers, refugees, the poor and lame, struggling along, gangs of these cowboys, adding to misery. Instead she hiked along an empty trail, her peace interrupted only by the occasional alarms of crows. If there was war here, it was swallowed by the land itself.

But late that day she did discover traffic. Ahead was a man sitting in a glowing black-lacquered carriage drawn by two trotters. He plainly was waiting for her. He sat comfortably, holding his hot-blooded horses at bay, his carriage more than ample for his every need. She saw he wore a black suit, a white shirt with a string tie, and a black flat-crowned hat. He had dark muttonchops but no mustache, and eyes that followed her every movement as a predator's might.

She hoped merely to walk by with a nod, keeping her donkey firmly in hand as she passed the bay trotters. But it was not to be. Even as she nodded and started to maneuver past him, he urged the trotter forward until they were athwart the trail. She halted, wary of this man. He examined her as one might examine a carcass of beef, for weight and heft and marbling of the meat. She didn't feel herself in immediate danger, yet she sensed that this powerful man could casually change her life, and do so whether she wished it or not.

"Métis?" he asked.

He was reading her dress, which was certainly typical of the subdued skirts and blouses of the womenfolk. There was more, of course. Her flesh equally revealed her Cree and French bloods. Her blue eyes told him she was not a full-blooded Indian. The ring on her finger bespoke a Christian marriage. The duck-cloth panniers on the donkey were not what full-bloods would employ.

She chose not to answer. Let him think she didn't understand a word. That she spoke only the dialect of her people.

"I think you understand me perfectly well," he said.

She gave no sign of recognition, thinking this would pass if she was patient.

"I wonder what to do with you," he said. "I have several choices. Perhaps you could tell me what to do. You're here illegally, of course. You're a refugee from Canada, where your people caused endless trouble. Well, what do you think?"

She was able to translate that well enough. She couldn't speak his tongue well, but she could sound out each word and put it into her own tongue, so long as he didn't talk swiftly. And he was a leisurely man. And one totally in control.

"You understand perfectly, madam. It's in your face. One choice would be to confiscate the jackass and pack. Then you'd be without means and nature would soon relieve the United States of a small problem. Another would be to deliver you to the army."

"Please do," she said. "Fort Maginnis. My husband works there."

A faint smile lit his saturnine features. "I knew it," he said. "Your husband works there, does he?"

She nodded.

"That's peculiar," he said.

"A civilian," she said.

"Ah, now it is clear. Well, tie the mule behind, and I'll drive you there."

"I will walk."

"You will ride, madam. I would not think of depriving an army wife of amenities."

"I wish to walk. You will forgive me," she said.

"No, I think I would like to learn more about you. And your squaw man."

She slapped him.

He rubbed his cheek and smiled. "Ah, some fire in the squaw."

She tried to slap him again, but he blocked her small brown arm. She saw her chance and led the donkey around the trotters.

"An entertainment, madam, a story for the campfires."

She did not turn around, but felt herself flinching even so. Nothing more happened. After a minute she did turn around and saw him driving away, continuing his passage in the other direction. She knew, even without proof, that this man would make every effort to keep her church from rising. And would rue the day he let her pass him by.

Someday soon she would find out his name, and remember it.

She was sorry she had alluded to Dirk. It was deceptive. He was not her husband except in name only. But it had spared her further trouble and had surprised the man too. So she pardoned herself for deceiving him.

Ahead the road showed evidence of much use; there were ruts, the grasses were ground down, and horse droppings were scattered everywhere. She came to a branch and realized the heavily used trail would probably lead to the fort, where she didn't really wish to go. She took the less worn trail, hoping she wouldn't run into Dirk. He must be somewhere nearby.

The trail wound through pine forest, past rushing creeks, and through small parks where sun streamed onto meadows. But now she saw things that wrenched her. A broken-down Red River cart, its axle shattered, lying in pieces in tall grass. A skeleton of an ox, its bones picked clean. And then a new grave, the earth mounded over the body. At its head was a small cross wrought from two limbs, with a little pewter crucifix appended to it with thong. She paused, aching to find a name, but could see none. These wayfarers had been hurried away. From that point clear to the Judith Basin, she discovered constant signs of strife: an abandoned McClellan saddle, broken in two; a leather case, probably for field glasses. A blue campaign hat. Brass cartridges. Had there been shooting here, at the ford of a creek?

Here too were ruts where the rawhide-clad wheels of the ox carts had dug deep into the soft clay. She found a small petticoat, and a worn moccasin, and an empty burlap bag which she salvaged. Cloth was precious, even burlap. She came upon another grave, this one utterly unmarked. Was it one of her people? A cowboy? An American settler? It too was fresh; the clay had barely settled, and rain had not yet smoothed its surface.

She began a long descent, and the piney woods thinned and surrendered to grassland. She found herself in a valley hemmed by the most beautiful uplands she had ever seen, and knew, from things she had learned earlier, that this was the eastern edge of the Judith Basin, and the prospect would become even more beautiful with every step west. Still, in this entire leg of her trip, she had seen no one. But the signs of tragedy she discovered everywhere were telling her that she walked through a vale of tears.

From the brow of a hill late in the afternoon, she discovered the village of Lewistown, which had bloomed only since the Americans had quieted the Sioux and Cheyenne a few years earlier. She was able to see the town below, nestled snugly on a good creek, a string of false-front stores largely built of logs, a scatter of wooden homes with steep shake-clad roofs. Chimneys constructed of fieldstone and mortar leaked smoke. The place seemed preternaturally quiet. A ranch wagon was parked on the sole business street. Two or three saddle horses were tied to hitch rails.

It would be a beautiful place for a church. Fingers of green seemed to reach right into town, nurturing it. The mountains on the east and south supplied water and wood. No wonder her people had chosen this place over all others to resettle.

She spotted what was probably the wood yard of Armand Trouffant east of town just as she had been told. Stacks of pine logs, limbs, posts, and cut stove wood lay about. She hesitated. Did she wish to contact this man and his sons? She decided instead to continue through the muddy village to the millers on the far side, Poule Blanc and his wife Cherie. She could not say why. She descended the last grade, and into the sunny main street, and now she did see a few people, some of them cattle drovers staring at her with hooded eyes. She didn't care for them, but no one disturbed her. She discovered several gray board and batten saloons, some with no name at all, others with a crudely lettered sign above the door. The Stockman's Rest. The Mint. The Whiskey Jug. She saw very little glass; that precious commodity was not yet plentiful in Lewistown.

She felt herself being closely examined, but ignored the eyes that she knew were peering at her from doors and windows and shaded galleries. Instead, she continued west and was soon at a rushing creek crudely bridged with logs covered with planks. There were two log buildings, one with an undershot waterwheel beside it. The building closer to the road had a crudely painted one-word sign on its front: Blanc. She had reached this remote town, and she had come to the home of a Métis she hoped would help her build her church.

She tied her donkey to a hitch rail and ventured into the building that served as store and home for these people.

She was attended at once by a powerful jet-haired man, as lean and strong as a smith.

"Monsieur Blanc?" she asked.

"Do I know you, madame?"

"*Non,* but you will," she said. "I am Therese Trouville, and I have received a vision," she said.

"Vision! *Sacre bleu!* Not another," he replied. "My friend Louis Riel, he had a vision too. His was to return to Manitoba and treat with the British, and lead our people back to their ancient lands. But the church disowned him, saying his prophecy was not true, and then the Canadians hanged him. I suppose you'll share the same fate," Blanc said.

twelve

*S*he felt the miller's soft gaze on her, a gaze that was assessing in nature as if he were looking for signs of madness. Which he no doubt was. Not many Métis women would walk into his rough building and announce that they had received a vision from a saint—and would commence to build a church.

"You are with your husband, madame?" he asked softly.

"I am alone."

"And you have a place to board?"

"I will find one."

"There are none here—for respectable women. Have you means?"

"Nothing."

"You have a family, madame?"

"*Oui*. My papa, he is Montclair Trouville. My mama, she is Helene."

He shook his head.

"Our cousins are the Desportes. We have friends, the Lesages. We came after the troubles in Manitoba, and settled in this territory as soon as it was safe, after the Sioux and Cheyenne were defeated."

"And do they approve of this—enterprise?"

"I did not give them that choice, monsieur. I was instructed by a heavenly apparition to do this thing, and so I came here."

Blanc stared at her, his fleeting expressions mirroring his inner conversation.

"You have a plan for this church? A churchyard? Masons and carpenters and joiners and ironworkers?"

"*Non,*" she said.

"A place to pasture that donkey?"

"*Non,*" she said. "I was hoping to find refuge—here."

"Madame, my poor household can afford no more boarders. Several of our families, unable to take frail older people, or one or two deformed little ones, cannot take them to Canada, and have begged me for help, and I can offer nothing except a millroom, where there are some bags of grain, some seed, and too many mice."

"Is there a place there, where I may lay my head?"

"There isn't, madame. I am sheltering six, no seven, of those driven from their homes by the army, and I cannot feed them except a little flour."

"Would you need a servant? I am able and healthy, monsieur. I can do chores."

"Ah, *non,* my wife and petite ones are crowded into a single room, and I enjoy an excess of labor and am lacking none."

"Might I do better with the woodcutters—the other Métis?"

The brown-eyed miller drew up straight. "It would not be suitable, madame, with a man and two sons."

Therese felt herself sagging within. For all of the long walk, the thought of her vision, and building a church, had sustained her. But now she was facing reality. Here was a hostile town, barely tolerating two Métis households, a town of drovers and rowdies, men wearing six-guns, false-front saloons, a town unsuited to women of any sort. And here she was, intending to build a church for her people. She would need land. She would need a plan, and artisans. She would need money to pay them. And while all this was happening, she would need to support herself in some respectable way. And she would need to send word out to the Métis hiding in the countryside that here was their home.

She was hungry and worn. Blanc had been kind but could offer her nothing. She tugged the donkey along and traversed the rude town. It was raw; the main street was little more than muck. The foul cross streets were worse. There were no boardwalks to protect her skirts. But she was used to all that. She eyed the saloons, sleeping in the sunlight, and the hardware and general store, which advertised dry goods and groceries. She saw a blacksmith shop, and a harnessmaker. She spotted a livery barn. She saw no butcher or baker but did see a cobbler and a barbershop. There was a wooden residence of some sort. The general store would have some ready-made clothes, mostly for men; women would have to sew their own. She passed through, safe in sunlight, but at night this place would be dangerous for a single woman. Her silver ring would not spare her and her mixed blood would only invite unwanted advances. But for the moment, with a single wagon parked on the street, and a couple of saddle horses at hitch rails, it was serene.

She continued on to the wood yard and turned in. Here were heaps of firewood, cut and split and drying in the warmth. She discovered mossy logs that had been hauled by wagon to this place. She saw axes and long two-man saws, and a grindstone operated by a treadle, used to sharpen all the blades and axes and saws.

The rude log cabin seemed barely large enough for Armand Trouffant and his sons; there could be no place in it for a woman not connected to the family. And yet, she had no other option.

"Mademoiselle?"

She turned, discovering a blocky dark man in his middle years, with great mustachios curling from his lips and cheeks.

"Je suis Madame . . . Skye," she said, feeling she was using her soon-to-be-jettisoned husband. "You are Monsieur Trouffant?"

He nodded, his eyes roving over her every curve. It was all she could do to stand there, but stand she did.

"I am looking for a safe place to board; I would offer work in exchange."

"I don't believe we've met, eh?"

"Therese . . . Skye. My papa, Montclair Trouville?"

"Ah, Trouville! Red River, *oui?*"

She nodded.

"And he sends you here for what?"

"I came on my own, to fulfill a task given to me . . . by my name saint."

He laughed. "My name saint gave up on me years ago. But we salute each other now and then, eh?"

Plainly, he was waiting for an explanation, and she was afraid that when she revealed her purpose, he would laugh her away. But there could be no avoiding this moment, so she started in.

"Monsieur, I have come upon a sacred mission, and I pray your indulgence while I tell you."

His enormous eyebrows caterpillared up and settled, and he ushered her to some logs suitable for sitting. "You will entertain me here," he said.

That's what it would be. Entertainment!

She told him the story of her vision, and he listened with intense concentration and a small, wicked smile. He obviously wasn't accepting a word of it. She felt a little miffed, and continued piously. She had received a task from heaven above; she would persevere.

"Fantasy," he said. "Superstition, naïveté, silliness, and probably lunacy too."

He was enjoying himself. "I believe in nothing. My mama, she believed the Cree stories. My papa, he believed the church stories. Me, I read Voltaire and think all religionists are demented."

He laughed. "Naïve little thing that you are. And why do you wear a wedding ring, eh?"

"I am married. But I am going to have it annulled as soon as I can hire a church lawyer to plead for me."

"Who to?"

"Dirk Skye. He is a translator for the American soldiers."

"Skye? Ah, there's a name, *ma cherie*, known to the whole world, if this one is the sprout of Barnaby Skye."

"He is. His father was British, but lived here all his days."

"And you want to abandon the son?"

"I already have. He's—I loathe him."

"Come in here," he said, rising. He ushered her into the cabin. It was dark, it stank, it was filthy. Bunks lined two walls, rude projections from the logs. A kitchen was built around a hearth at one end.

"Welcome chez Trouffant," he said. "We will hire you to cook and clean."

"Here?" She was utterly repelled.

"Ah! I will hang some old tarpaulins and you will have your corner."

"Tarpaulins?"

"*Oui*, ratty old ones no good for anything else. You live here, keep house, feed me and my sons, and build your church, eh?"

She stared at the layers of grease, at the small room with no partitions, at the single window high up the log wall.

Trouffant was grinning. "Wait here," he said.

He slipped out and returned bearing an ancient canvas, which he soon hung up to make a dubious wall around a corner bunk. Then he beckoned. "See here. You get a buffalo robe and this, *oui?*"

"The canvas is full of holes!"

"The better to enjoy you, *ma cherie.*"

"But I don't wish to be enjoyed!"

"Well, then just endure it. We will enjoy you even if you don't wish to be enjoyed. You are young and delicious."

"But I must keep my virtue, monsieur. What are your intentions?"

"To be as virtuous as you wish, but not a bit more, eh?"

"Is that a promise?"

"My promise is like that canvas wall, madame. It is full of holes, but it will suffice in the meantime."

She reddened. She had never been in such circumstances. But oddly, she didn't really mind, if the sons were as entertaining as the papa here. "And will your sons respect my privacy?"

"Not unless you sew up all the holes, madame."

"Will you help me build my church?"

He smiled. "Who knows? Churches ruin people, eh?"

She was weary. Here was a bed, of sorts, in a cabin owned by a Métis, of sorts, with a shred or two of virtue, of sorts.

"I must take care of my donkey," she said.

"I'll do that. You start supper. At sundown, my boys will return and will be hungry."

He vanished outside. She stared, wondering what she had gotten herself into. She would soon be enslaved, compromised, and ruined. Or maybe not. If he misbehaved, maybe he'd be the ruined one. The odd thing was, she welcomed the test of wills. The heathen versus the pious woman. The libertine against the virgin. She could not imagine why she didn't just walk away, but she had no intention of that. And besides, Armand Trouffant intrigued her. She'd never met a rascal before, and now she probably would meet three.

She eyed the miserable stove, with a pot half-filled with dried, caked something or other. She didn't trust it, so she took it out and emptied it in some bushes. She'd start some soup, if she could find any ingredients. Soup was the heart of most Métis meals. Soup could be made of most anything and turn out just fine.

She found a nearby creek and rinsed the pot in it, and

then set to work. She discovered no meat, but there were carrots and squash in a root cellar, and those would have to do. But first, a fire. She collected some kindling and some shavings, and started to lay the combustibles in the stove.

"I'll do that," he said.

She whirled. Trouffant was carrying a slab of meat as well as some onions and potatoes.

"Good," she said. "We'll have a stew."

He set the food on the table and laid the fire in the stove, and lit it with a lucifer. A flame swiftly rose in the stove, and she felt its heat rising through the cast-iron top.

"Madame, we'll help you build your church," he said.

"You? The heathen?"

"This is the most important thing to come upon us. My sons and I, we will build it."

"With field stone?"

"*Non*, madame, log. Many logs. Hard work. And we will get others. We know a few. But we will make the church rise up, just like in your vision. And maybe that will rescue the people like us, eh? You are a special one, touched by something, eh? Who knows what is the truth. I don't. I listen to Cree elders, I listen to priests and French elders, and I don't know anything at all. But you came here, sent by Saint Therese, and I scratch my head and say, good enough. We're going to build that church, eh?"

She began peeling onions, stripping away the brown husks, and then cutting them into pieces, weeping all the while.

"It is not the onions," Trouffant said.

"It is the onions!" she snapped.

thirteen

irk Skye watched the horsemen vanish in the west, taking his two horses and his pack with them. It was very quiet. He stood on a two-rut road across a vast basin brimming with lush grasses, cured brown now. Lewistown was far to the east; Fort Maginnis quite a bit farther. Here were a few open-range ranches, a few farms owned by Métis—if anyone was still there—and an overarching silence.

He might, if he hiked all day and much of the night, alight in Lewistown, where he would get no succor and be taken for a vagrant half-breed, unwelcome in any establishment even if he addressed the occupants in good English. If he hiked another long day he might arrive at the fort and could get help, at least until they heard that Captain Brewer had done the unusual thing of discharging him during the middle of operations.

He studied the hoofprints in the dust, looking for anything that might make them unique in the crush of prints, and he did find a few things. A shoe that dug deeper on the left; a horse with large cleated shoes. Then he started west. The roving cowboys were going somewhere, so he would go that way too. He would probably end up hungry, but he knew a few things about living off the land gotten from his father and might keep himself fed.

This trail was familiar to him. One branch wound south toward White Sulphur Springs. Another plowed toward Great Falls. The whole area was open range, where branded herds sometimes intermingled and were sorted out in the fall in great communal roundups. Maybe he'd end up at a ranch this night. They were more hospitable to strangers than towns. They even welcomed mixed-bloods—sometimes.

This country was riven by cold creeks, and at each one he drank gratefully. He hiked slowly west, studying the prints in the dust, keeping an eye out for the cleated shoes, as well as the prints of his own horses. It was not hard. So long as it didn't storm, he would have a trail he might follow.

He forded a shallow creek and stopped to have a bite to eat. He pulled up cattails, washed the muck away from the knobby roots, and then cut the roots into small pieces with his jackknife. The bits of root tasted terrible, but they were almost pure starch and would sustain him. Then he continued, harvesting occasional berries as he went.

The heavens were an aching blue and the September sun warm, without the power to scorch him. It would be good to recover his pack as well as the horses, because the pack held a coat against sudden cold.

He continued in this leisurely fashion through much of the day, and then the hoofprints turned south toward the foothills of the Big Snowy Mountains two or three miles distant. There wasn't much of a trail now, but the horse with the cleated shoes was heading this way and so were his own. He proceeded cautiously. This was Tomorrow Country, where anyone with a sharp eye could see into the next day. For all Dirk knew, that bunch of cowboys was keeping a careful eye on him and planning a little unpleasantness.

As twilight approached, Dirk spotted a string of smoke rising quietly ahead. It was time to abandon the two-rut trail, so he slipped to the left and climbed, staying under the brow of a long ridge so he would not be skylined. He rounded a bend and found himself staring at a compact farm nestled in the foothills. There were extensive gardens and a log home with a generous porch and fieldstone chimney. There was a large woodpile. The owner had cut a large supply of cordwood. There was only a small pen, suited for two or three animals, but within it were seven horses, including his own two. Saddles were strung over the rail. He supposed his packsaddle and saddle were too, but couldn't see well enough to know. Beyond the pen he saw a broken cart, a wheel missing, lying in weeds. He looked for a dog and saw none.

This was a Métis farm, not a ranch building. But the occupants were cowboys from one of the ranches, and it was a good assumption they were occupying the place to drive away the owners should they return. A rancher was usurping the farm.

Dirk studied the surrounding country, looking for telltale graves, clay mounds, with markers—or maybe without markers. He saw none. The light was failing. He eyed the horses, three of which were staring at him. He located the gate, which was wide and would probably squeak loudly if he opened it. Everything the Métis built squeaked because they used wood.

His knowledge of the ways of the Métis might help him here. The pen would likely be bound together with rawhide which had been applied wet and allowed to dry to iron hardness. With a little patience, Dirk could cut through it and remove the poles from the rear of the pen—if the horses would not take alarm and bring cowboys boiling out of the log house.

He would try it. If he could not find his own saddles in the dark, any other would do. He might have to leave his pack. Getting the packsaddle and pack on his second horse would be pushing his luck to its limits. Maybe he could settle for a few items in his pack—if he could find it: his coat, the revolver, a bedroll.

One of the cowboys emerged from the cabin, lit a smoke, and sat down on the lip of the porch. He was followed by another, and a third. One of them tossed a cigarette aside, a small arc of orange light. Dirk thought he saw a fourth head for the outhouse in the murk. There was no dog.

The cowboys drifted inside. A lamp flared briefly and died a few minutes later.

Night settled and he felt the cold eddy out of the mountains. He knew enough to wait. It would be hours before he could move. He heard a distant wolf and an answering bark not far away, and smiled. The wolves seemed to be a good omen.

An hour passed. A cowboy materialized on the porch, did something, and vanished inside.

The chill intensified. Dirk stretched, worked his muscles to keep them limber, and waited. A quarter moon rose, supplying some needed light. He was in luck. There was just enough light to see what he was up to. He waited some infinity longer and finally stretched his aching body and began a quiet trek toward the farmhouse. The moon vanished behind a cloud, and he proceeded in blank darkness. He bumped into the pen, stirring the horses. He felt along the top pole to the post, felt the rawhide binding, and felt the bindings on the middle and lower poles. He sawed away the bottom two, easing the poles to the ground. Then he cut the bindings at the other side and removed the poles. Only the top pole remained in place. The horses didn't move. It was too dark to tell which were his own. He explored the top pole clear around the pen, stirring the horses a little. He saw nothing moving at the farmhouse. He found a saddle, but knew it wasn't his; this one had basket weave stamping on the skirts; his didn't. He found other saddles and narrowed the choice down to two with smooth skirts. His was not a stockman's saddle, and it took only a cursory sweep of his hands to decide which one was his.

Now the tricky part. He needed his own bridles, and there would be no time to adjust someone else's to his horses. He found none at all on the top pole, and realized they were all hanging over the porch rails at the log farmhouse. He was nerving himself to head that way when the moon reappeared, making everything suddenly bright. He spotted his own bridles, which were less gaudy than the cowboys' and scooped them up carefully, retreating to the safety of the pen, where the horses continued to stir. He bridled his bay and then the buckskin, saddled the buckskin, and led both horses to the far side of the pen, where only the top pole remained. He sawed that free with his knife, set it aside, and led his horses out. The other horses followed. He led his toward the ridge, rather than the road out to the valley, while the ranch horses stopped to graze.

He found himself in the extensive vegetable garden. A heap of empty burlap bags lay on the grass. Good enough. He stepped off his buckskin and loaded a sack with squash. He cut a neck hole and armholes in two other sacks and pulled them over his head. They would do for a coat as long as the wind didn't blow. He grabbed two more sacks for future use, stepped into his stirrups again, and rode toward the ridge. Just about then the light failed again, which suited him fine. He topped the ridge and set off toward Lewistown by dead reckoning, sensing only that the Snowy Mountains were on his right.

He had some decisions to make. Report to Fort Maginnis, as directed by Captain Brewer? Some good might come of it. He might be able to reoutfit. Head for Miles City? He had no reason to return there. She was gone.

He moved quietly through the night, pondering his fate. He felt like giving the bay a free rein, and let the horse take him wherever it chose to go—which would be to the nearest lush pasture. This Judith country was probably the finest ranch land in all the West; certainly in the West he knew. And that was why the Métis were being driven out. Why lordly ranchers like Harley Bain were stuffing cowboys into the homesteads of the evicted Métis. Keep them out!

He stopped the bay. The sky had cleared off, and now the whole bowl of the heavens glittered above him. He found his namesake, the North Star, the Star That Never Moves, in the stories of his mother's people. It was time to be North Star. Sometimes he was Dirk, loving his father and his father's European world. But now his mother's blood was riding his veins, coursing through his heart, pumping through his arms and hands and feet and legs. The mixed-blood Métis could well be his people, no matter that he was Shoshone. He would come to them, bond with them, do what he could for them. He would try to undo everything his employer, the army, had tried to do.

Then he laughed at himself. He lacked an outfit. He was wearing burlap. He had no weapons, little food, some loose change in his britches. He had only a passion for justice, and a tenderness toward those uprooted wretches whose lives and dreams were being destroyed. He knew then, in the icy cold of an October night, what he must do. If the Métis had been driven toward Canada, then he would head north. If they were hiding from the army, it might be in distant mountain islands rising out of the great plains, such as the Little Rockies to the north. Or the Highwoods. Or maybe the Missouri Breaks, those mysterious canyons so remote that few had seen them, where the hunted could hide.

He would head for the Missouri Breaks and somehow find a way to help these people, and help himself. He knew intuitively that's where he would find these refugees. The breaks stretched deep into the prairies back from the Missouri River. They twisted every direction, and branched into a thousand side canyons. They offered game, water, shelter, fish, concealment, firewood, and safety. And even escape down the river, if it came to that.

He suddenly felt just fine. The pall of indecision lifted,

and he spurred the buckskin north, straight toward the North Star, riding through a night so thick he could scarcely see where he was going. At the earliest crack of dawn, he stopped at an icy rivulet for a rest. He let the horses graze and pulled a squash from his sack. With his jackknife he sliced into it, cut out a long thin strip, peeled off the rind, and cut the cold hard meat into small pieces, which he could masticate and eventually swallow. Thus did he pursue a breakfast that was surprisingly pleasant, in spite of the lack of coffee or meat or cereal.

After an hour, with the sky well lit in the east, he climbed onto the buckskin and headed north again. He had gone only a short while when he topped a rise and discovered a ranch close by. He swiftly backed off, not wanting to skyline himself. A column of smoke rose from a kitchen and another from a bunkhouse. He eyed the place, knowing there would be dogs, but saw none. He was much too close, so he rode a wide circle around the ranch, crossing numerous horse trails where the riders had fanned out to do a day's work.

Ranch life was varied. Some days the cowboys worked hard, especially during calving, branding, castrating, and shipping. Other times, the cowboys seemed almost to loaf through the days. Some of those who toiled endlessly, such as farmers and woodcutters, thought that cowboys were lazy, riding horses all day and doing very little to exercise their muscles. Dirk thought it would be an easier life than bucking a plow, weeding, or cutting wood.

He continued north, struck the Judith River, and followed it as it wound toward the Missouri, through rough, anonymous country. Here were places where men with secrets could keep them.

At the nooning he worked more of the squash into bits and downed them. He found some prairie turnips and harvested them, adding to his sack. He had the feeling at times that he was being watched but he saw no one, so he rode wearily onward, toward whatever destiny lay in wait. Somewhere ahead would be an invisible border between settled country and wilderness, and deep in there somewhere would be the people he wished to reach.

fourteen

irk rode toward Canada. He was on a road to nowhere. He had no good reason to go north but neither did he have reason to go south or west or east. He told himself he wanted to help these people, but in fact he was the one needing help. He tried to list what he could do for them and it amounted to nothing much. He knew the English-speaking world and could interpret it for these French Canadians. But mostly he rode north simply because his heart drove him north; there was no logic in it. Who had said the heart has its reasons which reason knows not of? He couldn't remember. Pascal, maybe.

He sawed off pieces of raw squash and masticated them one after another, but felt more and more starved. He found occasional buffalo berries and cattail roots to vary his intake. But nothing allayed the deepening need in his belly. He wanted meat; a buffalo rib, sizzling hot, dripping fat. But the buffalo were gone. No one had seen a buffalo for years.

The weather turned. Gray clouds with iron bellies scudded over and lashed him with rain. His two layers of burlap were no defense against it. He rode into the Judith bottoms, looking for shelter in the willow brush or perhaps deep in the roots of a cottonwood. He was plenty cold, and getting more so every moment.

A noble bronze-leafed cottonwood beckoned. He rode that way as icy rain smashed into him and found what he was looking for: giant roots splayed outward, with deep hollows between. Swiftly he cleaned debris out, unsaddled the buckskin, unfolded the saddle blanket, wrapped himself in its blessed warmth, and wedged himself in. He lacked a picket line or halter for the horse, and ended up holding on to the reins.

"Sorry," he said.

The back of the buckskin, and also the bay, had blackened with rainwater.

But he was in a good spot, leeward of the drenching rain, under the canopy of yellowing leaves that soon would tumble to earth. He saw no break in the lowering clouds, and knew this ordeal would not end soon. He could have ridden south. He could be on his way to Crow Agency, where he was known. He could have started for Bozeman City. He might have found menial employment there, maybe swamping a white man's saloon where he could not legally have a drink. Something for his belly, anyway. He eyed the burlap sack of squash, thoroughly blackened now with rain, and decided simply to wait. He was more or less dry, and the thin warmth of the saddle blanket sufficed.

It all called to question why he was in a remote river bottom, hiding from the drumming rain, en route to—

what? To the Métis, of course. But why? He was a well-educated man with English running in his veins; he knew Shakespeare and Euclidean geometry. He could teach the aborigines. But he also knew the beat of drums and feared Owl, the most sinister of all creatures in his mother's world.

He was puzzled with himself and accused himself of following impulse rather than setting a rational goal. The honest to God truth was that he was adrift and hadn't the faintest idea how to take command of his life.

Instead he was dodging the freezing rain in the middle of nowhere. He was crazy. He was an idiot. It was because of the suffering Métis. The decision to try to find them had been made not with rational self-interest, but with his heart—and with a rage to correct an injustice. For now the enemies of the Métis, these white ranchers and their drovers, had become Dirk's enemies too, and what sent his blood pumping through him was a passion. It wasn't until this moment, harried by icy rain, driven here by a firing, and then by the casual cruelty of cowboys, that he understood. The Métis were his brothers and sisters.

It was a moment of recognition. Here in the protective shoulders of a cottonwood, he had come face-to-face with himself. He would expend his energies, and maybe his life, helping these unwanted, homeless, landless, persecuted people.

An occasional gust of wind laced his face with rain. He hunkered lower, stared at the miserable buckskin, black now with icy water. The horse stared back. This rain would not soon go away. Dirk decided to take a chance. He stood, pulled the bridle off, and turned the horse loose. The buckskin stood for a moment, then wheeled, rump into the cold, and began stripping brush with his big yellow teeth. Then he freed the bay. Neither horse would go anywhere very far.

Dirk retrieved his sack of squash, and began cutting tiny slices of one, and masticating the miserable food. It would help sustain him: what else mattered?

The pelting rain surrendered to drizzle, which surrendered to mist and occasional gusts of wetness. Dirk scraped what water he could from the buckskin, saddled up, collected the bay, and started north again. He was only an hour from the breaks, where the Missouri had cut deep into the endless plains, creating a mysterious hinterland of cliffs and gullies, hidden oases and promontories. It could hide a nation, and if Dirk was guessing right, that is exactly what it was doing.

The horses splashed through puddles that reflected the bitter ice of the heavens, and the land rose up around him until the prairie was hundreds of feet above. There were mysterious trails along the river, but tortuous ones with wide detours where the river churned tight against rocky cliffs. He would pursue these until he was discovered. A hiding people would make that decision; he would be found, rather than find these people. They were no great distance from the Judith Basin, from which they had been driven, and poised to return if they could.

He spotted several mule deer but could not make meat. He discovered mountain sheep staring at him from a bluff, and watched a black bear berrying in brush. He scared up marmots and foxes and coyotes. He watched trout leap in backwaters, and red-winged blackbirds flock. But he saw no mortal, though he supposed mortals saw him.

An hour later, with the air crisp and the heavens blue

again, he did discover a mortal, an armed Métis man, with a trimmed black beard and a leather jerkin, sitting on a rock beside the trail.

"Bonsoir," the man said.

Dirk slowed his mount and nodded.

"You are the one with the soldiers," the man said.

"I am here on my own. I work for no one," Dirk said.

"That does not disarm my mind," he replied.

"You are right to be wary," Dirk said. "As you can see, I need help."

The man eyed the two burlap sacks Dirk was wearing, the horses, and finally settled on the rain-blackened sack.

"Squash from a Métis garden," Dirk said.

He undid the sack and slowly lowered it. "All there is to eat."

"Then your visit is good for something," the man said.

"Monsieur, I am Dirk Skye, two bloods like yourself, Shoshone and English. May I tell you my story?"

The Métis nodded. "I might listen," he said. "I have nothing better to do."

Dirk did, in halting French. He knew the words, but had to translate from English. The discharge by Captain Brewer. The loss of everything to the cowboy gang. Tracking the cowboys to a Métis farm; fleeing with his horses and a bag from the gardens. And his decision to come here, where he was sure some of the people would be hiding, hoping for the moment they could return.

"The cattle herders occupy our farms?" the man asked.

"The one I visited, anyway. And I think others too."

"Why are you here?"

"I have two bloods."

The Métis smiled. "And nothing to wear or eat. So you come to get these from us—even though we haven't enough to warm or feed our own."

"Well, I'll trade that bag of squash for your jerkin."

The Métis laughed suddenly. "Come," he said. "That squash, *mon ami*, is from my garden. I am Lorenz Sylvestre."

Dirk dismounted, intending to lead the horses, but the Métis took the reins of the buckskin. They worked swiftly into a hinterland of gloomy cliffs and hidden valleys, deep below the surface of the plains. Then they rounded a bend into a bright meadow, barely beginning to yellow, where several Métis families had fashioned a refuge.

His captor, if that's what he was, swiftly collected the Métis around him, talking a dialect of French and Cree so fast that Dirk couldn't keep up, though he got the gist. These people were dressed in Métis fashion, the women in the drabbest imaginable skirts and blouses, the men gaudy and colorful and very hairy. Children clung to their mothers' skirts, eyeing him distrustfully. But it was plain to all that this man, with burlap for a coat and bare horses and a sack of squash, posed no great danger to them, and soon their caution became curiosity.

"Is it that you are the one who married the Trouville girl?" one man asked.

Dirk nodded. He didn't want to go into that.

"Ah! She ran out! Good thinking on her part!" the gent said.

The Métis laughed. More than laughed. They rollicked. He had not expected to see this desperate people enjoying a rowdy moment, but then again, the Métis had two bloods and anything could happen.

The women took the bag of squash and soon had some

split open and baking in a tin oven. They intended to feed him from his own stores, which suited him fine. The men turned the horses out among their own stock. There was no place to go, except up barren cliffs, and no reason for animals to run off, given the good pasture and water in this obscure place.

As the day waned, a few other Métis, from surrounding gulches, materialized. Apparently word had gone out. Dirk sat, warmed by small hot fires. No one had introduced him to all these people; not yet. But he sensed that this evening there would be a real powwow and a lot of questions. He sat quietly, trying to anticipate what might be asked and form some answer.

"Yes, monsieur, the army is still rooting out your people. No, monsieur, there is not enough of them to do much except send you on your way. They'll get tired of it and return to their posts. But you now face a worse problem: the ranchers have put their men on your homesteads and farms. Now that's the worst trouble."

But instead, these people busied themselves with their daily life. Two couriers returned from a hunt, dragging the carcass of a doe. They strung her up and swiftly gutted and skinned and quartered her, and soon venison was boiling in the great black kettles that blended the meats and staples of these people.

Now and then one or another Métis elder did sit beside Dirk, mostly to share small talk. It was as if there was nothing Dirk could tell them, and nothing they could say to Dirk, and so they mostly sat and watched the women hurry a feast together. These people had built sturdy shelters, mostly walled with sod and covered with canvas roofs. He marveled that they could create some semblance of a home, even while they awaited whatever the future would bring. He saw no Red River carts here, though.

Now at last Dirk was introduced: LaFontaine, LeSage, Langois, Cartier, LeBoeuf, family upon family. These men wore moccasins now; their cobbled boots had no doubt worn out in the exodus. And some of their corduroy britches had been replaced by deerskin pants and fringed elk-skin jackets.

They served him a steaming bowl of stew, which he was expected to sip and eat by tilting the wooden bowl. He ate gratefully, noting squash was among the roots and vegetables in the stew. He wasn't the only hungry person. The crowd drained off the stew with joy and lust.

After a cheerful dinner, while the bonfires blazed, the men lifted their precious fiddles out of their nests, tuned the catgut, and began a musicale, a gentle and plaintive melody at first, which gave way to heated bursts of song, French ballads mixed with drum sounds that must be Cree, which gave way to a firelit step dance, sweeping around in circles, in the remotest corner of the United States. And even the drabbest of the Métis women were transformed into beauties.

fifteen

*M*étis men put their fiddles away, and the people drifted to their separate camps deep in the Missouri Breaks. A hard white moon shone above. Dirk thought there would be frost before the sun struggled upward in the morning.

"Voyons!" Sylvestre said. Dirk wrapped his saddle blanket about his person and followed. Sylvestre simply led him to a rock ledge and settled there, legs dangling.

"You have come here, *mon ami*, for something," the Métis said.

"A free feed," Dirk replied.

Sylvestre didn't smile. Food was the most critical problem. He stared into the mysterious cold, a big, dark, troubled man.

"That little farm, ah, *mon ami*, I poured my heart into it. We arrived seven years ago. After the Red River troubles, when our holdings were ripped from us by the English Earl Selkirk, we drifted. Then we learned the Sioux and Cheyenne were no longer a menace, and we came. We found a well-watered place, next to timber. I made a farm. I hewed down the pines, plowed the soil, put in the seed, built a cabin, little by little. My wife, Maude, my girls, the boy, all helped. We worked, monsieur. We worked from before dawn until we could stand no more. There were no days off. We did not ride around like lazy cowboys yodeling at the moon, but we cut wood, we planted, we harvested, we built a root cellar, we made the good earth yield to us. We bothered no one. We traded for a few things in Lewistown. I bought bolts of gingham and velvet for the women, needles and thread, and thus we lived, eh?"

"You and many others, I take it," Dirk said.

"Some. We weren't many. Five, six families. Not until these last months, when all the Métis fleeing Canada flooded in here. And *les Americains,* they took notice, *oui?* They saw my people cross the line and try to take up land."

"And they got the army to drive you back."

Sylvestre shrugged. "There is no back. The border is watched. If Métis try to return to Canada, the Royal Canadian Mounted Police chase us. So here we are." He waved at the rugged moonlit cliffs. "Here we are. Trapped. No place to go. We live on game. But the game is being shot out. This winter we will eat the last deer, the last antelope, the last elk. We will eat the last fish, and then we will eat our last ox and last mule, eh?"

"How many Métis are trapped?"

"Who knows, eh? A few hundred maybe. We are scattered up and down the Missouri River, hidden away, trying to survive, waiting to die. We hope the army quits. We think it will. This thing, it was the ranchers that wanted us out. They want every scrap of land for themselves. The army?" He shrugged. "This did not come from Washington. The ranchers talked the generals and colonels and majors into doing their dirty work. So maybe the army will quit soon, eh?"

"You're mostly right, sir. Most of the officers and men would like to pack up. But there are a few—I was commanded by one—who think this country should be for English-speakers, and they are very serious about driving you away. They don't want anyone here who is not Northern European."

Sylvestre shrugged. "I am half, more or less, eh? So what do I get? Half citizenship? Half a homestead? Half a vote? Half a tax? Maybe half the justice, eh?"

"Half a brandy," Dirk said.

Sylvestre chuckled. "Half a wife, maybe."

"Less than that. Look at me. I've got two bloods and a runaway wife."

Sylvestre leaned over. "That was bad. That girl, forget her. How could you want her, eh?"

Dirk didn't feel like responding.

"The farm of mine. How do I get it back, eh?"

"It won't be easy, Lorenz. There's two or three cowboys living there, and they're armed."

"Ah! Cowboys are lazy. They sit on horses all day. They hate to walk. They can't even walk to the outhouse without whining. They can't hunt; whoever heard of a cowboy making meat, eh? They got six-guns, but that's so they can pound staples into fence posts. When the time comes, I'll chase them away."

"How do you know when that'll be?"

"We got runners. They're true wilderness men. *Couriers du bois.* They keep an eye on everything, and the ranchers never see. We know what's what. They come back here every few days and tell us what they see, and then go out again. Like, right now, the army's over near Square Butte. The runners tell me."

"What if you can't chase off the cowboys?"

"Hey, bonehead. You don't know how dumb cowboys are. They're from Texas and that makes them all the dumber. The cows are smarter than they are. I respect a cow. I respect a bull. I even respect a steer even if he's lost his eggs."

"They may be dumb, but they've got revolvers."

"Revolvers! That's so they can swagger. Hey! What smart man wants to be a cowboy, eh? What's there to do but talk to cows, eh? Once the army quits, and there's nothing but cowboys around, we'll show dem what's what."

"They can be quick with their six-guns, Lorenz."

"What good is that, eh? We make babies faster than cowboys. By the time a cowboy finds a woman he's forty years old and can't make babies. You know how many babies I've made?"

Sylvestre held up seven fingers. "And I'm not done yet, either. You marry a Métis woman, you make babies. Maybe that's why that one quit you. She didn't think you could make babies good enough. She's gonna find a Métis man and make lots of babies."

"How many babies are you going to make, Lorenz?"

"Two, three women's worth of babies. Pretty soon, there's Métis everywhere. Now you go look at one of them big ranches, like Harley Bain's got. There's no babies being made anywhere. You go look at the bunkhouse, no babies around there. You go look at the big house where the boss lives, no babies around there. Or maybe the wife is back East, so no babies get made. There's no babies in all the Judith country. No babies on ranches, no babies in Lewistown, no babies at Fort Maginnis. So what's gonna happen? Métis everywhere, pretty quick. The cowboys, all they got is lead bullets. So they don't make nothing."

"They make a lot of baby cows."

"Yah, they help mama cows. They got six-guns and help make calves. Some life! Now you take a Métis, he's gonna make babies. And then we'll get our land back."

It was getting late, and Dirk was cold. "You got a place for me to stay?" he asked.

"Not in my house. I got six girls in there and a wife. You can sleep out here somewhere."

"You got a bedroll for me?"

"Maybe you need a woman to stay warm. The Beauchamps, over there, they got a few your age, keep you warm. I'll go ask."

"Ah, I just want a couple of blankets."

"We ain't got blankets enough. And the buffalo robes, they're all gone. Buffalo gone. Let me find a couple of Métis girls. You're no cowboy. You like women. You get two, three hugging you and you stay real warm, eh?"

Sylvestre rose swiftly and padded toward a distant log and canvas hut. Dirk followed reluctantly through the hard-edged moonlight.

"Hey, Claude! I'm giving this here half-breed to you," he yelled.

A moment later a skinny Métis emerged into the white light. "Oh, that one. *Oui, oui,* he can come in. I got women all over the floor. Take your pick. You get to marry her, whichever one you choose. We get a priest sooner or later for you."

"Ah . . ."

"You only got to marry her for one night. You say, I gonna marry you this one night, okay? She says, well, dat's good. Just this one night. I don't wanna marry no stranger for more than one night."

"But I'm already married."

"Yeah, we heard about her. Smart woman, she change her mind and kick you out before you're in. You no more married than a steer is married."

"Who are you?"

"Beauchamps, with Claude in front."

"Well, Monsieur Beauchamps, I'm thinking maybe I'll just borrow a bedroll and sleep out here somewhere."

"No you don't; in the cold you get sick. I got daughters fill up the whole floor. You can't walk in there without stumbling on daughters, eh?"

It was going to be sleep out in the frosty night without a bedroll, or accept the offer. He chose comfort.

Claude Beauchamps led him into the pitch-dark hut, which badly needed ventilation.

"Who is it, Papa?" asked a female.

"This here's Dirk Skye. Maybe he'll marry you for one night and divorce you in the morning. He's got to say the word. I marry you tonight. Dat's what he's got to say."

"I just want to sleep," Dirk said.

"Tough luck for you," Beauchamps said, "You can't. You got too many women."

Dirk stepped gingerly into the black hut. Boughs had been laid thickly over the dirt, and ancient buffalo robes on top of those, keeping the dampness and cold at bay.

"You fight over him," Beauchamps said, and vanished into a corner.

Dirk thought of a plan. "I marry all of you for this night," he said.

There were a few squeals and several sighs.

"I'm Clothilde, me first," a voice said.

"*Non, non,* I am oldest, so me first," said someone with a sweet voice.

"*Non,* you will wear him out," said another.

Dirk needed to lie down. He was worn-out. He edged farther into the cabin, feeling his way along, bumping into flesh, until he found a bare spot, with soft robes under it. He settled down, amid much rustling and shifting and sighs. He edged his moccasins outward, bumping into something, and directed them to the left, which yielded space. He eased himself down, and laid back, brushing someone or other, but eventually he got himself stretched out, and began to relax. A shelter at last. Warmth, softness under him, canvas overhead, a chance to sleep, which he badly needed.

A small hand wandered over his chest, followed by more movement. He ignored it. But then someone kissed him soundly, a long, lingering, sweet kiss that settled on his lips, while the small hand caressed his scruffy beard and played with his grimy hair.

"I'm Clothilde," she whispered, "and you're my husband now."

"No he's not," said another voice, and there was a violent tug. Clothilde disappeared, and someone else was attacking.

"I'm divorcing you all," Dirk said. "I want to sleep."

"You can't marry us and divorce us the same hour. You have to wait until morning," a sweet voice said.

"I'm already married," Dirk muttered. "Her name is

Therese. Father LeBoeuf married us just a few weeks ago at Miles City. So you'll all have to wait."

"Therese Trouville," said a female voice that sounded more maternal. Maybe it was Beauchamps's wife. "I know who she is. Good family. We are cousins."

"All Métis are cousins. That's because everyone marries everyone."

He didn't care what he said. He just wanted to sleep. He had come a long way, in cold, that day.

"*C'est vrais,*" said Beauchamps. "These are country marriages. Madame and I, we have a country marriage. We marry and pretty soon the church gets around to blessing it. We have four daughters before the church comes around. That is the way of the Métis. Pretty soon a priest shows up and says the words, and we're married for good. But up until he comes, we have our country weddings. Like now. You can marry or not marry or try another, just like I say. You can try out one, and try out another tomorrow, petite country weddings, eh?"

"I'm devoted to the Coyote," Dirk said.

"Coyote!" whispered a voice. "You are a bad man."

"I am a friend of the owl," he said.

"Owl! Why didn't you tell us! Owls are bad luck," whispered the voice nearest to him.

"I am a heathen," he said.

"Then the church won't marry us to you," said another voice.

"Bad luck," sighed some young lady or another.

At long last, Dirk did not feel assorted hands crawling over him, and he fell asleep in a few moments.

sixteen

*D*irk Skye knew his very presence was burdening these desperate people, and yet he lingered day after day. He wandered up the neighboring gulches and canyons, and found other Métis families living hand-to-mouth, hiding from the United States Army and the gangs of white men roaming the Judith country.

The Métis were surviving on game, but that wouldn't last long. Their women were digging up any roots they could eat, harvesting berries, hunting turtles, and killing prairie birds, all for the stew pots. The men hunted, always fearful that their shots would alert the Yankees and send the army down upon them. But so far, the Missouri Breaks nurtured and hid them.

Dirk made friends. He traded the bay horse, which the Métis badly needed, for a good elk-skin coat, a hat and gloves, a buffalo robe to sleep in, and a flint and steel. He saddled his buckskin, borrowed a smoothbore musket, and hunted with the men. His horse gave him an advantage over the Métis who headed out on foot. He reached farther into the lonely canyons and was able to return with mule deer and antelope on two or three occasions. But the meat would only go so far among two or three hundred refugees.

He stayed with the Beauchamps, who had no sons and welcomed whatever meat he could bring to the cook pot. The days shortened and the frosts coated the grasses regularly, and the Métis cast worried glances northward, knowing the time of blizzards could arrive at any time, and they had no way to survive for long if they were trapped and shut in. Reluctantly they built fieldstone and mud-mortar chimneys for their sod houses and began laying in firewood. It had been their plan to filter back to their farms, or start new ones, once the army had retired to its barracks. But the army was still out, still patrolling hills and hinterlands, still evicting or catching Métis families, turning them north, and telling them to head for Canada—or face the consequences.

No one was quite sure what might happen if the army found the Métis gathered here, but everyone was certain it would happen sooner or later.

One day, out hunting, Dirk ran across a group of the newcomers, refugees from Saskatchewan who had headed south in May and June, and who now were trapped.

"What are you going to do?" Dirk asked one, named Paul Beaumarchais.

The man shrugged. "Maybe die, monsieur. Some went back. It's not hard to cross the border but it is hard to take up land. Hard to start over. The British Canadians will not let them settle, and they will wander until a winter storm drops them, and then they will lie frozen for the wolves to eat on."

"And you? And these people?"

"Wait, Monsieur Skye. Wait and wait and wait. Someday the army will go away. Then we will go south. We will go where it is warm. We will follow the sun."

"To Wyoming? Colorado?"

Beaumarchais shrugged. "Wherever it is warmer. Wherever there are field mice and birds and rabbits." He eyed Dirk. "You, monsieur, maybe you don't know hunger."

"I know hunger. I also know what it is to have two bloods. They will think you are worse than if you had one blood. Worse than Indians. Much worse than white men. And you won't speak their tongue, which makes you even worse than that."

The man grinned. "We don't think so good of the damn Yankees, either."

"What will you do if the army doesn't quit?"

"Freeze to death."

"I know something that might help. The army isn't pushing Métis out of the towns. Only out of the open country because the ranchers want the land. If you could filter into towns, like Lewistown or Bozeman City, and find jobs—maybe that would help."

"Ah! My friend Skye, now you talk. The Anglo-Saxons, they are lazy. We work. We work from dawn to dusk. We walk into the woods with our axes and we cut wood all day and half the night. Chop! Chop! Saw, saw! We take a tree, chop it down, cut it into pieces, and load the pieces. We're strong. We saw, we cut, we haul the wood. You take ten cowboys and give them work, and ten Métis and give them work, and the cowboys, they don't do nothing. Half hour, and they quit. They whine. They hurt. They want to go lie down. The whole batch don't make enough stove wood to keep warm for two days. But the Métis, ten of us go cut dry wood in a forest, and we bring back ten cords of wood ready to burn."

"Well, why don't you?"

"Nothing to haul with. We need good wagons."

That was a formidable barrier.

"I'm thinking maybe I could find men with wagons who'd employ you. Freight companies."

"We don't work for nobody! We work for ourselves."

"Good luck," Dirk said.

Dirk returned empty-handed that day. Game was getting scarce. The hunters were trying to feed too many people.

That evening Lorenz Sylvestre came looking for Dirk. "You are the one to talk to," he said. "I need to get to my farm and take something."

"Your farm? Way down there?"

"*Oui*, it is worth it."

"With armed cowboys guarding it?"

"Oui, like I say, it is worth it. You ride your buckskin and I ride a horse I'll borrow, and we'll go through the night, and get what I need."

"This must be something very important, Lorenz."

"*Oui*, that's for sure. Brandy. I got a cask of brandy hid there. We'll go get my brandy, eh? I'll give you some. And a few bottles of redeye too."

"Let me get this straight. We're going to raid your farm, dodge the guards, and get some booze?"

Sylvestre drew himself up and glared. "What could be more important, eh? What could help the winter go by, eh? Ten gallons of brandy, few quarts of whiskey.

Medicine for aches and pains, eh? Happiness for the Frenchies, eh? Hope for the hopeless, eh?"

"That's a long way, two days each way."

"If there's stuff in the garden, we bring it too."

"We'll need a packhorse."

"I got one. And we got some burlap bags."

"How do you know the cowboys haven't found the brandy?"

"I got it hid. It's hid so good my wife, she don't know where I got it. If she found it, it'd be used up. If my neighbors knew, if my boys knew, it'd be used up. So I got it where nobody knows nothing."

Dirk stared at the bright sky. "Let's go. Sleep by day and ride by night. I'd like to know what's happening in the Judith country."

"Ah! You a man like the Métis!"

"No, I'm crazier than you to think about doing this."

"No, you're more Métis than us!" Lorenzo said.

Within the hour they were outfitted. Métis hovered around them, looking uncommonly cheerful. "You bring dat stuff, I'll get out the fiddle," said old Raoul. "We gonna get a dance going."

Dirk sat his weary buckskin thinking his old man would understand. His pa, Barnaby, was a famous drinker who would share a bottle with his wives and howl at the moon. Dirk thought he was a little like his pa. A hundred-mile horseback ride to recover some booze to warm an October night or two would be something his entire family would celebrate.

Dirk and Lorenz Sylvestre departed amid plenty of well-wishing. There were more Métis gathered for the departure than Dirk had seen in the Missouri Breaks. The

moccasin telegraph had been busy. Sylvestre was leading
a bony mule with a pack frame perched on it, and a shovel
and a dozen burlap sacks tied to the frame.

They followed the Judith River out of the trench of the
Missouri, and out onto endless flats, awash in cold moonlight. It was a long, plodding, cold ride. At dawn they
splashed across the river to a forested island where they
could shelter all day. They scared up a deer but didn't
shoot it with Sylvestre's ancient carbine. They were back
into ranching country and needed to stay hidden. So they
picketed the horses on grass, laid out bedrolls, and dozed
in the wan sun, seeing and hearing nothing. One could
ride for weeks through that country without seeing another mortal.

At dusk, feeling sleep-starved in spite of the long rest,
they set out again, working up the Judith River. Now and
then they scared up cattle, which snorted and wheeled
away. They were riding deeper into the pastures of powerful ranchers. Still, it was a free country, and this was public
land.

They worked quietly south, seeing no one. The fall
roundup was done and cattle had been shipped. The
open-range ranches had slid into a quietness that would
not be broken until the first winter storm. Sylvestre took
the lead; he was in his own country now and knew how
to move silently through rolling grasslands. He steered
clear of the main two-rut lane to his farm and managed
to reach a hill overlooking his old homestead at dusk.

There were three ranch hands on the porch, smoking, enjoying the thickening and peaceful evening. Dirk
counted six horses in the pen and wondered if these hands
each had two, or whether there were more men. The

vegetable gardens had scarcely been harvested. The cowboys probably preferred beef. Rows of potatoes, squash,
beets, beans, somewhat frost-damaged and browning,
spread from the farmhouse eastward.

"It gets dark, you dig; I get the brandy," Sylvestre said.

"You sure it's there?"

"I alone know where the cask is."

"You'll have it half-drunk before I even see the cask."

"Maybe you're right, Skye. I will tell you this: we will
take three, four days to get back to our people, eh? We
will make sure the brandy is in good condition, eh? We
will hide in brush and try it out, eh?"

"You'd better tell me where it is. Just in case something goes wrong."

"I damn well ain't going to tell you."

"What's to keep the horses from talking?"

"The horses stay here behind the ridge. I'm gonna
carry le cask."

"While I dig potatoes?"

"Then don't if you don't want to. Try the root cellar,
eh?"

That sounded better to Dirk. He wasn't sure he'd even
see any potatoes he dug up on a dark night.

Then some visitors showed up, clopping along the trail
to the farmhouse. Three more on horseback. There was
light enough left so Dirk could see the newcomers were
cowboys, with big slouch hats and holstered revolvers.

The newcomers ran their horses into the pen, unsaddled, and settled on the broad porch with the others even
as night descended. Dirk watched them light cheroots,
and watched the tips glow orange, and then watched the
whole lot go inside. A lamp flared, and Dirk could see the

newcomers toss bedrolls into corners. After a while, it became clear how this night would go. The ranch hands had settled around Sylvestre's kitchen table and were playing cards and sipping brown stuff. There would be some monthly wages traded before the evening ended. And the game would last most of the night.

It was black and chill now, and Sylvestre was ready. "You go fill some sacks; I'll get the brandy, eh?"

"If there's trouble, I'll meet you on the Judith River, up two or three miles," Dirk said.

Sylvestre grinned. "Trouble? They're getting sauced in there. We got the night to ourselves. Yeeow!"

seventeen

*D*irk felt a little foolish, but fun was fun. He slipped past the homestead with the poker players studying one another and reached the root cellar. He found the door and opened it slightly. It squawked. He eased it farther and peered in. The interior was pitch-dark, and finding any edibles would be a joke. Who could say what was in there? Rattlesnakes, maybe. He glanced behind him. The moon hung just below the northeast horizon, lightening the sky, but it would be a while before it would cast its pale beams into the cellar. He eased the door shut and decided to fill his empty burlap bags from the garden.

He didn't know where Lorenz Sylvestre had made off to; this was the man's homestead, and he could probably find his way around in pitch-black. Dirk stumbled, heading past the pen, and knew every horse was staring at him. But so far, that was not important. He found the garden and found squash that the cowboys had ignored. Well, he'd take some food back to the Missouri Breaks, anyway. The moon topped the horizon now, fat and yellow, casting its jaundiced light across the whole place. He saw something he didn't want to see: Sylvestre leading that bony mule with the pack frame on it, the cask of brandy firmly nestled into the crossbuck.

And every horse in that pen was staring at Sylvestre and his mule.

The mule started it. He lifted his snout and whickered.

Three of the cowboy nags whinnied. The others snorted.

Sylvestre's mule cut loose with a long, loud blat and some snorts.

The light in the cabin died, swiftly snuffed by the cowboys. Then the cowboys tumbled out the door and spread out on the porch, some of them rounding the house and heading for the pens. Two of the cowboys were armed; maybe more. It was hard to see anything in the shadowed porch.

Sylvestre trotted toward the slope, his mule behind him, the cask bouncing on the back of the mule. Dirk kept low, abandoned his squash, and dashed toward the safety of the ridge and his tied-up buckskin.

The cowboys were shouting, "There! Something over there!"

A shot. Two more. Lead hit something hard. Sylvestre abandoned the mule and ran for the ridge, as Dirk was doing. The mule picked up speed and soon passed Sylvestre, topped the hill and vanished beyond the rim.

Dirk heard a couple more snaps and some distant voices. He sensed that the cowboys didn't know what they were shooting at and didn't much care. Most of them stood on the dark porch, studying the surrounding country, which was more and more visible in the light of the rising moon. Dirk didn't tarry; those cowboys would shoot anything that moved.

He slipped over the ridge to safety, and moments later his Métis friend did too, and the two stared at each other, and at the mule, which had joined the horses down a bit. Had they made it?

Sylvestre was smiling so broadly Dirk could see his teeth white in the moonlight. They climbed onto their mounts, and Sylvestre picked up the lead line of the mule, and they rode hard and didn't slow until they had topped the next ridge and could escape.

"Ah, monsieur, this is a moment of joy! A moment of revenge! A moment of paradise," Sylvestre was saying. Now that they were more or less free, he was becoming talkative. Dirk wished the man would hunker low and stare at a night-world filled with menace.

The moon continued to climb, and the moon-shadows shortened.

They reached the Judith River and forded it, hoping to shake anyone following. The cowboys were good trackers and would follow as soon as they had daylight. Then Dirk headed north through the brushy bottoms and forded again, reaching stony ground that would leave no tracks. They continued for miles more, hiding their trail wherever they could, and finally spotted a brush-choked island ahead, where the river braided.

"Ah, Monsieur Skye, I think the time has come for a delectable repast, a chance to enjoy the fruits of our adventure. There rests the cask, fat and heavy, groaning with cheer. Don't you agree?"

Dirk decided he wouldn't mind that one bit. They

slipped into the river again and worked upstream for half a mile in shallow, hock-high water, and then climbed a bank and onto the island. It looked just fine. The brush stood high enough to hide the horses; and there was cured grass everywhere for the weary nags.

The night had grown chill. Dirk slipped off the buckskin, and Sylvestre dropped from the bay, anticipating a medicinal hour of refreshment and rest. In fact, Dirk had been anticipating this moment for most of the night, and now it would come to pass.

Dirk heard a moan that rose out of the earth and gained volume and ended in a wail. *"Sacre bleu!"* Sylvestre whispered. *"Sacre bleu!"*

Dirk headed his way. The mule with the cask lashed to the crossbuck stood patiently. But Sylvestre was groaning, slapping his forehead, and emitting something that sounded suspiciously like sobs. He pointed.

The cask had been perforated amidships, right at its lowest point. The brandy had gurgled out, soaking the saddle blanket, working its way down at the girth strap, and dripping from the belly of the mule. Dirk ran a hand under the belly of the mule, and found wetness there. He was tempted to drink whatever soaked his hand.

"Sacre bleu!" Sylvestre said. "It is the fate of the Métis. We are doomed. We will become extinct. God has quit us. We will all turn sterile and croak."

Dirk untied the straps holding the cask in place and lifted it, hoping to find some brandy remaining— somewhere. But the shot was well nigh perfect, emptying all but a little, and the jarring trip had drained the rest. There was nothing but a faint, enticing odor remaining.

"So where's the redeye you promised?" Dirk asked.

"Those graverobbers found it," Sylvestre said. "We are as dry as the Sahara. I will die of thirst."

"We didn't do very well collecting vegetables either," Dirk said.

"The whole world is against us!" Sylvestre announced. "The heavens are against us. We offended God Himself. We are a doomed people."

"What are you going to tell your people?" Dirk asked. "They're all waiting for the cask. They'll have people out on the promontories looking for us, and the moment we're spotted, they will collect around us, and their thoughts will be only upon that cask."

Sylvestre groaned. "It is too much to bear. I will not return. I will ride to the end of the earth and tumble off. The visage of Lorenz Sylvestre will vanish forever, and the name given me by my parents will be scrubbed from memory."

They didn't have anything to eat. They had counted on purloining a few vegetables and not even that had worked out. Sylvestre settled on the ground and turned sullen. He glared at Dirk, he glared at the mule, he glared at the empty cask beside him. Dirk knew exactly what was in his mind: eat the mule that had betrayed him.

"You need to save the mule for food next winter," Dirk said.

"Next winter won't ever come," Sylvestre said. "There is only now."

"You would waste meat."

"Who cares, eh?"

But Sylvestre did not slit any throats that twilight hour.

Dirk discovered some cattails on the lee side of the

island, pulled them up, washed the knobby white roots, and sliced them into tiny bits. He handed them to Sylvestre, who scorned them with an imperious wave. So Dirk gnawed at them. They were miserable, tasteless food, but food even so.

So passed a miserable night. But it wasn't raining and the cold didn't bite.

They started north even before dawn, with Sylvestre lost in his own dour thoughts. They rode through deep silence as the sun climbed and drove the frost off the brown grasses. They were leaving the Judith Basin when they encountered a black victoria drawn by two trotters, driven by a burly, well-dressed man. Dirk knew exactly who it was. He had seen this man and this rig once before, when Captain Brewer's column was riding north. It was Harley Bain, owner of three enormous ranches, two in the basin, one east of it, all operating on open range owned by the government.

Bain sat quietly, his trotters held at tight rein as Dirk and his Métis friend rode up.

The victoria shone blackly. There wasn't any road grime on it. The trotters looked as if they had just been groomed. The soft quilted leather of the seats looked inviting. Resting on the seat, next to Bain, was a handsome fowling piece, side-by-side barrels shortened to about sixteen inches, blued to perfection, with a checkered walnut stock.

Bain said nothing for the moment; not even a greeting. Instead, he was studying faces and cheekbones and the color of flesh.

Then, staring at Dirk, he broke the silence. "I know you."

"Captain Brewer's column from Fort Keogh, sir. I was the translator."

Bain's black brows arched and settled. "Yes, but I want a name."

"Dirk Skye, Mr. Bain. That's your name, isn't it?"

"Son of the squaw man. There are stories floating through the West about him."

"Barnaby Skye, sir."

"Deserter, womanizer, bigamist, on the wrong side of every white man's law."

Dirk refused to be baited. That side-by-side, no doubt loaded with number ten buckshot, spoke loudly.

"That one, does he speak English?"

"A dialect of French."

"Métis, of course. He has no business here. Neither do you."

"I believe this is public land, sir."

"You are not citizens."

"What you mean is, we're not white men."

"Exactly. The army came at just the right time. We were busy with the roundup, and that took every man I own, and I hadn't the means to stop the carpet beetles. But the army did our job. The army was thorough. We've cleared the entire country of red men. Except for you. What brings you here?"

"I think, sir, that is none of your business."

"Oh, it's my business all right. I'll ask again, and you'll answer, unless you need additional persuasion."

Sylvestre was puzzled. "What is this man, eh?"

"He wants to know our business."

"My business is to turn his carriage upside down and dump him in the river."

Bain was smiling. He understood Sylvestre's dialect well enough.

"Canada, my friends. Canada. My men are free now. Roundup's over. We've shipped the beef. My men have nothing to do. But I can put them to work. A few of this man's relatives—they're all related, you know—are lurking about. It might be fatal to be mistaken for a buffalo or a grizzly bear when my boys go hunting."

"Who's lurking?" Dirk asked.

"The Mounties tell us that only a few Métis returned. Pity, isn't it?"

"You're in touch with the Mounties," Dirk said.

"Of course," Bain said. "Now, I asked you what your business is here, and you've not given me an answer."

"Brandy, Mr. Bain. We came to unearth the mother lode, the source of all joy, the fountain of perpetual comfort."

"Brandy! Brandy!"

"Alas, it is gone. This country was the brandy-fountain of the universe, but the spring has dried up, and the brandy is no more."

"Brandy!"

"We came to fill our thirst. We came to load a barrel upon that sawbuck. We came to collect the elixir of the gods, but the spring has been plugged, Mr. Bain."

Bain rubbed his hands, tugged at his walrus mustachio, scratched his black hair, and eyed his shining two-barrel weapon.

"Where is this alleged spring?"

"Where are the heavenly vineyards, sir? Brandy is grape. Look for grape and you will discover the brandy works."

"What does he want?" Sylvestre asked.

"I want you to ride north and never return. If you return, your neck will fit a noose," Bain said. "We have our own ways with rustlers. There's no trial, and things happen very fast."

"He says for us to depart this vale of tears," Dirk said.

Sylvestre lifted his battered slouch hat, saluted Bain, clamped it down, and started north, leading the mule. Dirk lifted his hat to Bain, smiled, and joined Sylvestre.

eighteen

*B*oth of Trouffant's sons were small and wiry. Therese watched them wheel an overloaded wagon into the yard, put away the ox, and wander into the little cabin.

"Ah, madame, this is Beau and Martin," Armand said. "And this is Madame . . . Skye, is it? who will be helping us."

The sons eyed her sharply, plainly astonished by this turn of events. Beau finally smiled. Martin looked sullen.

Nothing more was said. The boys stared, and then settled at a trestle table wrought from split logs. Therese ladled her stew into whittled wooden bowls and served them. There was no tableware anywhere, and none of these males expected any. She served herself and settled on the floor next to the fire, where she knew a servant would sit. And they expected it and did not invite her to their table.

The boys didn't wait for the stew to cool; they downed it as fast as they could bear to slide it from their bowls into the mouths. They were half-starved, judging from the look of them. She rose, filled their bowls with the last of her stew, and retreated.

They were eyeing her furtively. They finally finished, wiped their mouths with their sleeves, and studied the cabin in the flickering light of the hearth fire. Their gazes had settled on the ratty canvas wall that would separate them from this woman. Martin, the dour one, eyed her thin silver ring. Beau's eyes seemed fixed on her breast.

Trouffant decided it was time to reveal a little more to his sons.

"Madame has received a vision," he said, mocking slightly. "She was minding her business near Miles City when Saint Therese of Avila decided to descend from the heavens and bestow a blessing and a task upon Madame here. I take it the apparition was festooned in white linen, and the air was perfumed, and there was unearthly light, eh? Ah yes, a vision. And our madame here was instructed to come to this place and build a church. Mind you, not build a congregation, but a church. With that, the blessed specter marched back up the golden stairs into heaven, and our new friend here, Madame, marched to this place and intends to erect a church."

Trouffant was enjoying himself, and pretty soon the boys were too. This was a fine story. One didn't hear a good story like this but once or twice in a lifetime.

"Now, Madame's husband is nowhere to be found, it seems, so Madame is on her own, protected by the vows of matrimony, but not by any husband lurking about. But I assured Madame that she would find protection here, more or less, given a few holes in the canvas that will separate us, and of course I assured her of the full cooperation of the Family Trouffant, which will fell the trees, skin the bark off the logs, and build a church around here, at a place where her divine inspiration directs her to build it. Now, I take it that she has not yet decided upon the spot, but she will put up stakes at the corners and then the *frères* Trouffant are going to erect this great edifice in honor of Saint Therese of Avila."

Beau was smiling and nodding. Martin was glowering.

"I work from dawn to dusk, until my hands bleed and my shoulders ache. How does she plan to pay us?" Martin asked.

"Why, that is a matter we've only started to discuss," Armand replied. "I proposed bigamy, and Madame said she'd take it under advisement. She said that the honor of serving the church would more than suffice, and I said we'd take it under advisement."

Therese knew she should gather her things and flee, but she didn't. In some odd way, she was enjoying this, and enjoying the danger of it.

"I think we should give it a try," Beau said. "I will want a kiss for every log I bring to the church."

She reddened. It wasn't even proper to talk about kissing. But she enjoyed it anyway.

"Maybe if we bring enough logs, she'll decide to talk to us," Beau continued. "I have yet to hear her voice. What sort of voice has Madame?"

"I received the vision from above, from God, speaking through my name saint, monsieur. I do not speak with my own voice. If you violate me or disparage my mission, you violate all the hosts of heaven."

"That would be entertaining," said Armand. "It gives a new dimension to being an atheist."

"It is for the Métis," Martin said quietly. "Her vision, it is for our people."

"There aren't any left around here," Armand said.

"But if they knew a church was rising just for them, what then?" Martin said.

She stared at this new Martin, whose glare had subsided. But his gaze lingered hungrily on her face and chest and then her skirts. Martin was the true seducer. The others were just bragging.

The hearth fire ebbed, and with it the energies of these men. She collected their bowls, took them out to the creek, and rinsed them out, and by the time she returned all three of them had taken to their robes, lying on the shelf beds they had hewn out of wood. That didn't surprise her. These men toiled until they dropped. That was the fate of the Métis, she thought. Ceaseless toil, just to survive in some small fashion. She eyed them in the subdued light and saw that Martin was watching her. The others had fallen asleep.

She slipped out again, this time to wash her face in the icy waters, flowing like quicksilver in the moonlight. After she had completed her toilet she returned to the cabin and its pungence of food and sweat and manhood. She could barely make her way to her cloistered corner, but she found the canvas and pulled it aside and settled, fully clad, on the robes that had been offered her.

She wondered what the night would bring. Her mood was not one of watchfulness or fear or suspicion, but rather surrender. Whatever happened to her this night, it would be something to bear in her mission; something she must endure for the sake of that smile and command she had received that electrifying moment weeks earlier.

She lay back rigidly, awaiting the brush of canvas and the groping hand. If she was to be a bride this night, at last, then that would be her fate. She had fled from Dirk Skye, so maybe this was all a part of what the stars held for her. But she heard no brush of canvas, and felt no rough hand caressing her or pulling her skirts up. No. What she did hear was a soft snore, which she somehow associated with Armand, not the boys.

She lay quietly for an hour, her thoughts tracing the memory of Dirk Skye. She drifted into a light sleep, and finally into a restful one, until the clatter of males filled her ears and a thin dawn light filtered into the cabin. She had been no one's bride that night, and her mood surprised her: she was vaguely disappointed.

She arose, slid into her moccasins and tied them, and peered out. The men were all dressed and Armand was stirring up something in a pot. She padded past them and outside, cherishing the sweet air and the frosty dawn. The world was clean and cold.

In time, the young men yoked the ox, gathered their axes and a saw, and rumbled off toward the wooded slopes. Armand began his daily stint of wood chopping, his great axe reducing the piles of deadwood to stove or hearth lengths. He seemed to work without pause, the steady thud of his axe shattering wood. Once in a while she heard the rip of a saw blade, but mostly the thump of his axe. She knew that this was how the Trouffants' lives were playing out. They toiled ceaselessly, no matter what the weather, heat or chill, snow or blistering sun. They were strong, not just of flesh but of heart. It took courage to spend a life metered by the thump of an axe.

She needed to wash clothing. Everything she owned

was begrimed and worn half to shreds. She had only a few spares of anything, which made her task all the more urgent. The men had no soap and she had no money, but she knew a thing or two. At the cold creek she beat the skirts and blouses and camisole with a makeshift paddle, twisting out the water and repeating the process, and then she spread them over naked bushes, devoid of leaf now, to let the wan October sun and the breezes dry them. Then she returned to the cabin to begin that day's stew. Her days would be as toilsome as those of her hosts. But she welcomed the work.

She discovered moldering heaps of their clothing, and set out to wash and mend it, using the same routine on these work-stained trousers and flannel shirts as she had employed on her own. They needed mending, so she approached Trouffant, who paused and leaned into his axe, waiting for her to speak.

"I can mend your things, monsieur," she said. "But I lack the means."

He smiled, hastened into the cabin, and showed her a stash of thick black cord and two coarse needles. There would be no delicate repairs on any of those trousers or shirts.

"*Bien,*" he said, and retreated to the outdoors, where he belonged, and soon she heard the steady whack of his blade splintering off yellow chunks, which he periodically tossed onto a growing heap.

At midday someone with a high-sided wagon drove into the yard. She watched the driver and Trouffant negotiate, and then the pair of them tossed a great heap of wood into the wagon. It was not stacked in an orderly way, but simply tossed into the yawning cavity between the high sides. She saw no money, no pay, exchange hands, and the driver turned his draft horse away, and toward town.

She wondered how many days of relentless toil by the father and two sons had gone into that single wagonload of firewood, and whether they earned much of anything from it from all those English-speaking ranchers and saloon men and storekeepers. It would buy a little food, for men who needed mountains of it to sustain a labor so bitter and hard.

And so the day passed. By evening, she had another stew simmering, some of the men's clothing was mended, and her own was dry and stored in her canvas alcove. Once or twice she had retreated there to lie down for a few moments. She cherished her small private nest, the generous buffalo robe beneath her, the sense of safety and sanctity she had discovered in this austere corner.

At dusk Beau and Martin appeared once again, their wagon groaning under the day's harvest. She stirred the stew and readied it for them when they entered. They eyed her curiously, but she hadn't the slightest idea what they thought of her or how they felt about the woman their father had installed in the cramped cabin.

Still, it didn't take long for them to discover their cleaned and mended britches on their bunks, or the flannel shirts freshly washed, the worn-through elbows sewn tight. She sensed that whatever else they felt about her, her womanhood, the anguish and temptation she forced upon them, they had at least discovered her utility. A mended shirt was a blessing, especially as winter lowered.

She served them and again didn't sit at their table, but sipped her stew seated before the hearth. The men were too weary to talk, and nothing meant more than filling their bellies.

Then Beau turned to her. *"C'est bon,"* he said.

She had found a few seasonings: rosemary, thyme, pepper, basil. Almost anything would improve a stew. The very fact that these work-worn men kept a few spices told her something about them. About the Métis.

Armand stuffed tobacco into a pipe and lit it with a lucifer, and smoked awhile as she cleared away the bowls.

"I've been thinking about the church," he said. "We will begin tomorrow."

This was a wonder. These men were much too burdened to be thinking of her church.

"I don't know how to start," she said. "But you do."

"Oui, I do. First we must claim land."

"Merci, but I have no head for it," she said.

"The Americans don't either. This is all government land. It's not surveyed. You cannot claim anything with a legal boundary, like a quarter of section twenty-seven, township thirty. There was a fur post here, and the town's grown around it. These people simply claimed land. They decided on fifty-foot lots, and drove their stakes, and someday a surveyor will come along and make it legal. It's called preemption. Sometimes the government accepts, sometimes not. Usually the government sees that there is a town and the squatters need legal title, and it is all settled. Eh? See where I am driving?"

"I don't know a thing, but I'll learn."

He sucked until the pipe crackled, and he exhaled a blue plume. "Tomorrow, we will pick a place outside of town, where the people won't care what you do. You'll pick a good place for your church, and we'll drive in the stakes and leave a claim in a bottle. We'll give the church two hundred feet, eh? Not that the crooked church deserves an inch."

"I have nothing to measure with, sir."

"I do. I have a cord with fifty knots in it, each knot a foot."

"How do you make a rectangle?" Martin asked.

"The distance from the opposing corners must be equal," Armand said. "From upper left to lower right, and from upper right to lower left. Make those the same, and you have a rectangle."

"Where did you learn that?" Beau asked.

"Geometry, taught in the schools at the Red River colony, by the miserable priests."

"Tomorrow, my church will have land under it?"

"*Oui*. As good a claim as any merchant in town has."

"I am blessed," she said.

He smoked a moment. "At the Red River colony in Manitoba, the Earl of Selkirk, Thomas Douglas, said that our ancient claims along the river, upon which our fruitful farms rested, were not good. The land must be surveyed into square miles in the British manner, and we must leave. And so we did, with a little help from their bayonets. The British are as bad as bishops."

She couldn't think of anything to say about that.

nineteen

After a breakfast of oat gruel, Trouffant asked a question:

"Would Madame wish to show us where the church is to be?"

It startled Therese. She had thought the time for that would be weeks, months, seasons away. She stared. "I don't know."

She didn't have the slightest idea. She had only once passed through the cluster of rude buildings calling itself Lewistown. She knew there was a road heading north, and another heading west, and one heading east.

"I have a site in mind, with your permission."

"Yes, of course!"

Trouffant collected his knotted string, some stakes, a hatchet, a small brass compass, some foolscap, and a pencil. These he tossed into the ubiquitous burlap sacks of the frontier.

He turned to his sons. "Do you wish to join us?"

"I'll cut wood," Beau said.

"I'll come," Martin said.

Soon Armand Trouffant, Martin, and Therese bundled against a sharp wind and braved the dawn. Lewistown was slumbering. The saloons were dark. The various residences around them, which housed gamblers and saloonkeepers and tarnished women, slept in the rising light.

Trouffant strode so fast that Therese couldn't keep up, but then he slowed. He took them through the trash-filled town and out into the open fields west of it, until the road began to ascend a long grade. And there, just where the road rose, was a flat on the south side of the two-rut trail, a little higher than the valley yet easy to reach.

"Voilà," he said.

She felt the power of the place, yet wasn't sure. "It looks right, but is there any place on the other sides that might be better?"

Trouffant shrugged. "The choice is yours, madame."

"There are no creeks here, no bridges to build," Martin said. "The land is high and will not flood. It's far enough from the town so no one will scheme against us."

She turned to him. "You've given this some thought," she said.

"Much thought," he said.

"Are you in the faith?"

"No, madame, I don't believe a word of it." He smiled softly. "But a church will be good for the Métis."

"If any are left here," his father said. "Very well. Madame, let us choose a corner."

Martin strode to a spot south of the trail and stopped. "The west and north lines from here, eh?"

It seemed fine to her. Could it be? Was this the beginning? She watched as father and son drove a stake at that point, and measured eastward four lengths of the fifty-foot cords, and drove a second stake, also back from the road. While she watched, they staked a rectangle two hundred feet wide by four hundred deep, and made it true. Then they built fieldstone cairns at the corners.

"Now, madame, where will your church rise, eh?"

"And how big?" Martin asked.

This time she had a sense of the right spot; close to the road fronting the property, and midway between the stakes.

"I like it here, but I know nothing about size, messieurs."

Martin turned to her with a faraway look. "Grand enough for all the Métis."

"Yes! That grand."

The father and son drove four more stakes, but they seemed very near to one another, and she thought this church would hardly hold a dozen.

"This is a big church, madame. It will hold all the Métis," Armand said. "Now, we must leave a claim here. What are you going to name the church?"

That was easy. "For the blessed one who came down the ivory stairs from heaven and told me to begin this task. Saint Therese."

"Maybe Saint Martin?" Martin asked, one eyebrow cocked.

"Aren't you full of conceits," she replied.

"There were two Saint Martins," he said. "So my name is holier than yours." He was smiling for the first time.

Armand nodded. "It is yours to choose, madame. The only thing I am going to do is write the claim in English. Then it will be respected because it can be read."

"Do you know English?" she asked.

"The priests at the parish school on the Red River taught me."

He settled on the frosted grass, turned his back to the bitter wind, and pulled the foolscap and a bottle from his sack. Then he penciled a claim. "This lot claimed by Saint Therese Church, October 14, 1885." He thought a little and added "200 ft by 400 ft."

He rolled up the foolscap and jammed it into the bottle. Then he and his son built a small cairn of fieldstone and set the bottle into its top layer.

"*C'est bon*," Armand said.

The men studied the ground where the church would rise, noting the topsoil, the presence of stray rock, the lay of the land.

Therese stood in the wind, blessed herself with a soft articulation of her hand, and the three stared at their handiwork, which had consumed so little time that the distant town was not yet awake.

Martin strode beside her, and she sensed it was no accident.

"Madame," he began, "ever since you arrived here, I have been curious. I have been awash in speculation. I have weighed and pondered. And I am just as mystified now as I was the moment we met."

She knew what was coming, and knew she had to give some explanation.

"Madame," he continued. "Would it be rude if I were to satisfy my curiosity? Would you forgive a young man's boldness?"

"I think you are wondering how I arrived here without the protection of my husband."

"Yes, those are my very thoughts. And what he thinks of all this. This amazing vision that you speak of. This mission to this place."

She weighed her response. But there could be no concealing of the truth. The Métis gossiped, and gossip would soon reach this boy's ears, and if she lied now, she would be greatly embarrassed soon.

"Martin, my husband does not know of this trip. He does not know of my vision. He probably wouldn't believe me anyway. So he has no opinion about what I'm doing."

"But how can that be?"

"I am married in name only, Martin. And someday I will have my marriage annulled. It was . . . I am . . . not yet a wife. Is that enough for you?"

She was annoyed. He surely had a right to some answers. A Métis woman traveling alone, a great distance, was unthinkable.

He plainly was not emptied of his curiosity. "Madame, what does your husband do?"

"He is a civilian translator with the army."

"Ah! Does he translate our dialect for them?"

"He understands it, but not as well as several Indian tongues. He speaks French. He can speak Shoshone, Crow, Hidatsa, some Sioux, Blackfoot, Cheyenne, and he's learned some Cree too."

The wind was picking up, and it was chill. Winter stood at the gates.

"And you quarreled about this?"

"No, not a word. But the moment the priest was blessing our marriage, I knew it was a mistake. I could not go on. I—walked away."

"And him?"

"He loves me. He is a good man taking pay to destroy us. I mostly don't like him, but he's a good man."

"And your vision, it came afterward, after you had walked away?"

"Yes, while I was staying with cousins near Miles City. That's where the heavens opened up to me."

"And when this church is built, what then, madame?"

"I have no life in me after that, Martin."

He glared at her, turned away, and walked toward the Trouffant wood yard keeping his distance from her. She didn't feel sorry. She had told him everything he wanted to know, not sparing herself. She glanced at Armand, who was feigning disinterest. Well, now they knew. Maybe they would toss her and her small possessions out the door.

The thought of her wedding, and her flight from Dirk Skye, troubled her. Could he be in this area? She dreaded the thought of running into him. Fate had brought her here. An army mission had brought him to the Judith Basin.

She hurried up to Armand.

"Monsieur, perhaps you can tell me. Where are the soldiers now?"

"In their forts, I am told. They are done."

"The big campaign, to find us and ship us away, is that finished?"

"Yes, madame. They succeeded, you know. They intercepted many Métis fleeing from the Northwest Mounted Police, and sent us back, and followed our people for many miles to make sure."

"You're here."

"*Oui.* The Métis that found hiding places in the towns, they are here. It was the ones out in the country that got chased away."

"Did any die?"

"A great pity. Some old were buried. But many more will perish in Canada. They have nothing and winter is here."

"Who will come to my church?"

"It will be a congregation of ghosts, madame."

She felt the wind cutting through her coat. Did things only go from bad to worse?

"The soldiers, the ones from Fort Keogh. Are they still here?"

He shrugged. "They don't tell me much in Lewistown. If I didn't sell firewood, they would have sent us packing too. But I hear a few things, whispers in the night. *Oui,* the column from Fort Keogh left. That was Captain Brewer's column, and it was the worst. It was the one that awoke people in the night, and sent us out into the wilderness, half-dressed, with nothing to spare us our lives. They were like a plague over the land, the finger of death. Be grateful they are gone, madame. Some of us lie in our hasty graves now."

She felt the stain of bitterness. How could he? What lies did he tell the people? What did she ever see in him? Gone from here! And now he was many leagues away, and she was glad of it. If God was just, he would send Dirk Skye another thousand miles away. She hoped Dirk Skye would leave the territory. She hoped he would vanish from her mind. Only she knew he wouldn't, and that only made it worse.

"Madame, it would be wise to remain very quiet. We

will build the church, but we will do it by fits and starts, by the light of the moon. We will draw no attention to ourselves. You must say nothing. Tell no one you are here. Do not talk about the vision you received. Do not walk the streets of Lewistown. Learn a few English words, and never speak our tongue."

"Why do you say this?"

"Because you will be a lightning rod. You will draw down the wrath of the heavens. You will endanger the people you wish to help. And you might be in danger. There are men who hunger for land and will commit any crime to have it. Men who want more and more grass for their cattle, and intend to have it. Men who would see you as a menace."

The prophecy chilled her.

They reached Trouffant's yard, and he wordlessly began his chopping, splitting one piece of firewood at a time, which is how he would expend the rest of the daylight. Martin stopped briefly at the cabin to bag a lunch, and then walked away, going to wherever Beau was, to fell trees and saw them into rounds, which could be split and turned into firewood.

And Therese wondered what madness had brought her to that place.

twenty

*S*ylvestre was morose. He rode northward lost in gloom, muttering to himself. That keg of brandy was the Holy Grail. Dirk watched him mutter and sigh, and wondered whether the others hidden in the Missouri Breaks would regard the loss as bleakly.

He turned to other thoughts, not wanting to rail against his fate. The encounter with Bain actually was valuable on two grounds: they learned that the army had quit and was now in winter quarters. And they learned what fate the big ranching outfits had in mind for stray Métis they came across.

Maybe it was time for these people to filter back and simply brave the threats of the ranchers. Or maybe not. Let one Métis man be hanged, while his weeping family watched, and these ill-starred people would be plunged into an even deeper pit.

On the other hand, each day these people waited, surviving in their rude huts in the Missouri River hinterland, the closer they came to starvation. He slowed his buck-skin, letting Lorenz draw up beside him.

"We've got to do some thinking," he said.

"Don't ask me to think! Give me some brandy, and then I'll think."

"The army's gone. The soldiers are wintering. Maybe this is the time to come back."

"And get hanged."

"I know something about these big open range out-fits. They don't do much in the winter. The cattle survive or not, pawing through snow to get at grass. The cowboys just hole up and play cards until spring. And they mostly hole up at the ranch headquarters. They don't winter in the line camps. They'd go crazy, two or three in a camp, trying to make the weeks go by. The line camps are empty all winter. Are you following my drift?"

"As little as possible, *ami*," said Sylvestre.

"They might not even be in your place, when winter hits. The army's gone. They think your people are too. So why would they stay? When it gets a little colder, they'll pack up and move. Never trust a cowboy to cut firewood or wash dishes if he doesn't have to. You following my drift?"

"So we slip in, take over our old places, and eat their cattle all winter, *ami*?"

"And get hanged in the spring, while you are fat on borrowed beef."

Sylvestre laughed. "That is a good Métis plan."

"You can starve in your huts, then."

"You got some money, eh?"

"Some loose pocket change."

"Ah! You ride to Lewistown and buy a bottle of brandy, eh?"

"You won't find brandy there. Redeye whiskey, maybe some beer."

"Here's what you do, eh? You ride to Lewistown. You take my mule, and you buy enough stuff, long as it's got spirits in it, you load dat stuff on the mule, and we'll have us a party. Then, after some festivities, when we don't got any more headaches, we'll come down here and move into our farms, and all the ones from Canada, they move into the line camps, and eat beef, eh?"

"And then what?"

"We all get hanged."

"Your choice, I suppose."

"Hey, Skye. You got it all wrong. This is justice. If I'm gonna get hanged, and I ate none of their beef, that would be unjust, eh? I eat none of these steaks and tongues and ribs, and get hanged, and they take me out to the cotton-wood tree, and I'm hungry and skinny and angry because this hanging's unjust, and they string me up even if I'm innocent, then it's unjust. It ain't right. So what's just? If I'm gonna get hanged no matter what, then I should eat all the meat I can find, and get fat, and feel good, and en-joy all that beef in my belly, and then if they hang me, it's justice, right? Then I got no reason to be angry. Then I got no reason to be bitter. I got no reason to shake my fist and say they's making a mistake and strangling an innocent man, eh? I get fat, keep my family fat, and then if they hang me it's all good and just."

Dirk was laughing. But he had the awful sense that this was the future.

"I'm gonna tell them up there, we should all go get fat and get ourselves hanged," Sylvestre said. "We'll eat good first." He rode a while in silence, and then added one more thought. "A good steak, it'd sure taste good, eh?"

Dirk didn't go to Lewistown on a booze run. He and Sylvestre followed the Judith River north until it plunged into the mysterious canyons of the Missouri, and then they followed barely visible trails until they turned into the one that Sylvestre called home. About the time they left the high plains the weather turned. The deeper they rode into the great trench of the Missouri, the darker the clouds and the colder the air. By the time they reached the great river, the wind was carrying ice crystals, which stung Dirk's cheeks and numbed his hands. He saw a rime of white forming on Sylvestre's black hair and collecting in the mane of the bay.

In the remaining two hours of their journey deep into that secretive haven, the world turned white. It wasn't much of a snow, just the crystalline kind that coated the last leaves of fall and the grasses and the north sides of cottonwood trees. Time had run out for the Métis.

They turned at last into that anonymous gulch that hid several Métis huts, and now the people poured out of their log and canvas shelters, all of them eyeing the mule with the empty packsaddle riding it. They saw more than the empty saddle, devoid of the cask, devoid even of a few burlap sacks of squash or cabbage from Sylvestre's farm. What they saw was ceaseless hunger, starting this very hour, a hunger for which there was no respite.

Nothing needed saying, so these people just stared as the whipping crystals of ice coated their shawls and scarves and leather coats. Dirk and Lorenz put the horses out with the oxen and mules, which were kept close in a box canyon.

"I hope I'm welcome chez Beauchamps," Dirk said.

"They got no food. They thought you'd bring some."

"None?"

"They ready to eat worms."

Dirk thought that things couldn't get harder. He found the Beauchamps family inside their hut, but they did not welcome him. They sat in the cold, because they lacked firewood. Clothilde and two other daughters huddled under a worn buffalo robe.

"We were chased away," Dirk said.

No one responded. There was no welcome here.

"I'm going to the river. I'll see what I can do."

Dirk abandoned them and headed for Sylvestre's hut. "I'm going to look for food. You got some fish hooks and line?"

"Naw, but if you ask real polite, I'll bring you a few spare buffalo, eh?"

"Mind if I borrow your musket?"

Sylvestre shrugged, handed the ancient weapon to Dirk, along with a powder horn.

Dirk headed into a swirl of ice crystals. This wasn't the sort of snow that accumulated, but it was mean and mocking, and seemed to howl its delight in making Dirk feel its icy fingers down his neck.

There would be an hour before the daylight faded. At the river he turned east, hoping to find some backwater with cattails in it. Or some ducks or Canada geese. Or anything. His feet were numbing. He did come upon a slough that stretched into an arm of dead water, running into a gulch. That was as good as he could hope for. The

gray heavens cast gloom over the place. He studied the
water, looking for anything with fins, and that's when he
did see a massive dark shape of a fish, lounging near a
bank. The fish had a huge beak in front, shaped like a
long spoon, and Dirk thought he knew what it was, but
he had never seen a paddlefish and couldn't be sure. If it
was, it would be heavy, around five feet long, and would
not be caught with bait. The fish survived on the river
debris that filtered through its teeth. It was usually caught
with a spear or by hooking a fin.

Dirk eased back from the bank. The fish did not stir.
He headed up the slough until he found a willow limb
that he might turn into a weapon. He had only his jackknife. He whittled his spear, hoping the fish would stay
put. It took most of the remaining daylight to fashion his
lance, but in time he had a six-foot pole shorn of twigs
and sharpened. Then, his hands numb, he headed back to
the bank and found the giant fish lazing there, sucking in
whatever filtered past its teeth. It seemed prehistoric, like
some monster out of the vasty deep. Its rear fin was wide
and looked to be the way to pinion that monster.

Swiftly Dirk climbed out of his britches and leather
shirt. The only way he could hope to bring this monster
to the table would be to get into the icy river and creep up
on the fish from behind and run that lance through its
tail.

He eased into the cold, feeling the water bite, feeling
his feet purchase traction on muck and sticks and rocks. He
eased forward, the cold thunderous on his legs, until he
rounded a soft corner and saw the monster ahead, its
tail idly switching to hold it steady as its dinner filtered
through its mouth. He would have one chance. If he

failed, the fish would turn away with a single flip of the tail. He knew too that water was a distorting lens; the tail might not be just where his eyes saw it through a foot of water.

His own energy was failing. He didn't wait. He lifted his harpoon and plunged its point down, aiming at the fin, and saw the fish lurch even as his lance pierced something and buried itself in muck. The fish thrashed forward, yanking the stick with it, but Dirk pried it back, and the fish twisted to the left, taking the stick that way, but Dirk righted himself just before the stick twisted him all the way into the back water. And so it went, even as the light faded and the ice crystals on the wind numbed the last sensation from his flesh. He lacked the strength to land the fish and yet he had to.

He spotted a gentle grade a dozen yards away where he might drag the fish from water. He felt it throb and tug and twist, but the stick held firm. He lifted the stick, got his hand under the fin, and eased the stick from the muck. The fish turned passive, letting Dirk pull it step by step, his hands on either side of the giant fin. Dirk stumbled backward, gaining the bank, and sat there, tugging the fish a few inches at a time, inch by inch until the heaving thing lay on the weedy ground. Dirk wasn't satisfied and dragged it two, three, five feet back, until he was sure the paddlefish wouldn't leap into the river and vanish.

He sat motionless, his heart throbbing, his body numb. He felt the ice on his flesh. He rose, found his britches and shirt and leather coat and moccasins, and put them on, and felt a thin comfort from them. He did not know how to get the fish back to the Métis. It was too heavy to carry. He was too worn. If he went for help, he would never find this place, and likely would never see the fish again. Night creatures would demolish it.

He took the stick and tugged. The fish slid. He tugged more. The fish slid. The coating of ice on the ground suddenly became his salvation. He struggled along the Missouri, a few yards at a time, and then turned up the gulch where these people lived, even as light gave out and he was traveling by sheer instinct.

The ice was his savior. It lubricated the land, so that Dirk could sometimes travel a hundred yards before he was forced to sit, recover enough for another stint, even as the crystals fell from the black sky, and night enveloped him. It took forever, it seemed, and he lost all feeling, and scarcely knew he was moving his limbs.

He stumbled into the clearing of huts, and found no light and no sound. These people were buried under their robes, enduring their empty stomachs, waiting for a worse day when the sun came up again.

He wasn't sure which of the huts was looming next to him, but he set down the pole and yelled hoarsely.

"*Oui?*" came a voice. It was Lorenz Sylvestre's.

"Help me," Dirk said.

"What is it that you have?"

"Paddlefish."

"*Mon Dieu!*"

He stepped toward Dirk, a shadow in the night. He stumbled over the fish, and on his knees ran a hand along its entire length.

"*Sacre bleu!*" He rose. "Maude! Maude! Get thyself busy and make a fire! We will eat!"

Dirk was too tired to help. He sat numbly while the family fanned a small fire into a large one, all the while gaping at the monster. Soon there were others rising out of the dark, until all the Métis collected there, at the tentative fire, gazing at the silvery fish.

Beauchamps appeared with some good knives.

"I have done this before," he said. "It is not easy. This fish is all cartilage and there's not much flesh, and the flesh is wrapped around the cartilage, eh?"

"Cut some for us to boil," Sylvestre said. "Quick! Quick!"

"Ah, even that is difficult, *mon ami*."

But Beauchamps didn't tarry. He slit the giant open and began wrestling the chord of cartilage running down the back, and as soon as it was freed the women began scraping flesh out of every corner, and throwing it into water heating in a pot over the wavering fire. It would take a long while, but this night every belly would be filled and every heart warmed.

twenty-one

The paddlefish was the true hoodoo. Elders squinted wisely, knowing that when a paddle-fish let itself get caught with a wooden stick, big stuff was happening. Fish stew found its way around the Missouri Breaks, food for the heart but more for the soul. It was a mighty sign. And with it came the news that the soldiers had retreated to winter quarters and all that remained to worry about was the noose.

But what was a noose or two among the Métis, eh? The people had thick necks and great prowess, and could make new Métis faster than they could be hanged. For every Métis the ranchers hanged, there would be ten little ones incubating in wombs. Voilà! And what would it matter if a few cows disappeared?

It was time for the Métis to abandon their hideouts and settle in their promised land. The few who had farms could probably return to them; the newcomers would have to find something else. Who could say where? The best thing was to start out and see where they ended up.

In spite of misgivings, Dirk thought it was a good idea for these people to hit the road. They had been one fish away from starvation. When some of them asked him where to go, he had phrased things in the negative: away from the open range ranches that spread toward invisible boundaries. Go into towns, hamlets, cities, where they could work and survive. But some had other ideas: occupy the line camps of the ranches, now that those cowboys were either clustered in their headquarters or were riding the grub line, as winter visits were called. That was tempting. Those empty cabins had stoves and bunks and corrals, and probably some stray beef not far away.

Thus began the migration. The Métis filtered south, traveling by night, riding the winds of winter, blowing with the snow, hiding by day. No leader directed them. No advance guards warned them away from danger. Yet they somehow knew the time had come to leave the Missouri Breaks—or die in their huts. They were mostly invisible, taking advantage of shifting winds and flurries that kept the ranchers and their hands huddled at their wood stoves. Who could say what the Métis ate? They could fish every stream, harvest frozen berries, pluck up withered roots, occasionally shoot a wild thing. Who could say what their oxen and mules ate? There was green cottonwood bark, that famous last resort for livestock. And yet, as long as the snow held off, and they could roll over frozen clay, the way was not difficult and the giant wheels of the Red River carts never mired.

The Beauchampses and Sylvestres rolled south together, and Dirk went with them, thinking maybe to find food for them. He had learned well from his father, but not all the wilderness lore in the world could feed starving people if there was nothing to turn into food. He thought the frosted earth at Sylvestre's homestead might still yield potatoes and whatever root crops the man had planted, and that might help these people survive. But it was a forlorn hope because there was no meat in that diet. He feared these people would soon be slaughtering a cow here, another there, just to keep themselves fed. And there was nothing he could do, and maybe he would share the guilt if it came to that.

It was a brutal trip, slowed by hunger and weariness. The children lagged, and could not be hastened. The wind bit necks and numbed fingers. Dirk, on horse, did better than those afoot. He spent much of his time keeping an eye peeled for trouble, but also hunting food. Anything at all. Not only for humans but for animals. One afternoon he found a wolf-killed deer, the carcass frozen and edible. He gradually pried it loose from the blood-soaked frozen ground and carried it to the straggling party, which welcomed it with joy. They would boil it into a stew that evening.

Moccasins wore out faster on the frozen ground, which lacerated the leather. There was little to repair them. One of Beauchamps's daughters fevered and had to be carried in the overburdened ox cart. At night, the men tried to find a spot that would hide a fire from distant eyes and usually succeeded. The valley of the Judith River was rich in small corners, out of the wind and under the lip of prairie. Yet in spite of all, these determined people were progressing southward to reclaim a home, a garden, a livestock pen, a root cellar, where once they had lived in peace.

They reached the long claws of the Snowy Mountains

at last and proceeded across the lonely land toward Lorenz Sylvestre's homestead. Late in an afternoon marked by glowering clouds that threatened more snow, they rounded a bend and beheld their farm.

But there was nothing there. No log home, no barn, no pens. Nothing but black ash, and a few forlorn black ruins. Scorched earth.

"Mon Dieu!" whispered Sylvestre.

The rest just stared mutely. There were ice crystals in the air, the threat of another storm, and no refuge from it. They led the weary oxen the last hundred yards and surveyed the ruins, seeing nothing but ash and broken dreams. Years of labor and hope lay charred. Comfort and succor lay dead. The simple hope of shelter, a wood stove glowing, a chance to endure a Montana winter, was gone. Dirk glanced at these homeless people, seeing the premonition of death in their sorrow. It was bad enough for the Sylvestres, but in a way, even worse for the Beauchamps women, whose dreams of safety and comfort had flown away in a trice.

Dirk stepped off his buckskin and walked the ruins, wondering if anything survived. But nothing combustible did other than the thick plank door of the root cellar. That hillside structure had survived. Then he realized the iron stove remained, a blackened hulk but a stove nonetheless. He motioned to Sylvestre.

"We have heat, if you have wood."

That galvanized them. They had a stove; they had their tarpaulins. They had good axes to cut frames and make firewood. The men immediately began wrestling the stove out of the field of ash, along with some stovepipe. Others began the task of erecting a canvas shelter out of whatever was at hand. Dirk pulled open the door of the root cellar and found nothing in it. It was perpetually cold in there. At the ruins of the barn he found nothing. No grain or seed, no harness or implements other than a shovel with its wooden handle burnt off.

Madame Sylvestre was out in the vast gardens, gesticulating.

They crowded toward her. There were still acres of food. No one of the cattlemen had thought to harvest any of it. Frost-covered squash, browned off potatoes, frosted beets, carrots, onions, stretching every which way. Food enough for the winter if they got it in before the frost dug deep into the earth. A feast this very night!

But they had only a single shovel.

"Dig! We must dig!" Sylvestre said. "Dig with the shovel. Dig with sticks."

The Métis seemed to organize themselves without command. The Sylvestre children unyoked the oxen and turned them loose to forage. Beauchamps and Sylvestre, the most powerful and muscular of them, set to work on the root crops. The Beauchamps girls found some burlap sacks and gathered squash and carried it to the root cellar, bag after bag. The men dug up potatoes and loaded them onto a tarpaulin, and dragged the tarp to the root cellar. Some of the women hunted for firewood and carried it to the stove, which now sat well away from the ashes of the home.

But the garden was the main thing. Dirk realized that these people could manage through the winter if they could harvest the entire garden, which ran several acres. And that full bellies would hearten them to rebuild, even through the bitterest days of winter. It was a task so daunt-

ing and complex that Dirk marveled that they would
even try. But the Métis had never shied from toil. These
people were hungry and cold but didn't pause to eat or
warm themselves. They were in a race against winter, and
they intended to win. Toil, the unending torture of their
muscles, would be their salvation. These people knew
this. They knew that they could chop and shovel and saw
and pull and carry on their backs, and the muscle of their
arms and legs and backs and necks would keep them safe.

Ice was in the wind. A deep cold that clawed deep into
the earth, or a blizzard, could ruin all hope. Dirk found a
row of cabbages, frozen and brown on the outside but
maybe still mostly usable, and he made it his task to carry
them to the root cellar. He found cucumbers that looked
mostly ruined, but who could say? He found frost-bit
melons, and who could say what might be saved? With
a stick he loosened onions from the earth. All these he
lugged to the root cellar and was amazed at how quickly
that hillside chamber was filling up. The daylight thinned
to nothing but the work continued, people somehow
finding their way in virtual blackness.

Light bloomed and grew. The women had a fire going in the stove and were filling a kettle with the fruits
of their impromptu harvest. A good stew this night, and
more to come. Even as the women prepared a meal of
potatoes, onions, carrots, and squash, the men collected
the downed corral rails and lashed them into a frame-
work to support the tarpaulins. There would be shelter
this night, a little warmth, and heaps of steaming vegetables.

They ate. There weren't bowls enough, but in time
they were all filled, and the Beauchamps girls fell asleep.

Sylvestre was whittling a pole to fit into the blade of the burnt shovel. Tomorrow there would be two shovels. Even with two, the harvest would run a week unless a ground-piercing Canadian cold ruined the rest of what lay out there. The tarpaulins rattled in the winter air but stayed the cold as long as the stove radiated its heat.

Dirk lay in his bedroll, unsure about the future. He would stay through the desperate harvest. He would struggle alongside these Métis to put every last potato into the root cellar. And maybe help them with a better shelter, enough to thwart the cold while the men set to work on a new house. There would come the moment when he would be an extra mouth to feed, an intruder among them. And then what? He would leave. He had been discharged not far from this very place. He had lost his livelihood and perhaps his vocation. Who needed a translator? Who needed a barely qualified teacher? Who needed a husband? Not these people.

At dawn there was a fresh white coating on the ground. An inch or two, but it was warning enough to set them all to frenzied digging and hauling, from the earliest light. Dirk pitched in, marveling at how much was achieved with so little. The men dug in shifts, and children carried burlap bags or dragged tarps loaded with the harvest. The women stored the incoming vegetables. There was a whole lore to it; ways to let air circulate; ways to slow the rot. Things to store low, things to hang high. And they knew it all. The smallest children, mostly the Beauchamps girls, hunted firewood. A single day would consume a great heap of it. A winter's supply was almost unimaginable. And if these people got snowed in, they would sleep cold and eat cold and maybe die cold.

Dirk's buckskin roamed freely, along with the oxen, sometimes drifting worrisome distances from the homestead. But it was finding good browned grass and recovering its strength. Each day, Dirk checked the horse that would take him the long trip down to the Yellowstone.

The day came when there was nothing left to yank out of the earth; the day when frost pierced deeper into the ground. The day when the Sylvestres and Beauchamps were secure enough to weather whatever came.

The summer leaves were gone. The aspen and cottonwood and alders lifted naked limbs to the darkened sky. It was time for Dirk to drift, to tumble along like the tumbleweeds, blown south by winter winds, his back to the cold, the icy fingers at his neck. It was time to be alone again, not part of these people, not part of the white world, not part of his mother's people, or his Crow mother's people, or his father's people.

It was time to ride, before snow blocked the way.

He saddled the buckskin, loaded his bedroll, embraced his friends, and rode away, a dot of flesh crossing a vast and bleak country, where there was no horizon but only endless haze.

twenty-two

*D*irk Skye rode the breast of the earth alone. He didn't mind being alone though it was not what he preferred. He enjoyed company. But now he steered his buckskin across an empty land, little changed from the days before settlement. A soft sun burned off the snow, which was a mercy to his eyes. He had what he needed: a bedroll, his jackknife, a flint and steel, and a burlap bag of squash that could be baked in their shells and cut open and eaten.

As long as the buckskin held out, he would. The world seemed large that November day, but that was because he was riding alone. He headed east, following the very trail his army column had taken months before. Company made the world smaller. Ride with friends, and the world collected around them. Ride alone, and one could see only the vast distances that lay hidden beyond the horizons.

He was at ease among all sorts, but not all people were at ease with him. Among whites, they noted his blue eyes, and then his strong cheekbones and a flesh darker

than their own, and there would be mysterious walls rising between him and them. He was more welcome among
Indians, but now and then they would see his blue gaze,
or hear the sounds of an education gotten in St. Louis, and
they would become very quiet, leaving him on his own
ground, which was not theirs.

And so the present world was large and he knew no
boundaries. He could ride east until he reached farms and
towns and railroads and colleges. He could ride south
until he was among Mexicans and adobes and flocks of
sheep. He could ride most any direction to the ocean, and
go most any distance to the ends of time. All that was because he was alone, and not living in a cloistered world of
friendships or family or children or neighbors.

He wished life could be different, but it could not. So
he rode across the Judith Basin alone, seeing no one and
hoping no one saw him.

He was not bored while long-riding. He was constantly
processing everything. He saw the roosting owl, the eagle
riding the updrafts, the crow perched on a limb. He saw
the hoofprints of elk on the road, the gathering of gloomy
clouds over the Snowy Mountains, the buffalo berries
that somehow escaped the frost. He was also calculating
the wind, and calculating his horse. He knew when the
buckskin tired, and then he would step off, walk beside it
for a while, let it graze the dun grasses, and then ride on.

He passed some stray cattle, dark dots against a snow-
patched hillside. They roamed freely. They could travel
from here across the plains, from here to Mexico, with
nothing to stop them. But they wore brands that said they
were owned, and those brands were carefully registered
in the territorial capital of Helena. He would not be eating

beef, even if the meat tempted him: those cowboys had taken his gun long before, and his sole weapon now was the jackknife, which he treasured as his most valuable possession.

He would find a good copse of cottonwoods or box elders or willows this night, and make himself at home in their midst. He didn't think it would snow; he thought the good weather might last all the way to Fort Keogh, six or seven rides away. Novembers in Montana were like that. Mostly sunny and quiet, but plenty cold.

Thus did his first ride pass by quickly enough, and as the sun began its early plunge under the lid of the world, he hunted for the small woodlands he wanted. He saw one at last, lying to the right, nestled between two claws of the Snowy Mountains, and headed that way even as the ground congealed under him.

He turned the buckskin toward the black mass of trees and reined up at once. There, catching the dying light, was a thin rise of smoke. Maybe his imagination. But no, he was staring at smoke, even though the flames were invisible behind that screen of woods. It was time for caution. He dismounted, making his profile lower, and started up the westward one of the two claws of the mountains, staying below the skyline. He heard or saw nothing, and thought maybe he was imagining things, but he persisted. The buckskin's ears cupped forward, and Dirk feared the horse would whinny. But that was a risk he would take. For after all, the odds were great that this would be a friendly encounter. The ranchers were at odds with anyone wandering through but the fire could signal a party of woodcutters or trappers or hunters or even prospectors.

Still, mindful that he was unarmed, he chose utmost

care. He actually worked past much of the woods lying in the valley between the arms of the mountains before he glimpsed flame, and spotted a dozen or so people near it. A wagon was burning. An ox that had been yoked to it was being led away by one of the horsemen. Several people were on foot, slumped on the earth, while several others sat their horses. And one more thing: there was the black victoria, Harley Bain's carriage, with the matched trotters in harness.

Dirk watched. Nothing much was happening other than that an entire wagonload of possessions was swiftly being reduced to ash. He saw no violence. He saw no ropes dangling from limbs. He saw no drawn revolvers. He heard no shots. But what was happening was plain enough. A family of Métis was being murdered. Not by bullet or knife or noose or beating, but by being left without a thing on the eve of a Montana winter. It saved rope. It saved bullets. It did the job in ways that would elude the law. Who could prove anything? The family's wagon burned, and they were breeds anyway.

Dirk quieted his buckskin and waited. It was a temptation to ride down upon them all and find some way to overcome this cowboy posse. But he knew better. So he waited, and after it was clear nothing in the wagon would survive, the man in the carriage stirred his trotters, and the ranch posse rode out of the forest and then out of sight.

Dirk urged the buckskin down a long grade toward the bereft family. He could see them better now, mostly silhouetted in the wavering light. There were two males, a woman and a girl, and the woman was kneeling in front of the inferno. He dismounted, not wanting to seem like a returning cowboy. He could not know how they might respond. So he walked, leading his horse, and paused at the edge of the clearing. In time, they saw him.

But there was music, or at least one clear sweet voice. The kneeling woman was singing. He walked hesitantly toward them, and they observed his progress, but did not welcome him. He tried to catch the music, to learn what absorbed them, and then he did. It was Latin.

"*Ave Maria, Gratia plena, Dominus tecum, Benedicta tu in mulieribus, Et benedictus fructus ventris, Tui, Jesus, Sancta Maria. Mater Dei, Ora pro nobis peccatoribus. Nunc et in hora mortis nostrae. Amen.*"

Dirk removed his hat. He well knew this sacred plea. The men blessed themselves. The woman did also, and then arose to face Dirk. She was pregnant. There were no tears in her eyes. The men eyed him and his horse. They saw his leather coat, cut in a style well known among the Métis. They saw Dirk's strong cheekbones and warm flesh.

"Is it that I can help?" he asked in French.

They stared. A man responded in a tongue Dirk couldn't translate but he heard some French in it. Michif, then.

He would try to get them to Lewistown. They could not survive in this place. He saw that they had intended to stay here, perhaps live Indian-style in a lodge, survive by hunting. Now they didn't even have rifles to hunt with.

He pointed to himself. "I am Dirk Skye."

A man pointed at the woman. "Marie." At the girl. "Josephine." At the other adult male. "Pierre." At himself. "Antony."

"We probably should go to Lewistown," he said, wondering whether they grasped any English.

One of the men, Antony, nodded. Dirk had the sense

that everything was being left to himself. He undid his bedroll and motioned to the woman to mount the horse. She did, hesitantly, her gaze shy. He gestured to Antony to pick up the girl and place her ahead of her mother. Antony understood at once and lifted the child. Dirk wrapped the ancient buffalo robe around them and drew the horse along with the rein. It was barely dusk. They might make Lewistown in two hours, maybe three. Before the town fell asleep, anyway.

The night swiftly turned dark and cold, with ice-chip stars. There was only his namesake, the North Star, to steer him. Somewhere ahead his path would cross the road to Lewistown, and he feared he might miss it.

The men walked silently beside him and the horse. Dirk wondered whether they were brothers. They seemed about the same age, young and just starting out. The steady hiking was pleasant enough, except for the cold wind. After some while, one of the men muttered something and stayed Dirk. It was Antony again. He knelt and wanted Dirk to do so also. He had found the rutted road wending its way east toward the village. Dirk's hands traced the ruts.

"Thank you," Dirk said. They turned toward the town, the North Star riding Dirk's left shoulder now. Nothing else could help them. They were working across a long plain, tunneling through an unknown and unseen world. Then, about the time Dirk thought he was hopelessly off in his estimate of where they were, they began to descend a gentle grade, toward a single glimmering lamp in a distant window. He wondered what they would find. It was quite possible that Lewistown would be colder than the natural world.

Marie sat quietly on the buckskin, shrouding herself and Josephine with the old robe, her calm as ancient as the world. Another half hour or so took them into the bottom of a valley, and then into a street with darkened buildings, mostly false-front log structures that snaked back from the artery. One saloon was still open. He knew all about saloons and Indians and breeds, and decided simply to ignore all that. He helped Marie and her daughter off the horse. The men looked uneasy.

Dirk peered through the single grimy window at a row of ten or twelve men, still sipping at the bar, lit by two overhead lamps. Some wood smoke swirled down on him. They were ranching men, which didn't help any.

He nodded to his friends, but they held back.

"I want them to see you," he said.

They still held back. There could be big trouble in there. They stood outside, in the wind, unwilling to step indoors.

"All right," he said.

He pushed open the door, against the night wind, and let the lamplight spill out. He entered and found himself facing curious men. Cowboys, apparently. Young men, devil-may-care types whiling away a night during the slack season, when open-range ranches simply waited out the winter. They were dressed in coarse woolen shirts and wore their hats indoors. The thin warmth of the saloon barely kept the Montana night at bay.

The bald barkeep wore a white apron and black sleeve garters. The man squinted at Dirk, his gaze studying cheekbones and flesh, but Dirk trumped the gaze.

"There's a family outside in trouble. I've come to get help," he said.

"Who are you?" the keep asked.

"Dirk Skye."

The rest of the crowd said nothing. These were late-evening drinkers, and they had run out of conversation hours earlier. They were simply sucking redeye because that beat going to sleep somewhere.

"Hey, Dirk, you a breed?" one of them asked.

Dirk didn't respond. "I need to get a desperate family sheltered and fed. The woman's expecting. There's a daughter. Two men."

"Dey speaka da English?" asked one cowboy.

"No, not a word."

"Canadian breeds?"

"Someone burned their wagon. Everything they possessed. Their shelter, their food, their clothing, their weapons. They need help."

"Yeah, I'm sure they do. Maybe we should burn a few more wagons," said another cowboy.

"I'd like to pass the hat," Dirk said. He pulled his off and handed it to a young one holding down the end of the plank bar.

The cowboy handled it gingerly, grinned, and passed it to the next, who whipped it to the next, who turned it upside down and shook it. Nothing came out. They laughed. Dirk's hat traversed the row and halted at the last, where an older man who looked none too sober eyed it seriously.

That man rose, returned the hat to Dirk, and nodded.

"These bloomin' Métis are in trouble?" he asked.

"They have nothing."

The man eyed the rest. "I guess I can give a hand. They up to walking two, three miles? I got a place north of town, foothill of the Judiths."

"They can manage it, sir. And you would be saving their lives."

"Hey, don't do nothing like that!" yelled a younger blond cowboy.

"I'm Pap Reilly," the man said to Dirk. "I raise a few sheep and other stuff. My buckboard's out there, if the nag ain't fallen asleep on me."

"You've spared their lives, sir."

"I know how that is, lad. I know all about that."

They left the staring cowboys and plunged into blackness. The Métis huddled in the wind, fearful. Dirk beckoned.

"This is Pap Reilly," he said. "These are Marie, Josephine, Pierre, and Antony. I haven't got their last name."

The buckboard held the women and Reilly. Dirk offered the buckskin to the men, but they refused. And so the parade started, due north from Lewistown, bucking the wind.

twenty-three

*R*eilly set the horse at a brisk pace, and Dirk soon lost all sense of where he was going. The stars told him northeast; that's all he knew. He couldn't see the ears of his own horse.

"Do you think maybe we're going too fast for the men walking?"

"Ah, lad, it's good for them. Keep 'em warm. If they lose us, they freeze to death."

The women huddled in the robe, rocking with the wagon.

"These here people, they may as well be Swahili. It's a pity I can't talk to 'em. I like to talk. So you're it, Skye. You can get every bloody word I say, so I'm going to talk."

"That'll make the trip go faster," Dirk said.

Reilly laughed. "You're an optimist. You'll want me shutting up pretty quick now, but I've got ye caught, and you'll listen unless you fill your ears full of fingers."

Dirk heeled his horse forward. He actually wanted to hear Reilly.

"No man alive's lacking a story, Skye," Reilly said. "We all work on our stories, and perfect 'em, and use 'em. I got a story or two. Now let's take this story and get on with it. There I was, a poor boy in Waterford, and my poor pa, worn down by all the care he was givin' his brood, my sainted pa, he says, Pap, me boy, I can't afford to keep ye a day longer. I can't keep the children in food. I can't feed your ma. I can't earn enough sweepin' chimneys to keep ye. So, boy, I'm saying good-bye now. You're on your own, lad. I've scrimped up a little change, and it'll buy passage in steerage on one of them sailing ships down in the harbor, and it'll take you to wherever you're going. So, lad, your ma and me, we sez be off and quick, so we can get along."

"That's a sad story, Mr. Reilly."

"Oh, it gets sadder, Skye. I got me steerage, and ended up in Boston, and began doing most anything needed doing, just for a bit of food, and pretty quick I came west, got a few sheep, and here I am."

"That's inspiring, Mr. Reilly. You started at a tender age and survived. I hope you've made contact with your parents, just to let them know."

Reilly laughed. "You're a gullible feller, Skye. I made up the whole bloody yarn, and there's not a thread of truth in any of it."

"Then why tell it?"

"A man lives by stories, lad. And anyway, I just wanted to see how much a fool ye be."

This was an unexpected turn, but Dirk figured it would all work out. If these Métis got sheltered and fed, it didn't matter what sort of nonsense Reilly was full of.

They rode awhile more through a close night, with

the blackness coming at them, bearing down on them like the ceiling of a low cave.

"All right, Skye, I'll tell ye the true story. Me folks, they weren't sainted at all. My pa was a mean bugger, especially when he'd downed a few pints. That's when he'd pinch my ear until I was yowling. That's when he'd send me out to steal anything I could get away, so's he could trade if for another pint of ale. And my ma, she was worse. She kept a hickory stick she used to beat on me, just for the pleasure of it, boy. She'd send me out to steal, just like Pa, and beat me black and blue if I didn't come back with something real quick, and outrun the coppers too."

Dirk thought that the real story was a lot sadder.

"So there I was, boy, getting beat on, and all. My parents, they weren't fit to bring a child into the world. They ruint me and a sister and buried two brothers from the milk sickness. They thought children, getting lots of children, that would keep them in feed and ale. They called me unholy things, and I was getting to where I called them unholy things, but then one day I just took off. Why go back? I had rotters for a ma and pa, and things couldn't get worse, and if I did their bidding I'd be tossed into some gaol soon enough. So I get my skinny arse out, and headed to the water, and stowed away on a clipper, and got my skinny arse to Boston. How's that for a story, eh?"

"I'm sorry you were so unlucky, sir. We can't choose our parents. They're ours whether we want them to be. But you escaped, which says something for you. You're not living your life penned up in some rotten jail; you're here."

"Skye, you're a naïve idiot. There's not a word of truth in what I just told you. Not one damned word. I made up the whole story, just to see what sort of bloke ye be, and truth is, you're so gullible you'd believe anything. You're lucky I'm not some confidence man, because you're a natural victim. Anyone with a hard-luck story, you'd be their first mark. You're nothing but a mark, Skye, and anyone with a little cunning can see that."

Dirk didn't reply. Reilly was rubbing him raw.

"Take this bunch here, Skye. You've been had. They saw you coming and played you for a sucker."

"No, sir, I witnessed their tragedy."

"It's a racket, finding someone to take care of you."

"Then don't."

"Oh, a little edge on ye, eh?"

Reilly steered his wagon through the night, ignoring the deepening rancor that was exuding from Dirk, on horseback beside him. The women sat quietly. The men paced silently. They were far away from the saloon where they had met.

"The true story, me lad, is that I'm a bounder," Reilly said. "I fled Waterford with the law on my heels. I was a purse-snatcher, a cut-purse, plying the cobbled streets. I could outrun any old bummer out at night, and I had me a sharp razor to slice the bag away before the old cob knew what hit him. My pa—ma was dead—he gave up on me, told me to get away from little house and not come back. I snitched my way onto a freighter lying to, and went across as a stowaway, having cut what I needed to keep alive. It was cold, living in a lifeboat, but pretty quick Boston Harbor rose, and I crept off in the dark, inside a packing crate, eh? Pretty quick I cut me a pile of cash—hardly any cut-purses in Boston, so it was easy. Then I bought me a ticket west and stole a few sheep, eh?"

"Can you prove it, Reilly?"

The man laughed. "By Gawd, I'll make a skeptic of ye, yet."

Reilly sat comfortably, holding the lines, and then asked a question. "Every man has a story, Skye? What's yours?"

Dirk scarcely knew whether to say anything. Whatever he said was going to be as plain and true as he could make it.

"My father was a deserter from the Royal Navy. Jumped ship at Fort Vancouver. He took my mother, Blue Dawn, as his second wife. She was Shoshone. He called her Mary. I'm his only child. I had a Crow mother, he called Victoria, as well."

"After the queen?"

"Barnaby Skye was a good Englishman all his life, and became an American citizen only when he was old."

"There's no such thing as a good Englishman, Skye."

"My father was a good Englishman."

"So, then what?"

"Not much. Schooled in St. Louis. Taught at an Indian school on the Wind River reservation. Buried all my family. Worked for the army as a translator until I got into trouble. Married for about one hour to a Métis woman."

"Ah, now there's something worth telling, Skye."

"She vanished that very hour."

"Did ye get yourself into a rage and do her in, lad?"

Dirk started howling. Of all the possible conclusions one could draw from his confession, that was farthest from mind.

"She decided she didn't like me, Reilly."

"Well, she's one smart woman. I'll give her that. You're too gullible to be marrying anyone."

Dirk didn't have a reply, so he focused on riding his

buckskin through the cold night, while his travel companion snorted and cackled.

Reilly slowed the wagon suddenly, hunted about in the darkness, found what he was looking for—faint ruts off to the right—and turned onto them. The palest of sliver moons was finally yielding a ghost-glow to the night.

"Another half mile, laddie, and we'll put these refugees to work."

"To work?"

"You don't think I'm going to give them a free pass, now, do ye?"

"In the morning, then."

"No, right off, my boy. They can night-herd my livestock and keep the coyotes off."

"They've lost everything, Mr. Reilly. I'll do the night-herding. That woman beside you's far gone with child. The others have come on foot for most of twenty miles."

"You've got no sense of humor, Skye. You absolutely would not qualify as an Irishman."

"You're right. I haven't got a funny bone in me, Reilly. I'll night-herd, and then I'm taking these people off your hands. We'll be gone at sunup."

Reilly wheezed and snorted and spat a few times. "By gawd, Skye, it's the English in you."

The awful truth was that Reilly amused Dirk, but he was damned if he'd let the man know it.

A substantial log house loomed out of the gloom. Dirk saw some sheds and a rail-fenced paddock of some sort, but nothing else.

"Here now, laddie. You put my nag out in the paddock, along with yours, and I'll take these refugees inside and get a fire going and some patooties heating."

Reilly helped the woman and the girl step down, and motioned the men to follow, and took them all toward the bleak, dark building. Apparently Reilly lived alone.

"Now you come along, here, you elves. This is Tara, home of Irish kings, and I'm the King of the Universe," Reilly said.

The Métis couldn't understand a word, and Dirk thought that was just as well.

In the moonglow, Dirk led Reilly's dray to the gate, unhooked it from the tugs, and led it through the gate. He could find no rag or brush to wipe down the horse, but he did see a runnel leaking from a spring; the horse would find water. He brought his buckskin in, unsaddled it, wiped it down with his hands, for want of a brush, and turned it loose. He hunted for hay, found none, but did see some thin grass still standing. He carefully latched the gate behind him and headed for the cabin. Lights shone through the two small windows now.

He entered.

"Did you find the hay, laddie?"

"No, but if you show me—I'll take a bait to each."

"I'll do it. You get these people settled."

Reilly vanished into the night. Dirk found himself in a comfortable one-room structure. The new-laid fire in the stove would soon drive away the cold. A single kerosene lamp cast orange light onto the weary faces staring at him.

He tried French, which was closest to Michif of anything he knew.

"There will be food and shelter for us, *mes amis.* This man is from Ireland and he raises a few animals. I think he will offer you food and shelter, for some work."

"*Bien*," said Antony. He translated that for his people.

The woman, Marie, blessed herself and sank to the floor, collecting her daughter. They sat, backs to the wall, relief and weariness etching their faces. The men joined her, their backs to the wall. They were worn down to nothing.

Reilly returned, shook some loose hay off, and examined the stew, which was in a Dutch oven on the stove.

"Pork stew," he said. "Some tooties, some pork, some turnips."

"Pork?"

"What did you expect? Mutton? Laddie, you don't get the twist of it. I raise hogs. I confess to raising sheep down there at the saloon. Cowboys don't like sheep, but they respect a sheep man. Hogs! Now, if I told them I raised porkers, they'd not sip a glass of redeye with me. So in Lewistown, it's sheep. Here, it's hogs."

"Why hogs?"

"Mean devils. A catamount or a wolf thinks twice about going after a hog. I've got about a hundred, maybe twice that—who knows?—and mostly they root up a living for themselves, and I don't have to do much except haul one to the butcher now and then. I've got a prize boar too. Meanest in the lot. His name's Richard. Don't ever trust Richard."

"I never did," said Skye.

"This boar, Richard, he keeps an eye out. He'd eat that little girl."

"You should find a way to tell her parents, Reilly."

"You still calling me Reilly? How do you know that's my name, eh?"

"That's how you introduced yourself."

"Well, it's not. It's something else. A name that's well kept from cops and constables."

"Reilly, or whoever you are, you belong in that stew-pot," Dirk said.

"By Gawd, Skye, you'd make a good Hibernian."

The Métis sat wearily, waiting for the stew to heat. They hadn't eaten that day. But soon they would.

twenty-four

Therese made herself useful. Not only did she have a stew ready each evening, when the weary woodcutters returned, but she fashioned a broom of reeds gathered on a stick and swept the cabin daily. She began washing their clothes as well. They had no tub, but she heated water in a kettle and scrubbed their britches and flannel shirts and drawers as best she could. She mended the clothing too with some stout black thread and needles Armand got for her at the mercantile.

Armand also brought some rope, which she strung in the wood yard, and hung the washed duds on it. She was well aware of the passage of days and the steady advance of cold that often slowed down drying the clothing she'd scrubbed. Sometimes she would drape the clothes around the wood stove on whatever was handy.

This toil wasn't leading her anywhere, and least of all toward the great task she had been commissioned to do. And the days were long and lonesome. Sometimes all three men were out in the hills collecting wood. Other times Armand sent his sons out and stayed close, sawing and chopping mountains of wood into stove lengths. Other times he loaded a wagon with his wood and delivered it somewhere. Even a small place like Lewistown seemed to consume mountains of cordwood.

It was a mean life she was living; lonely and weary. Beau and Martin were usually too worn from their long days of hard work to do much more than devour their supper and fall into their bunks. But now and then Martin hovered about, curious about her, eyeing her small cubicle, his yearnings plain to her. Sometimes he was sullen; other times he was bold and opinionated and given to bragging. Once he put a hand on her hip; she firmly removed it.

"I am married," she said.

He laughed smartly at that. She wished she had deterred him in some other way.

But he was helpful too. He fashioned clothes pins from sticks he cleverly channeled, and after that she could entrust her washes to a windy day. The others barely noticed her face and figure, except to puzzle her solitude in their minds.

Nothing more was done about the church. That agitated her, but she was helpless to make things move. She apologized to all the saints in heaven for letting them down. She wondered if she had been given a false task, a delusion she would laugh at someday if she ever escaped this drudgery. Her people always worked hard, but the time always arrived when they tuned up their fiddles, poured some fiery drink, and danced the night away.

Then one day work found her. Arnie Campbell, who owned the Lewistown Mercantile, saw scrubbed clothing hanging from a line in the wood yard and came calling. Fortunately Armand was present, because Therese could understand very little of it. But Armand soon translated the whole meeting for her.

Campbell wanted her to wash his clothing. There wasn't any washerwoman in Lewistown. The only ones who washed anything were the sporting women, but they didn't wash for others, just for themselves. The men of Lewistown wore clothes so foul they got stiff with grime. If the little lady would wash Campbell's clothing, he'd give her a metal tub, some soap, and a good corrugated washboard, and she could repay him out of her services. If she'd wash other men's duds, he would act as her agent; collect the stuff and get it to her, and pay her two cents a shirt, one cent for britches, and one cent for underdrawers. And if she could mend, he'd pay her one cent for each rip she sewed up. He'd charge his customers more, of course, but she would get business and he would profit from the trade.

Armand didn't press her, and she was grateful for that. "If you do, the money's yours," he said.

"What money?" she asked. It would take a long time to earn one dollar.

He laughed. "Firewood is better. We're doing pretty good."

"I will do it," she said. "I've never been afraid of work. I do good work."

Armand walked over to Campbell's store and returned a while later with a galvanized metal tub, a washboard, an orange box of Fels Naptha, and more clothesline.

Then he pulled a heavy item out of the tub. "He sent this along too. For his shirts, even if no one else wants it."

He handed her a small flat iron. "One extra cent to iron each of his shirts," Armand said.

She rubbed a hand across the smooth bottom of the iron and clasped her hand around the wooden handle. She would need to be careful with it. But it would earn a little more toward the building of her church.

She immediately had more washing than she could handle and spent her days scrubbing and rinsing and twisting water out of clothes. Each day, Campbell brought her loads of clothing, sometimes in a burlap bag, other times loose. On good days they went outside; on the cold, dark, snow-spitting days, she draped them over every surface in the cabin, which often annoyed the men. But they didn't object. She was earning a little. Pennies, dimes, and two-bit pieces began to fill her spare moccasin. But it wouldn't buy a church.

Martin teased her, usually after he had demolished more of her stew.

"You should have stayed married," he said. "Now you got three men to feed and five hundred to keep clean."

"Well, you could wash your own clothing," she replied.

"I like for you to wash mine. I'll keep you plenty busy."

There was something possessive in his tone. She thought that when she could, she would move to a cabin of her own. She lived with three men in the same room, and she was depending too much on their restraint.

One sunny November day she grew weary of the endless toil, wrapped a shawl over her, and headed into a pleasant day. Her feet took her to the churchyard. The stakes were still present, but the small cairn with the claim in it had been demolished. She looked for the jar with the claim in it, but it was gone, and the rocks were scattered. Did someone want the land? It was well west of town. On the other hand, someone had trenched the foundation, so that there was a rectangle cut into the soil, and the rectangle was level. Fieldstone could be laid into it for the foundation of the church. So someone had been busy. But who? Beau and Martin? She didn't know. They seemed so busy harvesting and cutting dry wood to feed the town's appetites that she scarcely imagined they would find the energy and will to proceed.

She sat down on dry grass, directly over the point where the altar would be.

"Madame," she said. "Someone builds your church. And I have earned a little. But I don't have the means to build an entire church. I can only do a little. I do not know what you wish of me, but I am willing to do whatever I am directed to do."

She heard only the rustle of dead leaves.

Almost immediately, she grew aware of a commotion of hooves and discovered a two-horse ebony carriage toiling slowly up the grade from Lewistown. This carriage had a folding top that formed a hood, and that was up this day, even if the November sun warmed the afternoon. There was a sole driver, dressed in a long winter coat of gray wool, and a wide-brimmed felt hat, also gray. The carriage shone in the wan sun, as if it had not a speck of dust or mud on it. And the matched bay horses were perfectly groomed, with roached manes. They were in a handsome harness.

The man saw her lying just there, upon the place where the altar would be, and tugged the lines. The carriage stopped quickly. The bay horses heaved a little, having pulled the heavy carriage up a long slope.

The man didn't get out, but studied her for some while, saying nothing. She saw he had great wealth and thought maybe Saint Therese might have heard her pleas and was sending someone. But no, this probably was the same man she had met on the trail when she was coming to this place. She did not like him.

The man seemed very distant and probably didn't speak her tongue. She arose slowly, dusted off her long coarse gray skirt, and drew her shawl close around her. She didn't like being inspected, but that was what was occurring. It seemed rude of him.

"I don't suppose you speak English," he said.

She knew only what he was asking: did she speak the *Anglais*?

She shook her head.

"Then, madame, we will converse in French. You are a Canadian, is that not so?"

"Long ago," she said, reluctantly.

"From Saskatchewan, then."

She marveled that he could know so much.

"And you and your family arrived in 1871 or so."

"*Oui*, monsieur."

"And what is your name?"

"Therese Trouville."

"And your husband?"

"I am not married anymore."

"I've heard all about you," the man said. "You are the laundress."

She nodded.

"And this is the churchyard."

"It was given to me," she said.

"Ah, so I have heard, madame. You received a vision.

A French saint came down an ivory stairs and there was the scent of roses in the air, and you were commissioned to come here and build a church."

"She is not a French saint, monsieur. Therese of Avila is Spanish, and she was given the great task of reviving the Carmelite Order."

He smiled. "Forgive me my error. I do not know anything about these things. I'm not even a Protestant, having abandoned all thought of religion from the age of twelve or so."

He was conversing easily with her, and she knew most of the French, even though it was not quite her tongue. He seemed at peace, as if he were the lord of all creation here.

"You are?" she asked.

"Pardon me. Harley Bain. I manage a little property hereabouts. Manage is the correct word. It is open range, belonging to the government, and my actual property consists of a few acres." He lifted an arm and swept his hand in a broad arc. "But I manage the rest."

"You know something of me?"

"Certainly. It is my business to know everything. I know where you are living, in somewhat questionable circumstances. You are with the woodcutters. They are useful men. The whole town and half the ranches would freeze to death without them. And of course there is the miller over there, who is harboring several of your people. It happens we need him. And we need you: my men are filthy and need their clothing repaired. And it has come to me that the Sylvestres have returned to their home, even though they are not citizens, and are camped there with still more of the Métis. And I've heard about another family that showed up in the night a while ago, and is sheltering with that drunk who runs hogs north of town. And that's not all. One of my riders reports that a Canadian family of about twenty has occupied one of my line camps, stuffed six deep in bunks on every wall, and all of them without privacy. It is not something that white people tolerate."

Therese thought that this man would not contribute to her church. He sounded more and more like one of those who had supported the army, and sent all the people back to Canada.

"I will wash the clothing," she said. "And build my church."

"The clothing, that's fine. But building the church? I don't think so."

"And why not?"

"I think I want this land," he said. "It's close to town, and valuable. And I'm a citizen."

"I made a claim, in the name of the church."

"I'm afraid you didn't. You had no status as a citizen. Now if a bishop had made the claim, and he was a citizen, then I would say that the church would have some squatter's rights—a sort of preemptive claim until the land can be surveyed."

She didn't grasp all of that, but she got the idea.

"This is where my church will rise. It is given to me to build it," she said.

"Madame, I'm afraid not. It is not possible."

"It is not in my hands; it is in the hands of God," she said.

"Ah, I seem to have a powerful opponent, then. And here I thought it was merely the Métis I was facing. This little church was simply an instrument of you Canadians. Well, stern resistance requires stern measures. I think it is time for you to move on, madame. You will not want to live in Lewistown, especially one like you who is single and vulnerable."

He smiled, the gentle creases of his weathered face crinkling up slightly.

"*Au revoir,*" he said, and clapped the lines over the rumps of his trotters. The bays lowered into the tugs and drew the carriage upward and finally over the brow of the hill.

Therese knelt at the altar again. "I ask for help and what do you send me?" she asked her patroness.

twenty-five

*E*ven before the fullness of dawn, Dirk heard the thump of an axe. He knew intuitively what that was about. Pierre and Antony were out at Reilly's woodpile chopping firewood. Reilly had barely stayed ahead of his needs, but now the Métis were determined to help the pig farmer. They were good at it. It took skill to chop wood into stove lengths.

Dirk rolled out of his worn buffalo robe and found Marie and her daughter quietly at work at the stove, heating water and measuring rolled oats.

Reilly awoke with a start.

"A man can't get some shuteye around his own house!"

"Go back to sleep then," Dirk said.

"What're they chopping wood fer? We don't need it yet."

"Certainly we need it. You were out."

"I'm never out. When I need wood, I chop it."

"How long have you been in Montana?"

"Long enough to have second thoughts about it, is what my answer is to your nosy question."

"What are you going to do with all those hogs out there when it gets really cold and snowy?"

"I'm not going to nursemaid a bunch of pork."

Dirk laughed.

"They can fend for themselves or I'll haul them to town in my wagon and let 'em face what's coming."

"You've just started a hog ranch, Reilly. It's not a pig farm anymore. You've got some hired hands and some domestic help."

"I knew the good times would end if I brought you out here. Now I don't have a house to meself."

"Let the bad times roll, Reilly!"

The hog man eyed Dirk, and then subsided. "Maybe for a few days," he muttered.

"You think Fort Maginnis would trade some feed for some hogs?" Dirk asked.

"What do I need feed for?"

Dirk wasn't sure for a moment whether Reilly was just being ornery or whether the man had no idea what a Montana winter would do to his hogs and sheep, not to mention the chickens and ducks roaming outside the window.

"You wash your face, Reilly, and we'll load a couple of hogs into that wagon and see what we can do at the fort. Meanwhile, these people will look after your place."

It took a while, but Reilly finally downed some of the oat gruel that the women had boiled up, and the available males hogtied two porkers and set them into the spring wagon box, and then Reilly and Skye set out for the army post six or seven miles away.

"They going to throw you back up to Canada?" Reilly said.

"I'm not Métis. And I'm a citizen."

"Don't make any difference to soldiers. You look Métis, so off you go."

"I'm British and Shoshone."

"You think maybe those gents would stick around? I mean, hire on for help?"

"Food and shelter is all they seek for now."

"They got more coming?"

"Hundreds if you want them."

"They work pretty hard."

"They work from dawn to dusk, and they do the tough jobs that cowboys avoid."

Reilly was lost in thought as his plug horse tugged the wagon eastward, through a pine-girt pass and then out upon the broad plains. The hogs struggled and whined, knowing their fate, but they had been tied up tight. The day proved to be cold and clear, and the eddying air lanced the heat away from Reilly and Skye.

"What's your story today, Reilly?"

"I haven't got one. And if I did, I wouldn't tell you."

"Your story's about the change, Reilly. You've got some hardworking people who'll turn you into one of the biggest ranchers in the Judith Basin. Hogs, sheep, whatever."

"I don't want to be a big rancher. I just want my pint of ale, Skye."

Every now and then the spring wagon careened as the hogs fought their ties, but the wagon didn't tip.

They raised the post midmorning. It stood whitely, smoke drifting from a score of chimneys, operations largely suspended for the winter. Dirk steered the wagon toward the headquarters building, where a frostbit flag hung. Dirk had been around army posts for years and thought he knew how to proceed.

"I hope you know what you're doing, because I sure don't," Reilly said.

Dirk braked the wagon, stepped onto frozen ground, and into the board and batten structure. An orderly greeted him.

"I'm looking for the quartermaster or officer of the day. Got some hogs out there we'd like to trade for some feed."

"Hogs? Pork? Bacon?" the aide said. "You just stay right there."

He returned in a moment with a sergeant.

"Beadle here. Let's see the porkers," he said.

Beadle studied the writhing hogs, lips pursed.

"Guaranteed fresh meat," Reilly said.

"Pretty thin," the sergeant said. "Not much on those two."

"Well, if you don't want them, we'll go," Reilly said.

"I want them. I just want to whittle down the price to what it should be, and not what you think it should be," Beadle said.

They dickered. Dirk stayed quiet. If Reilly didn't like the price, Dirk would hear about it all the way back. But in time, they worked it out. Soldiers hauled the hogs off and loaded the wagon with fat bags of oats and barley and some molasses for sweet feed.

Dirk thought it was a good haul.

"Bring two more in a week or so," Beadle said. "We're tired of beef."

"We'll think about it," Reilly said, eyeing the mound

of burlap bags in the wagon box. "If the price is right. If you're going to ream me, I'll take my custom elsewhere. It's a long way from there to here and here to there."

Beadle lipped a cigar and smiled.

It was a long ride back, but the trip was joyous. When Reilly drew up at his ramshackle place, he began muttering. "What's that?" he asked.

"Looks like a hay pile to me," Dirk said.

It wasn't much of a pile, but it was native hay, scythed from the dried brown grass on the foothill slope nearby.

"What do we want that for?"

Dirk laughed.

"Waste of energy. We could all be lifting a tank of ale in Lewistown."

"You're stuck here," Dirk said.

It seemed scarcely possible that these people could have cut so much native grass hay, but there it was. And there were some grimy-looking sheep feasting on some of it.

"How many sheep and hogs you got here, Reilly?"

"Beats me. When they see me coming, they hide."

"These Métis are good at sheep shearing. Next spring, you'll have some wool if you don't eat the sheep."

"Are you trying to tell me how to run my own place, Skye?"

"As a matter of fact, that did occur to me, Reilly."

"Well, you're fired. They're all fired. I want them off my place."

"Guess you're stuck with them for a while."

Reilly threw up his arms, growled, and stomped off to the cabin.

Dirk didn't see Pierre or Antony, but he didn't doubt

they were making other improvements on Reilly's place. He spotted some hogs in a nearby pasture, feeding on something. The Métis were apparently collecting the feral beasts and luring them in with food.

Dirk entered the cabin and found Reilly in a sour mood. "I don't have a corner to myself, Skye. You did this to me. I can't get a moment's peace around here. Look at 'em! Cooking and cleaning like they own the place."

"Poor devil," Dirk said. "It's so hard to be taken care of."

"I can take care of myself, thank ye. All I need is some ale at the pub, and I'm a happy man."

"Your duds need mending, Reilly," Dirk said.

"I can mend 'em myself. I don't need a thing!"

"Well, your boots are falling apart and that coat's got a rent in it and those britches are an embarrassment around women."

"You've ruined me, Skye!"

Dirk looked around. In the space of a few hours the Métis mother and daughter had transformed the befouled cabin into a sweet-smelling, clean home. Reilly, if that was his name, would get used to it. And the place would feed and shelter the Métis until they could settle somewhere when these troubles had passed.

"Reilly, I'm done here. In the morning I'm heading for Miles City to get my stuff and then somewhere else."

"Where you going, Skye?"

"Wherever there's a job."

Reilly stared and relented. "Cheers," he said.

It wasn't until full dark that Pierre and Antony returned, and with them came the sounds of livestock. Dirk stood in the cabin door, listening. There were scores of hogs, and some sheep were blatting too. And the yapping of a dog.

He peered into the night and made out a long-haired herding dog of some sort, which was circling the hogs and sheep as if born to the task. Where it came from Dirk had no idea, but the Métis could walk up to any mountaintop and come back with much more than the Ten Commandments. A herding dog would help the Reilly ranch more than any other creature.

As soon as the Métis men came in, Marie and Josephine began serving more of their stew, giving the first bowl to Reilly.

"What am I going to do with all these people, Skye? I don't have a corner to smoke a pipe. Them and me, we can't speak a word."

"You don't need to speak a word. They'll take care of you."

"Skye, you blithering idiot. I live to talk. All I want is my mug of ale and some ears to hear me."

"Well, talk away, Reilly. It's a good thing they can't understand a word you say. That way they won't be bored."

"Insulting me now, are ye? Me, who gathered you up in the cold, and saved your lives. No sooner do you move in on me than you start in on me. Well, out with you!"

"In the morning, Reilly. I'm off at dawn."

"You deserting me, are you?"

"Yes. I have to get my own life squared away. The army fired me."

"And right they were too. They should've fired you straight off, Skye."

Dirk had come to the same conclusion, so he just nodded and smiled.

Sometime in the night, Dirk was awakened by the barking of that mutt outside. The incessant barking woke the rest too, and in time, the women got an oil lamp lit. Dirk thought it might be wolves. Whatever it was out there, there was noise.

Reilly was the first up, in his long johns, and opened the door. There, on his stoop, were half a dozen people, one of them an elderly woman, who collapsed even as the first warmth of the doorway reached her. The others waited abjectly in the cold until Reilly helped them in. Three burly men, a young woman bundled in a blanket, two little girls, and an ancient man in rags stumbled in and fell to the floor, too weary to stand.

They were Métis.

Marie and Josephine rushed to help these people, while Pierre and Antony checked outside to see whether there were more. The newcomers began some sort of talk with the other Métis people, most of which Dirk couldn't grasp. But there was just enough French in the dialect to give him a sense of what was being said.

"What are they yammering about?" Reilly asked.

"Night riders jumped their camp, burned every possession they had, including their tents, and left them to die in the cold."

twenty-six

*P*ap Reilly looked like a trapped rat. He watched sourly as the rest helped the Métis who had stumbled to his door. The cabin swarmed with these people, and they were babbling Swahili as far as Reilly knew.

Dirk helped to settle the newcomers. They needed warmth most of all. They needed hot food and a refuge where they could weep. They filled the whole cabin, filled its floor, filled its few rough chairs, filled its bunks, swarmed its hearth, surrounded its stove. And through it all, Reilly muttered to himself and looked about to explode.

There wasn't much to be told. These people had abandoned the Missouri Breaks as game diminished and hoped to find shelter among the Métis who had settled in the Judith country. Instead, they were left to die in the cold and everything they owned was ash.

That didn't soften Pap Reilly one bit. He glared at the mob in his cabin. He paced. He swung the door open, stared into the quiet night, and slammed the door shut. Finally he corralled Dirk.

"I'm going to have me a mug of ale in town. Get some peace and quiet. I want them gone when I get back. They're like dandelions; let in one and they take over the lawn."

"I'll help you harness," Dirk said. "And we'll catch a hog and you can take it to town. You'll get there before dawn."

"Now what would I do that fer?"

"These people need tools. Axes, saws, hammers, spades."

"Tools! I trade a good hog for tools? All I want is a quiet ale, talkin' with people who talk my tongue, not these pissants."

"You trade that hog for tools at the mercantile, and all these Métis'll get busy making themselves useful. You've got the farrowing shed, the lambing shed in your yard. Those are going to be your bunkhouse. The whole lot'll move into them. Oh, get a sheet-metal stove and some pipe too."

"Bunkhouse! Stove! Tools! What are ye babbling about, Skye?"

"You're about to become the most prosperous rancher in the Judith Basin. You'll have more hogs and sheep than there are people in the whole area."

"Prosperous rancher? Are ye daft, Skye? I want me a pint of ale and a bar stool with my name on it and the devil with the rest. Let the hogs and sheep take care of themselves, for all I care."

"Say, what does Pap stand for?"

"Pappy. Like in father."

"You a father?"

"Don't ask questions I won't answer."

"I'll get the wagon hooked up," Dirk said, sliding into the night. The well-lit cabin threw lamplight toward the pen and sheds. He fumbled around, found the bridle and harness, found the wagon dray, threw the collar over it, and buckled the rest in place. Reilly stood in the dark mumbling unhappily.

"They've robbed me of a night's sleep. They're taking over; they're multiplying by the hour, Skye."

"They're going to give you the skilled labor you need. They're going to put food and ale on your table, keep your house, do your chores, keep you warm."

"Do my chores? I don't have any chores."

"Well, now you do. You've won the jackpot, Reilly. You're a rich man."

"Rich, am I? All the way to the poorhouse."

"The saloons won't open until noon. But you can trade a hog for tools. Now, let's corral one of those porkers."

Dirk found a lariat on a peg and easily dropped it over a giant hog.

"Not that one, Skye. That's Richard, my boar."

"You should name your next boar Barnaby, after my pa," Dirk said.

"My next boar'll be Thomas Francis Meagher, after a patriot I know."

Richard was in no mood to be caught and tugged away, almost tipping Dirk. But Dirk handed himself down the rope, managed to slide it off the boar, and dropped it over a fat sow, who oinked piteously. Dirk always believed that hogs knew their fate. But with some help from Reilly, they got her tied up and into the spring wagon.

By the time they got the wagon hitched and the sow

hogtied and settled and Reilly into a good warm coat, the eastern heavens were showing early light.

"Shovels, axes, hammers, nails, canvas, a couple of tin stoves, some pipe," Dirk said.

"I'm going to spend every cent on ale, damn you, Skye. I'm going to drown in ale as soon as the saloon opens its doors. I'm going to tell them I got evicted from my own house."

With that, Reilly smacked his lines over the croup of the dray, and it tugged the wagon through the frost, while the bacon oinked and whined.

Dirk watched him go and soon the dawn light swallowed him. Reilly didn't know how lucky he was. He'd inherited some skilled labor, the most valuable commodity in the territory. There were ranchers across the whole area who dreamed of building homes or barns, dreamed of having skilled ranch hands, skilled gardeners, skilled cooks and wheelwrights and millers and harness makers and saddlers. But here he was, getting these riches for the price of a little food and shelter. It was better than a gold mine—if Reilly would figure it out.

But the man was just boneheaded enough so it might elude him. Either that or Reilly just didn't want to try anything out for size.

Dirk found the newcomers collapsed in corners of the room, lying everywhere but on Reilly's bunk, which remained property beyond their reach. Marie and Josephine were serving the newcomers any way they could, but most of these exhausted and half-frozen people wanted only to curl up in a robe and rest. The room couldn't hold them all, and the air was increasingly fetid. Marie handed Dirk a bowl of the stew, which tasted just fine as the new day brightened outside. He ate gratefully and weighed what he might do. He wanted to saddle up and head for Miles City, as he had intended. But there was trouble here, and he alone could mediate between Reilly and these worn and desperate people. Dirk decided to stay another day.

He heard the sound of chopping outside and realized that Pierre and Antony were already busy cutting wood for the hearth and stove. The old man was falling asleep. The two younger ones were propped up against a log wall, staring mutely into the smoky room, too worn to talk.

Dirk squatted next to the one who looked the most able to talk.

"I'm Dirk Skye," he said in French. "And you?"

The Métis stared, and then talked slowly in that tongue Dirk had so much trouble grasping.

"Alain Boulez," the man said. "All Boulez. Saskatchewan. Our *maman*, she is *mort*."

"Last night?"

"*Oui*. She saw the fire burn all we had, sat down in the snow, and perished."

"I am sorry. She was the spouse of him?" Dirk pointed to the old man.

"*Oui*. Now the wolves will have her."

"I'll go get her. I'll need to know where she is."

"Follow our tracks, monsieur. We walked all the way through snow."

Dirk got their story, bit by bit. These people were newcomers, refugees from the Northwest Territories, hoping to find the Métis who had settled earlier. It was their sole hope for surviving the winter. They were camped in a pine glade near a creek, their Red River cart laden with all they possessed, their two oxen finding a little grass through the crusted snow. And then the night riders had come, men on horses, men wearing slouch hats, chaps, thick leather coats, boots—and six-guns.

"What did they say?" Dirk asked.

"Who knows? They talked *Anglais*; we could not understand. But they made themselves clear, monsieur. The made us get away from our fire. Then they pitched everything we possessed into the fire. We watched our clothing burn. Our tents, our tools. We watched our venison turn to ash. Our few sacks of roots. And then they tipped the cart onto the fire, and the flames went high into the night, and the wheels burned, and the shafts and the axles and the wooden sides, and it was warm for a little while. Then they found our oxen and took them away so we would not have them to eat, and the *Anglais*-speakers, they rode away driving the oxen before them. And it was very quiet and soon very cold, and *maman,* she lay on the snow, her life taken from her, and we could do nothing. We could not carry her. We could not cover her. And soon it was dark and cold and bitter, and all life was bitter, and we would soon join *maman* unless we found refuge."

They bundled up in what little they had and started walking, not knowing how to get to Lewistown. They had only a creek to guide them. Travel down a creek and it would take them somewhere. For much of a bitter night they walked, stumbling through the inkiness, no moon to help them, and then one of the men smelled smoke, and his keen nose led them to Reilly's doorstep.

The cowboys probably assumed these people would be dead by now, lost in some obscure pine forest, never to be seen again. And their ranch would be richer by two oxen.

The story galled Dirk.

"You people rest. I will go for your mother when I am able," he said.

"The wolves," said the man. "Go quickly."

They simply stared at him, so worn by the night wandering the wilderness that they could do no more. Marie and Josephine were toiling quietly at the stove. So many mouths, so much work to feed them all.

"I'll be back as soon as I can," he said.

He dressed as warmly as he could. He was ill-dressed for winter, but the days were still mild. The cabin was as silent as death, but the people were watching him, those who could keep their eyes open.

He stepped into a sharp cold. Pierre and Antony were over at the lambing shed, shoveling the manure from it, leveling the ground. Dirk realized suddenly that they were starting to turn the sheds into a shelter, eventually a bunkhouse, a refuge for these people against the terrible winter that would soon be upon them.

He saddled his buckskin, found a hatchet and some twine, and headed out, the blood-specked trail in the patched snow easy to follow. Those people had stumbled and crawled, gotten up and stumbled on through the night. Dirk saw resolution in each step. The trail led slowly down to a creek flowing out of the Moccasin Mountains, and then to a thick pine woods.

The old woman was lying in the patchy snow, her face eaten away. Dirk was too late. Even as he approached, raptors flapped upward and brown animals streaked away. She faced upward, her face gone, her clothing the subdued and modest attire an old Métis woman might wear. A crucifix hung from her neck. Thousands of footprints dimpled the soiled snow around her.

He took off his hat, feeling the bitter air eddy through his own dark hair.

"This is where life ended for you, mother," he said.

Nearby was a mound of ash, gray and black, some small bits of iron lying about. A family's entire wealth reduced to nothing. It was as they had told him: the prints of shod horses told the story as much as the softer prints of moccasins and boots. This was murder. Not with a six-gun or knife, but with fire and ice.

He tried to lift her and found she was frozen tightly to the ground. He managed to pull her loose, bit by bit, tugging on her calf-high moccasins, until he freed her. But she was frozen stiff, awkward. He had hoped to carry her back to her people, but knew he couldn't. He needed to do something else that would honor and respect her. There were willows along the creek, and he knew he would honor her as her Cree ancestors might have. He would give her to the sun and the wind and the heavens.

She was very light but awkward to carry. The creek wasn't far, and he would find a place for her in the willows. He made his way to a noble willow with two horizontal limbs spreading out like wagon spokes. It would be her grave. He set her down gently and hunted for saplings, which grew abundantly there. These would give him the thin poles he needed to build a scaffold. Reilly's hatchet was dull, and it was hard work, but eventually he felled a few saplings and limbed them. The miserable hatchet sometimes bounced back rather than bit into wood. He tied two of the saplings to the willow limbs, as crosspieces, and the rest of the saplings he arranged in a row. Here she would lie until the sun and the wind and the snows and the eternal world took her home.

It took longer and wearied him more than he had expected, but the moment came when he had a scaffold. He lifted her gently and arranged her there, and wrapped twine over her to hold her there. Then he lifted his cap.

"Grandmother, this is your resting place. It is the way of our ancestors. I don't know your name but maybe you are related to Therese, and maybe you might have been my own grandmother by marriage. So I will grieve for you as I would one of my family. That is what you are, one of my family, the family of people of two bloods. And so I give you to God. I will tell your husband and your family that you are buried the ancient way, and you are not alone. You will never be alone."

He couldn't think of anything more, so he collected his hatchet and climbed onto the buckskin and rode through an utterly quiet autumnal morning.

He would start for Miles City now. He was done here. He had helped these people. He had his own life to look after. He headed back to Reilly's haphazard settlement, intending to return the hatchet and say good-bye. Reilly would soon come around to welcoming these people, and these people would in turn offer Reilly the labor that was required to make a home and an enterprise out of a patch of foothill land. Dirk was not needed here anymore.

twenty-seven

*D*irk was being shadowed. A rider was following, maybe a third of a mile back, and making no secret of his presence. It boded ill. Dirk was unarmed. Still, the rider was making no effort to catch up, and that counted for something.

Dirk stopped a while at a creek, but the rider never approached. Dirk rode on, and the rider reappeared. Dirk was heading toward Reilly's foothill hog ranch and wondered whether he should head that way or head straight for Lewistown. He decided to continue back to Reilly's place, collect his stuff, and leave.

This was lonely country. Reilly was situated in a land of long gulches that other ranch outfits didn't much care for, which was a reason no one bothered him. Dirk knew there would be no help if he should need it. This was one of those corners of the territory that embraced a lot of nothing.

But then, when Dirk reached a two-rut road heading out of Lewistown, he spotted the black carriage, its hood up, the trotters quiet in their harness. Waiting, waiting, waiting for him. It didn't surprise him. Harley Bain ghosted across this country, choosing the places he wanted to be and the times he wanted to be there. And now Bain was ahead, and Bain's business would be with Dirk Skye.

Dirk continued. The man behind was following along, keeping his distance. Bain's man.

He rode closer to the ebony carriage and could see Bain sitting patiently, dressed in a gray alpaca coat. Dirk steered his horse straight toward the carriage and then tugged on the reins.

"You want something from me?" he asked.

"Come sit in here," Bain replied.

"I'd rather not."

"I would like you to. My voice doesn't carry and I don't like to shout. I don't even like to speak up. It's not my nature."

"Do we have business?" Dirk asked.

"We do."

"Then I'll dismount and talk to you. Provided you tell your man out there to steer clear."

"He already knows that." Bain did have a soft voice, so soft that Dirk could barely hear him. Bain slowly surveyed Dirk, as if he were a piece of beef. "Yes, you're the one," he said. "I believe we've met. Not once but twice. Most recently, a few days ago on the Judith River. I've made some additional inquiries about you. You're Dirk Skye, translator for the army until Captain Brewer sacked you out in the field."

Dirk nodded.

"Ah, they tell me it was because you were exceeding your office."

"Captain Brewer was not pleased," Dirk said.

"And it was because you were siding with the quarry."

"The what?"

"The partridges and pheasants and prairie fowl."

Dirk had no idea what Bain was saying.

"All those Métis invaders the army was moving out of the area."

"Pheasants?"

"Game birds, Skye. The army sent out beaters to scare up the birds so they could be shot."

"What is your business? If this is it, I'll be on my way now," Dirk said.

"You're a mixed-blood yourself, Skye. Shoshone mother, British father, a deserter I'm told. Not much of an inheritance for you."

"I don't think we have any business, Mr. Bain."

Skye turned toward his buckskin, intending to ride away.

"Wait. I'm offering you a job. I've ridden all this way to employ you."

"I don't think I want that job."

"Hear me out, Skye. This whole business of driving the flotsam and jetsam of life away from here is melancholic, is it not? It is. I am saddened by it. My riders are instructed not to take life if they don't have to. But winter finishes off the very people whose lives I have spared. It killed the old woman you just buried. I use the term loosely. The old woman bearing a crucifix that you buried savage-style on a scaffold. She would have preferred a priest and a funeral, I'm sure. But she had to settle for you. Now, Skye, you don't see my men abusing these illegals. You see them merely building fires here and there and burning their possessions, which means they have nothing at all with which to establish themselves in the States. That's all I can manage. The army tried humanely to drive them back to Canada, but the army lacked the manpower, and these illegal half-breeds settled into the Missouri Breaks and now they're swarming my land once again. That's where you come in."

"Federal land, not your land."

Bain smiled for the first time, a gentle shrug. "The land belongs to whoever is willful enough to hold it. I am, and I do. It is mine and will be in the foreseeable future."

"You done? I'll be on my way."

"Not done, Skye. As I say, I am hiring you."

"I don't think so."

"You haven't heard my proposition. Aren't you curious about what I would pay? And what you would do? I'll start with the latter. I'm melancholic about all this. I don't like to cause suffering, but I am forced to inflict it to protect my grazing land. So I thought to hire you. It will be your task to intercept these people, tell them to head for Canada. You're a mixed-breed and they will listen. That would lift my sagging spirits, Skye. I am a sensitive man, you see. I really don't wish to trouble those people. So I've thought of this approach as a way of relieving my pain. You will receive a bonus for each family or travel group you turn back to Canada."

"Sorry, I'm on the other side. I'd like to see them settle here. They're good, hardworking people."

Bain smiled. "But you haven't heard my proposition."

"I don't need to."

"Yes, I'm afraid you do," Bain said gently. "Your pay. Aren't you curious about your pay?"

Dirk in fact was curious.

Bain nodded gently, stared up at the overcast. "Your pay will be life."

"Your pay is life?"

Bain smiled blandly.

It took a while for Dirk to register it. Bain was reading him.

"You can start by evicting that crowd of Métis that Reilly's got. Then you can evict the Métis in Lewistown, including the girl who's started building a church. You will tell them to head north at once."

"A church?"

"A Métis girl says her mission is to build a church, and this was handed down to her by some saint or another, and she's stirring the pot there. Evict her."

"I'm on my way to Miles City," Dirk said.

"Then I can't pay you," Bain said softly. "Pity, now, isn't it?"

"And what of the bonuses you are offering?"

"Two dollars for every Métis you persuade to head north, with no thought of remaining south of the border. You're a half-breed and a translator. Ideal for the job."

"Cattle are selling for more per hundredweight, Bain."

"Exactly. Cattle are worth more."

"I'm on my way to Miles City."

"What a pity." He eyed Dirk carefully. "I can read you well. You've just decided to stay. You're throwing everything away. You could winter here for a five-hundred-dollar profit."

"I don't buy or sell human beings, sir."

The rancher smiled. "Well, then, till we meet again, eh?"

He slapped his lines over the croups of the trotters and the ebony carriage rolled away, swaying slightly in the rutted lane.

The outrider waited awhile, and then followed Bain westward.

So a hundred-pound Métis was worth two cents a pound. That was the price for breeds, apparently. Dirk figured he'd be worth three dollars in all.

It was very still. Midafternoon, actually. Time enough to make Reilly's place before dark. Nonetheless he heeled the buckskin hard and put the horse into a mile-eating jog. He would alert those people to the threat. And he would ask them about Bain's strange story of the Métis girl in Lewistown heeding a vision from a saint. Dirk had heard odd stories, but this was oddest of all.

What sort of man was Bain? A gentleman who spoke softly and found a way not to call murder what it was. And obviously, a man of iron who would impose his will upon the great basin, no matter the cost. And also a lonely man. There apparently were no women in his life, no mothers or daughters or sisters or a wife. There must have been once: he knew his manners and was unfailingly civil, even when he was threatening death.

"Pay me with life," Dirk said to the buckskin. "They treat horses better."

The return trip was uneventful although Dirk kept a sharp eye for trouble. He didn't know what he would do since he was not armed. But nothing happened. He reached the long gulches of the Reilly place and followed one toward the home place, halfway up the foothills. He scared up some wild hogs, which bolted with surprising speed. Reilly was richer than he knew, after years of neglecting his livestock.

Reilly's spring wagon stood in the yard, unhitched and empty. So Reilly was back. The Métis males were hard at work on the lambing shed, and some of them had new axes. Others were working wood with a new saw. So Reilly had traded the hog for tools, in spite of all his folderol. A tin stove stood inside the shed, along with some stovepipe and a roof jack. Dirk smiled. A trapped loner like Reilly would do all he could to usher the Métis out the door. But not too far out the door. Reilly was eating better than he ever had in all his bachelor years.

Dirk unsaddled and brushed his buckskin and let him loose to graze.

That's when Reilly steamed out the door, looking irate.

"Now look what ye got me into," he said. "The butcher, Carstens, wouldn't pay me a fair price for the hog and I had to sell cheap. The mercantile, they charged twice too much for all this stuff. And I hardly had a dime left over to buy me some ale and a little Jameson's at the saloon, and now ye cheated me out of a hangover, but maybe one's coming on. How can a man go to town without payin' a price the next morning, eh? You've ruint me, Skye."

"I'll hogtie another porker and you can go soak at the bar for a week, Reilly."

"You think that's funny, I suppose, but you don't have twenty Indians robbing you of sleep."

"Métis are mixed-bloods."

"Whatever they are, I'll thank the stars and the saints when they're outta my house."

"What's the word in town?"

"It's all them Canadians. Few more families got burnt out of all they have. A couple bunches made it to Lewistown. There's a regular Métis hotel some woodcutters are running, them red ruffians crowded into there like so many communion wafers. And that reminds me, Skye. There's a saint in Lewistown. Some say she's Saint Mary come down from heaven in the form of a Métis girl, and some say she's Saint Therese, and you know what she's up to? She's building a church. She says it came to her in a vision straight out of heaven. Go build a church for her people there in Lewistown. She's either a loon or sent by God or both.

"I can't fathom it. I don't suppose they'll let a drinkin' man through the door, but maybe I'll help. She's got them Canadians working on that thing. It's west of town on a rise, and they got some rock in for the foundation and are working on a floor. Them woodcutters are bringing in logs and the Métis are shaping them with drawknives or whatever, and laying in the floor. And she's sort of wandering around there, never smiling, just watching, like she's God's messenger.

"I drove by there and I saw more than I wanted to see. There were a mess of Métis, but also a mess of spectators, half of the saloon men and merchants in town, watchin' like they'd never seen a building going up before. And I'll tell ye, Skye, I didn't like the smell of it. The Métis building the church and all them others, they looked like they needed a few rounds of whiskey to get themselves properly stirred up."

"I heard about the girl."

"How could you? You weren't there."

"Harley Bain wants her out and offered me the job."

"You breeds are up to no good," Reilly snapped and walked off.

"I didn't take it," Dirk yelled at his back.

twenty-eight

*D*irk Skye was torn. Part of him wanted to get out, go find a job somewhere. The other part wanted to stay here, help these refugees find food and shelter and safety. He didn't know what he could do to help. He was a schoolteacher, a translator, and a man at loose ends. But he would help. He was like his father, a man with no past and no future, adrift in the New World, looking for some way to get ahead.

The New World wasn't so new anymore. The West was mostly settled. There were territories, counties, sheriffs, governors, ranchers, and towns here and there. Barnaby Skye had taught him to take care of himself in the wild. But this wasn't wilderness, and every county had its sheriff and every territory its governor and legislature and courts. Harley Bain used public land and drove others off of it, and the reasons weren't obscure. He wanted his neighbors to be English-speaking white men, not mixed-bloods who spoke strange dialects. This was not about the land; it was about neighbors. The right kind of neighbors.

And that's why Harley Bain was purging the Métis from Montana. It wasn't quite genocide. It wasn't quite war. It was all clothed in legality: send the Canadians back to Canada. They were illegal immigrants. And now Dirk found himself drawn into a conflict in which he had no stake. Maybe it was the weariness and desperation he had seen in the faces of the refugees. Maybe it was Bain's offer of "employment." Maybe it was Bain's thinly veiled threat against Dirk's life. But there was more here, something that had to do with good and evil, justice and injustice, right and wrong. And Bain and his ranching friends were wrong. This was a good land and it could bear all sorts of fruit: not just beef, but gardens, wheat farms, orchards, children, schoolhouses, peaceful villages, churchyards, people living in harmony with one another.

He did have something to offer. He had a foot in each camp. He was at home among Indians and whites. He could help people talk to one another, understand one another, do business with one another. He could bring the beliefs and thoughts of the Métis to the Yanks. He could also convey the unhappiness of people like Bain to the Métis. Maybe he could mediate, get them to talking, find ways to make this bountiful territory welcome the refugees from the north. He had the advantage of possessing two bloods, and that might help him.

"You leaving now?" Reilly asked. "Quitting me now I got a house full of strangers and I can't understand a word?"

"No. I'm going to ride into Lewistown and see how the war's going."

"And then come back and mooch on old Reilly, like everyone else. You'll eat me out of house and home."

Dirk laughed. "You're stuck," he said.

The buckskin was weary but Dirk saddled up anyway. He steered toward town, across a quiet country, seeing no one. This land was so big it could absorb thousands of people and still not be too full. This was big country, big enough for sheepmen, cattlemen, truck farmers, wheat growers, shopkeeps, livery barn operators, blacksmiths, and the skilled and unskilled people of all the world.

Lewistown snugged sleepily in its valley, its many chimneys curling smoke into the November sky. All those stoves and hearths were being fed by Armand Trouffant's strong arms. Without woodcutters, Lewistown would be a cold and miserable burg.

He rode quietly through town, noting its peacefulness. There was nothing amiss here. He turned west on the main street, that being the way to the new church. It was easy to spot, somewhat higher than the town. There wasn't much to see. He reined the buckskin and stepped down. A lot of sandstone had been collected and roughly dressed and fitted together into a dry wall foundation. It was going to be a small church. Dirk wondered if it would seat more than fifty people. But the sandstone rectangle stood ready to receive the weight of a church. Some roughly squared logs had been laid on the rectangle, and rough-hewn joists spanned the rectangle. They would support a floor. Whoever was building this church was doing it without planed lumber, and much of the pedestal had been squared with an axe and drawknife.

There wasn't a soul around, and Dirk wondered what the fuss was about.

He found a small cairn, a location marker of some sort, and a document in a bottle. He pulled it out and read it. The land had been claimed by the Diocese of Helena and would be the future home of Saint Therese Catholic Church.

And the document had been signed and dated by Armand Trouffant.

Dirk stared at it. Where was the signature of the Métis woman? She probably couldn't read or write.

"You wondering about that thing?" a man asked. "You ain't the only one."

Dirk found a black-bearded Yank, rawboned and small, with eyes that burned like coals.

"New in town. I heard a church is going up."

"And coming down," the man said. "It's not a church. It's just a meeting house for them half-breeds from Canada."

"Who are you?"

"I'm the mayor, Phil Stoltz."

"You have a business?"

The man pointed. "That saloon." He stared at Dirk. "You Métis?"

"No. I'm a citizen."

"You don't look like one."

"Citizens come in all shapes, I imagine."

"At least you talk English good. You drifting through? We don't let breeds stay in town overnight."

"I won't be here tonight."

"Neither will this be here by morning. There's going to be a little party here this evening."

"It's church property."

"It ain't anyone's property. The priests don't know it exists."

"Who signed this claim?"

"Woodcutters on the east side of town. They got a strange woman living there, and not married either. She's putting them up to it. I wouldn't mind woodcutters around here but not her. They keep the town in cordwood, and no one else wants to do it. But she's different. She's got some sort of magic hold on them, so they do her bidding. Like a witch."

"What do you mean, magic hold?"

"That stuff's all hoodoo. She tells them that some saint came down some stairway from heaven and told her to come here and build a church. If you ask me it's just bunk. But it's got a few breeds around here all stirred up, so they spend an hour or two every evening, laying up the foundation and dressing logs and all that. But it's all gonna stop this night."

"What's her name?"

"Beats me. But I hear she's naming the church after herself. How about that, eh?"

"Theresa?"

"Who cares? She's a half-breed."

"Where does she live?"

"The woodcutters. But we'll get rid of her quick."

"What are you going to do with her?"

"Sell her to the madam, I guess."

"With her permission, of course."

The mayor shrugged. "She's a breed."

"Would you sell your daughter to a madam?"

"I don't have any—that I know of." He laughed. "Now, you hightail outta here. No vagrants in Lewistown."

"What about white vagrants?"

"There's no such thing."

Dirk said nothing, boarded his buckskin, and rode

slowly toward town while the mayor watched. But Dirk wasn't interested in the saloons or the mercantile. He continued until he spotted a wood yard with heaps of firewood, some cut to length. A black-haired man was rhythmically chopping, his axe rising and falling, knocking limbs and trunks into stove wood. Dirk paused to watch. The man never paused, and never wasted motion. He had sawn rounds of trunks or limbs on end and shattered them, sometimes managing to cut several pieces loose in two or three blows. He didn't rest. He didn't seem weary. He didn't pause or wipe his brow. He had, actually, a huge heap of stove wood, enough to feed Lewistown's needs for weeks ahead.

The man appeared to be a Métis, with the ruddy flesh and stocky build and jet hair of those people. There were stacks of uncut logs, which suggested others were out collecting the wood from the surrounding jack pine forests. There were wagon ruts into the wood lot, and they showed signs of steady use. Smoke curled from the log home beside the spring creek flowing past the yard. And laundry hung from a line nearby. A woman was caring for this man, and the others who must live in this place.

The steady thump continued as the Métis shattered log after log, with a hand so practiced that he rarely failed to sever pieces of wood. Once in a while he picked up his fresh-cut stove wood and tossed it into the growing heap. Was this how the man spent his waking hours? Was there nothing else in his life? Did he awaken at dawn and eat some sort of porridge and then spend a whole day feeding the needs of Lewistown?

Dirk turned in. The man saw him coming, but didn't

pause until Dirk reined the buckskin and slid off the saddle.

"*Oui?*" the man said.

Dirk chose French. "Are you Armand Trouffant, who signed the claim?"

"*Oui.*" Trouffant leaned into his axe and waited.

"I am Dirk Skye. I was just there. I was curious. A man who called himself the mayor approached me. Stoltz is his name. A saloon man. He asked me to leave by sundown."

"And you're looking for a place to stay, *oui?*"

"No, I am welcome at a ranch north of town."

"A cowboy, that is what you are?"

"No, a teacher. I taught at an Indian school, and then I was a translator." He let it go at that.

"Then you are with the army."

"Was. I was a civilian translator. No more."

Trouffant's demeanor changed. "I have no business with you."

"That is true. I came to warn you of something."

"I hear warnings every day. They mean nothing."

"The mayor said that this night there's going to be a little party at your church. And before it's over there will be nothing left of it."

Trouffant squinted at Dirk, uncertain.

"It gets worse. You have a woman here."

"*Oui.* A saint, I think. A messenger from God."

"I think you'd better spirit her away while you can. She is in grave danger."

Trouffant lifted his woolen cap and ran thick fingers through his hair. "*Non,* these people, they may not like the Métis, but they need me and they know that there is no one else who can keep them warm. My boys and I, monsieur, we are secure here."

"The woman isn't. Métis, is she?"

"*Oui*, she is one of the people."

"By dawn she will be employed in a place where she would not wish to be."

Trouffant stared, doubting. "The hand of God protects her. She comes and goes unharmed. She washes clothing for many. The men of Lewistown, they bring her soiled clothing and she cleans it. She is safe, monsieur."

A young woman stepped from the cabin, a wicker basket filled with washed clothing in her arm. She hung each piece carefully until the line was burdened with shirts and union suits and drawers. Then she turned to face the guest.

Dirk stared. It could not be.

She stared, hesitated, and approached.

"Therese?" he said.

"You, Monsieur Skye?" she asked. "How can this be?"

"You—look well, Therese."

She seemed flustered, ready to escape to the cabin.

"You know each other?" Trouffant asked.

"He was my husband," she said. "But that is the past. He is a stranger now, employed by the army."

"*Sacre bleu!* Now I connect the ring on your finger to someone!"

"*Non*, monsieur. It lasted only an hour. Now the ring is for my true husband, the church. I am married to the church, forever."

twenty-nine

*T*here was something so final in her pronouncement that Dirk could only believe it was time to go. She stood there, cold and unmoving, like a bronze statue, her gaze upon far shores.

Monsieur Trouffant intervened. "Madame, the monsieur has come to warn us that there might be trouble at the church. It was very kind of him."

"Warned—or threatened?" she asked.

Trouffant seemed disconcerted. "Threatened?"

"He is a translator for the army."

"No, Therese. I have no employment."

She stared at him, her face a wall.

"Monsieur came here to warn you away, madame," the woodcutter said. "I think you should heed what he says. The mayor himself gave the word."

She stared at Dirk, and at the woodcutter. "We will go to the church. Your sons will be there and will need us."

Trouffant hastily explained it all to Dirk. "Each day, my sons bring in the firewood, and then go fell a tree and bring a log to the church. There are several families now. Eight, ten, maybe more Métis, filtering in, living in the shadows. They send their sons and fathers, and we square the logs with drawknives and prepare for the moment when we'll raise the walls. Now is the hour. We will work until night overtakes us."

"I will help," said Dirk.

Trouffant grinned. "Even a man of words can square a log with a drawknife, *oui?*"

"I would prefer that you stay here and guard madame," Dirk said.

"There is no need to guard me," Therese said. "And why do you discuss my fate as if it were not my choice? Some husband you'd be."

Chastened, Dirk kept quiet. Trouffant was grinning.

There would be an hour or two until twilight; time to prepare several logs for the walls of the church. Lewistown seemed preternaturally quiet.

"Come meet my sons, Beau and Martin. Good sons, bringing strong shoulders to their lives."

"I will help square logs," Dirk said.

Therese wrapped a blue shawl over her hair and about her neck. Its ends fell loosely over her gray dress. Somehow, the sight of her stirred Dirk, and he couldn't say why.

They walked through town while Dirk led his buckskin. There didn't seem to be anyone out on the road. When they reached the church on the slope, they found a dozen people working steadily. Some were bucksawing the planks that would rest on the floor joists. Others were working the great logs, peeling back the bark and squaring them and smoothing them. When they had enough of these, they would lay up the log walls. But there were many logs to go, and Dirk wondered whether this church would be roofed before spring. Still, here were the burly dark Métis, magically present, quietly hiking miles from their obscure cabins and huts, to build this edifice to their faith—and their presence in the territory. As they approached the church lot, the Métis men stopped their labors and crowded toward her and stood silently, awaiting something.

Dirk watched, uncertain what all this was about.

"The blessings of our Lord are upon you," she said.

"Blessed be the Lord," they replied.

They nodded, tugged at caps, eyed her tenderly, and returned to their labors. They worked hard and fast, shaping wood into useful forms. Two teams of strong-shouldered men were buck-sawing thick planks. These were cut from logs resting on a rack of some sort. Others were sitting on great logs, drawing their knives over the surfaces, peeling away bark and flattening the side that was facing upward. Others were sawing rounds or splitting them into shakes for the roof. They were toiling hard, as they had night upon night, devoting the final hours of each day to the task, even after they had done all that needed doing to advance their own survival. The Métis worked and worked and there was no end of work for them.

Dirk marveled. They pulled their drawknives along the trunks, peeling away bark. A single blow of an axe produced a shake for the roof. Dirk thought he saw one or two of the men who had found refuge at Reilly's hog ranch, but he couldn't be sure. These Métis wore woolen caps pulled tight over their jet hair, and it was hard to tell one from another.

"Therese, I will help," he said.

She eyed him levelly. "I don't want your help," she said. "I will help anyway."

"You are not one of my people. You are not one of my faith."

"I honor your people and I respect your faith."

"You talk too much," she said, and turned away.

Trouffant eyed him and shrugged.

The rattle and creak of the carriage changed everything. Harley Bain's ebony vehicle rattled down the long grade from the west, pressing against the croups of his drays. It crept closer to the church site and finally turned in. Behind Bain rode a dozen cowboys, armored against the cold in chaps and heavy coats. And armored against the Métis with holstered revolvers and some scatter guns. At almost the same time, a similar crowd, but larger, marched out of Lewistown and up the grade. These were saloon men and merchants and town toughs, armed with pikes and crowbars and sledgehammers.

The Métis watched and kept right on toiling. The Métis bore no arms; the gathering mob was well armed. Dirk watched uneasily, scarcely knowing what to do. He had no weapon and knew that possessing one at that moment could be fatal. He could only wait and see, and maybe as a translator he could mediate. But even as Bain steered his shining black carriage close to the church, Dirk knew there was nothing he could do, nothing anyone could do. Whatever would happen would be entirely at the whim of the rancher in his black suit of clothes and gray coat and cream-colored hat.

The cowboys rode outward, forming a broad line on either side of the carriage, and simply waited as the city mob climbed the long grade.

But the moment came when the whole crowd had assembled, and at last the dozen or so Métis stood and waited.

"Good evening, madame," Bain said, lifting his hat slightly and settling it again. "And you, Mr. Skye. Good evening."

Dirk didn't respond. Therese lifted her jaw, and let her blue shawl slide away from her smooth dark hair, and waited proudly.

Bain seemed almost apologetic. "I feel this is most unfortunate, madame, but you were told that you're trespassing on my property. I have filed on it. You were told that your church doesn't own it. So . . ." He smiled wanly. "You face eviction."

"I was first," she said in clear English.

Bain sighed. "It's a pity," he said. "Now you will kindly direct your illegal immigrants to vacate."

"They would not even if I asked them."

Indeed, the Métis stood rooted at their posts.

"It's a pity, madame. Do think it over."

Dirk watched the city mob spread wide. Some carried kerosene cans. The pikes and crowbars told him all he needed to know.

"Mr. Bain, if you have a dispute with her, then there are courts of law to settle it," Dirk said.

Bain stared at him. "What business is it of yours, Skye?"

"I side with my wife."

Bain was visibly startled. "Ah! Somehow that eluded me. My intelligence seems to be lacking. Is it so, madame?"

She stood icily, refusing to respond.

"So take it to court. The territory has justice courts to settle this," Dirk said.

Bain sighed again and slowly shook his head. "One never gets proper justice in territorial courts, you know. A man sometimes has to defend what's his."

"Or what he steals," Dirk said.

Bain nodded and stood up in his carriage. "Remove them," he said. His cowboys swiftly lifted their revolvers and shotguns. Now there were a dozen black bores pointing at the Métis, and two or three more directed at Skye and Therese.

"Tell them to leave the premises, madame."

"I will not."

Dirk was certain Bain was bluffing. He would not command a massacre of unarmed people building a church.

The seconds ticked by, and nothing happened. The Métis stared into the bores, unmoving. The townsmen licked lips and waited, anticipating horror and blood in the earth.

Bain waited, while nothing at all happened. Then he pointed. "Get her," he said.

Dirk saw two of Bain's men head for Therese and piled toward them. Armand Trouffant did also, and between them they caught the oncoming cowboys in a bloody brawl. Therese fled backward, while the Métis gathered around her, their saws and axes in hand.

But in moments, additional cowboys pinioned him to the earth, and it was over. Trouffant knelt, a dozen hands holding him.

Bain stood over Dirk, smiling down. "You see? Your salary for me was to be life."

Dirk hurt. Someone had kicked him in the ribs and bloodied his nose.

"Whose life?" Dirk said. "Yours or mine?"

Bain paused, registering that. "I'm glad you came clean, Skye. Know thine enemy is sound advice."

He nodded, and the townsmen swarmed toward the construction, a swarm of wreckers who wasted no time prying up the floor joists, wrenching the squared foundation logs, smashing the rock footings. More of them poured kerosene over the works, drenching shakes and squared logs and planks, and then light flared, and flame leaped upward, licking the dressed wood, even as the mob tossed more and more planks and beams into the inferno.

The Métis watched silently, still guarding Therese with their lives, a wall between her and Bain and the spectators. Bain settled in his quilted carriage seat to watch. He seemed to be in no hurry. The thump of sledgehammers added to the crackle of the giant fire as Bain's men bashed the rock foundation to bits and scattered the rock so it could never again be put to use there. The fire grew into a giant beacon that cast wavering light on the town a mile below.

No one moved. Bain was plainly going to watch until he was certain nothing could douse the fire or salvage so much as a twig. The Métis men stood sternly, axes in hand, ready to die for the woman they believed was sent from heaven. Now and then Bain eyed her, and eyed them, calculating whatever would come when the fire was beginning to die. The flames cast a ruddy and pleasant heat a great distance, warming Dirk as he lay on the ground, several cowboys keeping him there.

He wanted to rescue Therese. He had not forgotten the sinister threats the mayor had mouthed to him. But the reality was that he was helpless. He eyed the crowd and discovered a cowboy holding the rein of the buck-skin.

Maybe he could bargain. He had no chips. He had no weapons. His wife, if she could be called that, was safe for the moment behind a stern wall of outnumbered and unarmed Métis. So far, no one had died. Bain probably preferred it that way. Deaths were messy. Deaths created inquests and investigations and sometimes indictments. That was the only bargaining chip Dirk had.

The crackle and thunder of the flames blotted out conversation. What had started in quietness now was a roar shooting hot sparks into the last of the twilight.

When at last the flames began to diminish, Bain stirred.

"Madame, you will leave this area at once."

She stared stonily.

"If you do not leave, you will never see your husband again."

She glanced briefly at Dirk, who was still pinioned on the ground. "I will rebuild my church," she said. "This is where it will be. That is what I received."

For once, the smooth Harley Bain seemed nonplused. He stared at her, and then at Dirk, and finally shrugged. "You have condemned your husband."

"No, I have not. You have."

"It is within your powers to save him, madame."

"It is within your powers to release him."

The odd thing for Dirk was that he sensed she had spared him his life. It didn't make sense. But Harley Bain's threat was now public; everyone in that mob fathomed it. And however powerful the rancher who dominated the whole Judith Basin was, he would not escape the law of the territory.

But now much still hung in the air. A dozen or so Métis, wielding little more than axes, stood firmly around a woman they regarded as something of a Madonna, and they would die for her if they must. There were men out in the mob with blood lust in their faces, men with shotguns and pikes.

Bain sat quietly, content to let events continue as they might. The flames withered, and the roar diminished. There was nothing left of the church and the wood intended for it but char and ash.

"I think winter will do the job," Bain said.

He nodded. The cowboys released Dirk, who stood slowly. One gave him the reins of his horse.

"Scorched earth and Montana cold will do it every time," Bain said. He lifted the lines and slapped them over the croups of his trotters. The ebony carriage wheeled away, climbing the long grade out of the Lewistown valley. Bain's motley army of ranch hands and cowboys followed along behind.

The mob remained, the light playing across their faces. But then, slowly, something eased and it was over.

"Therese, I would be pleased to take you to your home," Dirk said.

She didn't object. Still surrounded by every Métis male, including Trouffant and his sons, she walked slowly away from the saloon men and their merchant friends, step by step, away from the firelight, through town, and finally to Trouffant's wood yard.

She reached the cabin and turned to them. She walked from one man to the next, clasping the hands of each. "Thanks to you, we will continue. Thanks be to God. Thanks be to each of you. Tomorrow we will begin."

She reached Dirk and peered up at him. "Thanks be to you," she said. She clasped his hands.

Dirk looked at her, standing before him. "You are beautiful," he said.

She turned swiftly away, and he could not see her face.

thirty

irk was filled with his aloneness. He made his
way back to Reilly's place, the only refuge he
had at the moment. The weary buckskin carried him through darkness that matched the darkness
within him.

Therese had softened a little, but what did it matter?
He didn't want her. He didn't want a woman who cali-
brated her affections on some scale of loyalty to her people.
He had wanted her because he loved her just as she was.
She had doled out her favors based on whether he was
sufficiently Métis to suit her. It would never work. He'd be
better off forgetting her but that wasn't possible. She was
there, and always would be.

It was a somber night, but the darkness allowed him
time to reflect on all this. Harley Bain and his gang of
ranchers and cowboys were embarked on something akin
to mass murder. It wasn't called that. They didn't shoot
anyone, so far as Dirk knew. All they planned to do was
drive the returning Métis out of their shacks and cabins,

burn their every possession, and leave them in their night-clothes, barefoot, in a Montana winter.

Dirk found himself no longer in that half world of the half-breed, half white, half red, half European, half native. He had reached a moment as sacred as repeating an oath. As sacred as marriage vows. As honor-bound as a promise. Tomorrow he would borrow a pack animal from Reilly, if he could, and load it with emergency supplies, food and blankets and moccasins or leather to make them, and set out looking for the Métis victims of Bain's extermination campaign. Maybe Dirk could save a few lives. There were scores of these mixed-blood Canadians filtering through the territory, maybe hundreds, wanting only one small corner of the world. They would encounter the night riders. He'd be lucky to save a dozen, somehow get them to Reilly's place, or maybe Sylvestre's, if indeed that family was still alive at their own homestead.

But then he thought of the futility of trying to rescue these people over a thousand square miles of land in the Judith country. They would be snow-covered, wolf-eaten corpses before he would happen on them. Tomorrow he would try something else. But what?

He knew he was dithering like some rustic Hamlet. Should he take up arms against a sea of trouble? Fight back against Bain, bullet for bullet? The idea was absurd. He was an unarmed schoolteacher. Those Métis who hadn't been burned out of their huts and homes had a few ancient rifles barely suitable for hunting. They could not fill their stomachs, much less fight a war. War was an absurdity. In any case, Harley Bain and his allies commanded powerful private armies of ranch hands.

What could a teacher do? What weapons did Dirk

Skye possess? How could he rescue these people from manslaughter? What chance did these refugees from persecution in Canada have here in the territory? Especially when they were mixed-bloods, whose crime was not being white men? Dirk mulled that as he steered the buckskin through the bleak dark, and it gradually came to him that he had some weapons, schoolteacher weapons. A pen, some paper, and a bottle of ink. The territory was well settled; even if the law ran thin in Lewistown, it was potent in the capital, Helena, and the burgeoning cities, such as Great Falls and Bozeman.

There was mail service in Lewistown, a thrice-weekly stage operated by Kinnear, from Fort Maginnis to Great Falls and points south. Dirk decided that on the next westbound stage some letters would be in the mail pouch. One would be to the territorial governor, Samuel Hauser; another to the federal marshal at Great Falls. And maybe he would write an additional letter to Major Brevoort at Fort Maginnis, urging a rescue mission to save lives, regardless of who and what were being rescued.

Those letters would describe the plight of the homeless Métis. They would describe Harley Bain's removal policies in the Judith country. They would urge immediate relief, regardless of blood or citizenship. And he would send fair copies here and there. That was a schoolteacher's response, but the pen could be mighty in its own right.

At last he felt the future open up to him. He was done playing Hamlet. Whatever his own fate, it would lie with the Métis he would try to rescue.

He rode quietly into the ranch yard and found a lamp still lit in the cabin. After caring for the horse, he entered and found it brimming with people, mostly lying everywhere in that fetid room. But Reilly was sitting bolt upright in his chair.

"I heard all about it," Reilly said. "All you people do is get me into worse trouble."

"Poor old Reilly," Dirk said.

Reilly squinted, ready to snarl at him, but Dirk's grin silenced him.

"You got paper and pen and ink?"

"What would I have that for, and why would I give it to you? I work my fingers to the bone, and you want everything in the cabin."

"Do you or not?"

"Of course I don't. What sort of idiot do ye take me for?"

"I'll get them in town. And you can load up your wagon with food and blankets and shoe leather and go look for refugees."

"Look for refugees! Why should I do that? I've got more than enough to ruin me."

"When you got off the immigrant boat, who helped you?"

"I helped myself."

"How did you come west?"

"They told me."

"Who told you?"

"The bloody immigrant aid society."

"And they got a rail ticket for you?"

Reilly stared. "I'll load up my wagon and be off in the morning, damn your hide. Nothing but bad luck since you showed up. I can't even talk their tongue."

"I'll suggest that one or two go with you."

"I suppose you're going to start teaching me their heathen tongue."

"You'll learn it. You'll pick up some new words every time they smile at you."

"Skye, you are a rogue."

Dirk made his way to the newly wrought bunkhouse and knocked. He discovered astonishing brightness and warmth in what had been a shack.

"Monsieur Reilly will look for refugees tomorrow, and wishes the company of someone who can talk your tongue," Dirk said.

"He is a man who steps down from heaven," one of the Métis said.

And so it was agreed.

It took some time to find pen and ink and paper and envelope in Lewistown. Dirk got the paper and envelopes at the mercantile, but had little luck finding pen and ink until he walked into the butcher shop, where the post office operated, and borrowed the writing tools. Then he settled down and scratched a letter to Governor Hauser first, and wrote similar ones to the rest.

He assumed they wouldn't know much, so he took his time to explain. The Métis were people arriving daily in the territory, driven out of Canada by Anglophone Canadians. They had settled in the Judith Basin in the 1870s. The newcomers driven out by the North-West Rebellion sought help there.

Dirk named no names. He didn't want the letters to be accusatory. They were a plea for help. He did say that the ranchers accosted the newcomers, burned their possessions, left them in the winter cold, without clothing, tools, food, or shelter. Métis were dying from exposure and starvation, this was occurring on public land, and that the situation was catastrophic. Immediate aid was required to prevent further death.

He assumed the territorial officers would know exactly whom he was writing about. Whether they would come to the aid of half-bloods from across the border was the question. Maybe they would. Anyone with half a conscience would. But the territory was full of men who lacked even half a conscience when it came to mixed-blood people.

That was the best he could do. He blotted his letters, sealed them, addressed them, bought two-cent stamps, and mailed them. There would be letters to authorities in Helena, Great Falls, and Fort Maginnis. He stared at the brass slot where he had dropped the letters, returned the ink and pen and blotter, and headed into the wind. He had used a schoolteacher's weapons. He had done what he could do alone; not what an army might do.

He felt vaguely ashamed. He wasn't his father, Barnaby Skye, and now he wished he could be.

Inside the cage, an elderly man with an arm garter and green eyeshade snapped up the letters and began postmarking them.

"Looks like you're writing to half the officials in the territory," he said. "Must be important."

"It could be."

"What's all the scribbling about?"

Dirk hesitated, wondering if the letters would ever leave Lewistown.

"A man needs a job, doesn't he?"

The postmaster eyed him. "Not likely you'd get one," he said.

Dirk had walked into walls before, so he shrugged. "I've worked for the government all my life," he said.

The postal clerk lowered his wire-rimmed glasses, stared, and sniffed. For him it was beyond fathoming.

Dirk climbed aboard his buckskin and rode out to the ruins of the church, which was now a forlorn field, a heap of ash, and loose foundation rock scattered across a wide area. One person was there, and he recognized her at once. Therese was collecting the foundation stones, rock by rock.

He dismounted and approached. She saw him and ignored him. He began carrying the scattered rock to a pile she was building, adjacent to one of the ruined footings. She eyed him, questions in her face, but did not speak. He worked steadily, in quiet cold air, under a bleak overcast, not stopping because she didn't stop. He tactfully lifted the larger stones, and she gratefully collected the smaller ones. The day passed and they carried the scattered stones without surcease.

It was amazing. By some miracle, they collected every stone in sight, and carried them all to the ruined foundation. He could not believe the amount of rock, but there was the evidence before his eyes. She had done it herself. He had only assisted at the last. She had worked from dawn until now, late afternoon. He had completed her task. The rock was back. The gifted artisans among her people could begin anew to lay up a foundation.

They stood, staring at their work, and then at each other.

"Would you let me brew you some tea?" she asked.

"I would be pleased," he said.

She led the way, down the slope to town, and out to

the creek, and the wood yard, where Trouffant was rhythmically shattering dead trees into cords of firewood.

She renewed the fire in the iron stove and set a teakettle on it, and then vanished to some place outside. When she returned, she was fresh and washed and her cheeks were rosy with the splash of icy creek water on them.

"I will come tomorrow and help," he said.

"You don't need to. It is for the Métis to do. It is for the congregation."

"I will come anyway."

She turned her back to him, lifted a pot and placed it on the stove, which was radiating heat into the cold cabin. "I am heating stew for you."

"I will eat it," he said.

"Why are you here?" she asked.

"I am staying with a hog rancher named Reilly—along with several of your people he has sheltered."

"And how did he find out about them?"

"I took them to him."

"He drinks at the saloons. He needs many drinks before he is happy."

He laughed. "He needs more than that. Your people have turned his cabin into a bright, comfortable place. It was a pigsty. That unsettled him."

"I have heard about him."

She added tea to the boiling water and placed a chipped porcelain cup on the stove. She poured the tea through a strainer and handed it to him.

"Black is what you get, Englishman."

But she poured some for herself as well and sat down at the rough-hewn table across from him. She sipped.

"I am married to the church," she said.

"You can keep the ring," he replied.

She fingered it, removed it from her hand, and dropped it into his palm.

"That would not be right," she said. "I'll have the stew warm soon. I am good at making stews."

"I know," he said. "I'm good at eating them."

The thin ring felt impossibly heavy in his hand. He put it in his britches because there was no good place to put it. It didn't belong there.

thirty-one

irk Skye heard Reilly's ranch wagon before he saw it. The cold had congealed its axle grease so that the wheels protested. He stepped outside, along with the Métis women who were among the refugees at Reilly's hog farm.

Reilly was steering the wagon toward the cabin. Dirk could see the wagon was burdened. Reilly and two of the Métis men had left with some cooked mutton and a heap of ancient canvas; he was returning alone with some bodies lying in the wagon box.

There were two of them. One wore an ancient gray union suit and his feet were bare. The other was a woman, also barefoot, wearing a thin cotton night dress. Dirk crowded close, along with the others. The two lying in the wagon were Lorenz Sylvestre and his wife Maude. Cold had killed them. There was little or nothing between the arctic winds and their flesh. It had been a slow, miserable, cruel death.

Reilly tugged the lines and the wagon creaked to a

halt. Some of the Métis women moaned.. The men stared silently.

"We found some of the half-breeds," Reilly said. "Eight of them, all froze solid. The boys with me, they loaded these two here, and they went looking for live ones, taking the meat and rags with them. So I came back with these two."

"These are Lorenz and Maude Sylvestre. They had a farm over in the foothills of the Snowy Mountains. Raised their own food, got burnt out but went back to start over."

Reilly jumped off the wagon. "I don't want their story," he said. "All I get is trouble."

The men stared. A woman approached timidly and ran a hand over Maude's cheek. The face was blue, the flesh frozen hard.

Lorenz had tried to walk her to some shelter, some-where. Bain's cowboys had burnt the place again. There were more people somewhere, alive or dead.

Reilly stomped into the cabin and slammed the door behind him. Whatever might happen next was up to the refugees crowded there.

The bodies would keep.

Dirk unbuckled harness, freed the dray, and led it to the pen. One of the Métis took over, rubbing the horse, forking prairie hay into a manger. But the bodies lay in the wagon, rebuking them all. Sylvestre's eyes were open; he stared upward at nothing. Maude looked simply to be asleep.

And so the wagon remained, the Métis caught in their own silence, and Dirk caught in his. No one wanted to make any decisions. It still was fall; the earth would not yet be frozen. A grave could be chopped out of the cold turf, a grave deep enough to keep Reilly's hogs out.

He remembered Lorenz, hearty and brave, he and his family refugees from the Red River Settlement, people who had been in the United States for many years. Their farm was operating even before the Custer battle of 1876. But the enemy turned out not to be Indians but Yank cattlemen moving in and usurping all the land. These Métis had been subsistence farmers, growing their own food, selling a little, harming no one, benefiting many.

One of the women brought an ancient blanket and tenderly drew it over Lorenz and Maude, tucking it in as if it would warm them. Another of the women brought a small dark crucifix, which she laid on Maude's breast.

Dirk still hadn't mastered the names of all these people, but one of the men he knew as Francoise addressed him in that mostly French tongue. "Pardon, monsieur, would you ask our benefactor, him who is in the cabin, whether we might use his ox or a mule? We wish to take our beloved to Lewistown, where they will make coffins and we can bury them in a blessed way."

Dirk nodded, headed for the cabin, asked Reilly, who glowered a moment and agreed.

A few minutes later, with an ox yoked to the wagon, the Métis, with Dirk along, headed south along an ice-patched road, the wagon complaining, the Métis men and women silent, wrapped mostly in black. With a slow ox, it would be a long walk. But the woodcutters could fashion a coffin, and maybe there could be some sort of service there. Some, at least, would know the Sylvestres, who had supplied produce to Lewistown its entire life.

By the middle of the day they had raised Lewistown

and steered the wagon directly to the Trouffant place—and Therese. He wished he might see her in happier circumstances. The procession had taken on the nature of a cortege, the Métis men and women walking on either side of the wagon with its cold burden.

Armand Trouffant was shattering firewood as they drove in, his woolen cap pushed back from his bronzed face. He stopped, then walked directly to the procession, a single glance telling him everything. He lifted the woolen cap from his head, let the ox-drawn wagon rumble by, and followed it to the door of his cabin, where Therese stood, waiting for whatever was walking in her direction.

"Sylvestre!" Trouffant said. "Ah, *Dieu!*"

"Would you build us coffins?" asked Francoise.

"At once. But tell me . . ."

The Métis shared the news. Dirk understood most of it. Reilly had found them, brought them back. The others of the household would be straggling in.

"Froze to death," Francoise said. "Sans shoes, sans shirt, sans dress, sans pantalones, sans fire, sans food, sans shelter."

"Who?" Trouffant asked, a wrath blistering his face.

"It is unknown."

Trouffant glared. "It is known perfectly well."

He eyed the assemblage. "Mesdames, my *cher* Therese will brew tea for you. Please warm yourselves. Messieurs, we must saw planks."

That's how the next hours went. Dirk and the rest steadily sawed planks from the logs, which rested on a high cradle so two men operating a bucksaw could chew through the wood. By late in the afternoon enough sawn wood was readied to build two coffins.

By late afternoon, others of the Métis had arrived. The miller, Poule Blanc, and his wife Cherie appeared, along with a dozen Métis refugees they were harboring. All of them paused at the wagon out front, made the sign of the cross, and entered the somber cabin. Still other Métis arrived, from who could say where? Dirk marveled. They seemed connected by some sort of moccasin telegraph. They filled Trouffant's cabin and wood yard. His sons Beau and Martin showed up with a load of wood, and eyed the burdened farm wagon somberly.

Dirk watched Therese welcome the Métis, boil more water, brew more tea. Her lips formed a thin straight line, compressed with sadness. She barely glanced at Dirk, and yet she was accepting him. Her anguish was palpable to him, and he wished he could help in some way, but she was caught in a grief that belonged to her own people. She who had come to build a church was burying its parishioners. She looked oddly beautiful to him, as if the more sorrow that was placed on her slim shoulders, the richer and sweeter was her face and upright bearing.

As the day waned, the Métis men fitted their planks into a double coffin, narrow and square but sturdy, fastened with mortise and tenon. It was as if these people were born to shape wood. By the light of lanterns, they lowered Lorenz Sylvestre and Maude Sylvestre into their casket and anchored the top. They eased the double coffin into the wagon.

But the task was not ended. The men gathered shovels while Therese wrapped herself in a cape and a black hat. Dirk joined them. He wanted to help dig the graves. It was important to him. Therese joined him without saying a word, and Dirk sensed that this was an important thing to her, as well as to him.

She led them all to the dark slope where the ruins of the church were scattered, and then to a far corner of the lot she had staked out.

"This will be the sacred ground," she said.

So there would be a churchyard cemetery, and the Sylvestres would be the first to lie in it.

The burly Métis measured a double width grave and scraped the topsoil away. And then each man present, in turn, dug a few minutes. It was a ritual. Each would contribute to the grave; each would partake of the mourning. The spade came to Dirk, and he bit into the cold earth, worked past a rock, and pitched the bitter soil aside. There was a strange power in it, as if this were a sacred act that bound him to the dead, and to these people beside him who were sharing the toil. And to Therese. With each shovelful of earth he unloosed from its primordial bed, he found himself becoming more Métis, and he could not explain it. Their blood was not his, and yet it was.

It consumed an hour. But when all was done, a rectangular hole pierced the earth in the rear corner of the churchyard, and the party walked quietly through an inky night, past the lively saloon district, to the Trouffants' wood yard to await the dawn, and that ceremony that would lay the dead to eternal rest.

There was stew awaiting them all, for the Métis women had been busy at Trouffant's stove. Outside, resting on the wagon, were the Sylvestres. In the morning, one of Trouffant's draft horses would be hitched. Poule Blanc and his people returned to their own place, and the rest settled down to a night on the floor, in whatever blankets might be found.

Dirk caught Therese just before she disappeared behind her wall of blankets.

"Have you a priest for tomorrow?" he asked.

"*Non*, Dirk. Maybe you will?"

"Me?"

"You are the teacher."

"But . . . me? I don't know anything."

She smiled. "All the better, Monsieur Skye. Just talk English. No one will understand a word. Like Latin."

"Some solace that is!"

But she had slipped into her alcove. He found a corner near the stove where he could stretch out. It was going to be a long night. And in the morning he'd follow Therese to some place and deliver a funeral to Métis who knew some French, plus some Cree, and very little English, and probably a little of the mass. Dirk thought he'd try French, if he could think of something to say. But it could be short. A prayer and a benediction.

Dawn was a long time coming, and the hard floor left him bruised. The dozen or so people in the cabin, snoring, coughing, rising in the night, didn't help matters at all. But he would endure.

No sooner had the sun whitened the eastern sky than the procession started through slumbering Lewistown. There was that about it. Few people were out and the mercantile was not yet open.

He spotted a man riding a mule, slapping its rear with his reins, while flopping about in a most unseemly manner.

The rider proved to be Reilly, who slowed the heaving mule and settled into a walk beside Dirk.

"Made it," he said. "I'll recite the service."

"You?"

"What do you think this is, eh?" He waved some sort of breviary or text at Dirk.

"You? Are you ordained?"

Reilly grimaced. "Don't ask. Don't say a bloody word. You're going to translate into French. I'm going to do it my way. And if you ask any more questions I'll consign you to hell."

They cleared Lewistown and headed up the long grade toward the churchyard. It would be a graveside service, then, Dirk thought.

But it wasn't. In the ruined rectangle where Therese's church had started to rise, the Métis had prepared an open-air altar, and below it rested the casket, the morning sun illumining one side of it.

Therese's church would serve for the first time.

thirty-two

The Métis men shouldered the rough-sawn coffin and carried it to the grave that had been cut into virgin sod hours before. Reilly followed along, the blue scarf that had wrapped his neck when he arrived somehow transformed into a stole.

He was looking more and more like some renegade priest, Dirk thought as he followed along. Maybe a deacon, long ago. The Métis gathered, Reilly consigned the remains to God, and the men lowered the coffin into the ground. The crowd stared at the box in the shadowed earth, not wanting to break away. The Sylvestres were in the earth now, soon to be covered over, but no one wanted to depart.

Dirk grew aware of a faint racket along the road and discovered the black carriage descending the long grade, and with it several horsemen. So Harley Bain had come for the funeral. The Métis eyed the descending carriage uncomfortably. Here was the instrument of the Sylvestres' death, in person, perhaps wishing to make sure the dead were dead.

Reilly squinted, tucked his breviary into a pocket, and nodded at Dirk.

"Tell them to bury the dead."

In French, Dirk suggested that they cover over the departed.

He and Reilly headed straight for the ebony carriage, which now rested on the roadway, flanked by Bain's private army. They were drovers, some of them with six-guns, others with sheathed rifles. Their collars were turned up against the arctic air lowering out of the north.

"Well, you have saved me a walk," Bain said.

He sat in a stiff black overcoat, comfortable on the quilted seats, a scattergun lying beside him.

"Why are you here?" Dirk asked.

"To cause trouble," Reilly snapped.

"Gentlemen," Bain said. "It's a simpler matter than all that. I'm afraid it's a simple trespassing matter. These people insist upon violating my land. I've informed them that it's not church land; it's my land, and yet they ignore me."

"We have buried the dead," Dirk said.

Bain sighed, despondently. "I'm afraid you'll have to ask them to remove the coffins. I'll have no cemetery on my land."

"The coffin will stay. We have just buried two people who died of . . . shall I say a crime? Exposure?"

"Of their own foolishness," Bain said. He sighed again, as if the burden were more than he could bear. "Please direct them to remove the coffins from my property."

"No, the Sylvestres are buried now."

"I was afraid you might be a little, shall we say, recalcitrant, Mister Skye." He nodded to his men. "If your people won't, then these gentlemen will."

"Ye bloody scoundrel, you let them mourn their dead," Reilly bellowed.

Bain ignored him. "You will instruct them to take the coffins with them to Canada. We will bury citizens here. Why, I have no objection to a graveyard, so long as it's for Americans."

"The Sylvestres were living on their farm longer than you've been in the territory," Dirk said.

"Ah, yes, squatting. Sorry, gentlemen. You will tell the half-bloods to remove the coffins. I will give you one minute. After that, my men will do it for them." He pulled a gold pocket watch on a fob from a pocket in his pants and held it up. "There now, see? The second hand crosses the twelve."

"I'll break your bloody neck," Reilly said.

But even as he spoke, the bores of Bain's scattergun found his chest. And two of the escorting drovers had drawn their revolvers.

"You can tell them yourself, Bain," Dirk said.

"No, Skye, you'll be my messenger. And then of course you'll remove yourself while you can."

Dirk did nothing. If Bain had bad news to impart to the staring Métis, standing at the grave, let him do so.

Bain leaned over the edge of the carriage. "My friend Nelson, the postmaster, tells me you've written letters to my good friends in Helena, Governor Hauser in particular. Now what might that be about, Skye?"

Dirk kept his mouth shut.

"About the removal of illegal immigrants, I imagine. A letter from a noncitizen about other noncitizens."

"Born here, Bain."

"Ah, but of a Shoshone mother. You're a ward of the government. You belong on the Wind River Reservation, where you will proceed immediately or be taken there by authorities. You're an Indian, and will be treated as such."

Dirk stared.

"But I'll give you credit, Skye. You chose peaceful means to get at me. The frontier's gone. We're all at peace now, and modern times require modern means. It's who you know these days, not who you shoot."

Dirk eyed the scattergun in the carriage, which didn't waver.

"There now," Bain said. "The second hand's gone around. Time's up." He nodded to the drovers.

Bain's men dismounted, headed toward the grieving Métis with pointed revolvers. The people fled, suddenly terrified, scattering down the slope toward town even as Bain watched.

The drovers reached the burial ground, stepped into the grave, and lifted the box out.

"I'll take it, damn ye," Reilly said.

"Back to Canada, I trust. Or perhaps you should be deported, Mr. Reilly? For crimes done in Ireland?"

Reilly ignored Bain, headed for his wagon which was near the foundation of the church, and drove it over to the grave site. The cowboys lifted the oblong box onto the wagon bed.

"There, you see, Skye? It was all handled peaceably. Now if you are not out of here by morning, there will be federal authorities looking for you."

Dirk's helplessness was all too familiar to him.

Bain smiled, nodded, slapped lines over the croups of his trotters, and drove off. His men lingered on to enforce Bain's will.

Dirk looked for Therese, fearful that harm might have come to her. She, above all, was the obstacle to Bain's vision of a white man's land. She was standing with the Métis, unharmed.

Dirk watched the ebony carriage roll away and could barely contain the tumult flowing through every ounce of his flesh.

Reilly settled in the wagon seat.

"I'll bury them on my plot of ground in this great republic that's welcoming all the poor of the world," he said. "Makin' a new world where everyone's got a chance."

He steered the ox toward town, while the Métis gathered around it, a cortege once again. Dirk thought to join the cortege too as it wended its slow way into Lewistown. He saw Therese walking beside the wagon, something fierce and proud in her bearing. Dirk stayed at the rear. This was a matter for the Métis people. They needed to come up with some place to bury the Sylvestres, a place that would suit their beliefs.

It surprised him that Reilly didn't steer the burdened wagon toward the hog farm, but continued toward Trouffant's wood yard. So maybe that would become a burial ground for these people. The weary people followed, and in a while were all collected there at Trouffant's place, surrounded by mounds of firewood and logs.

Dirk put his saddle horse in the pen and joined the crowd, which had gathered around the wagon, waiting for Therese to say whatever was on her mind. It was her church, her hallowed ground that had been violated. She was the one who had received a vision.

Dirk listened, straining to understand the broken French and Cree tongue of these people, but he got the gist of what she was saying. At twilight the Métis would return and bury the Sylvestres exactly where the grave had been dug.

"Are you sure, madame?" asked one.

"I was given a vision. We will build the church there. We will build it no matter that they tear it down. We will build it again and again. We will replace every stone. We will shape every timber. We will build a house of God, and our people will worship in our house."

"They have guns, madame," said a young man.

"Then some of us who are building the church might die," she replied.

It was an oddly tender statement, and Dirk could see it settling over these people.

"If I die, bury me there," Reilly said in English.

They stared at him, well understanding his words.

"Well, we may as well enjoy ourselves while we wait to die," Trouffant said.

The Métis were smiling.

Trouffant addressed Dirk. "Monsieur, would you slide into town and make some purchases?"

Moments later Dirk walked toward Lewistown, some dollar bills in hand, and purchased two quarts of redeye and two quarts of brandy, and didn't much care that the barkeep would sell to him only through the rear door because he was an Indian.

By the time he returned, the Métis had already begun the party. Two fiddlers were tightening their strings. The women were preparing a kettle of stew. The men were chopping firewood to help Trouffant pay for the party. But not until Dirk unloaded his gunny sack of bottles did the party begin. It was an odd time, midmorning, but what difference would it make? One could party at any hour and bury the dead whenever the moment came to carry them back to the churchyard.

Miraculously, still more Métis arrived from somewhere, and Dirk marveled. These people slipped across the country unnoticed when they chose to. Trouffant's cabin bulged, and the party spilled into the chill afternoon. By afternoon the stew was ready, the bottles were lined up, and the fiddlers were all tuned up. The Métis men drifted in from the wood yard, washed, and settled around the room.

The fiddlers struck a note or two, then burst into dizzying music, too fast and spicy for Dirk to keep track of. He watched Therese, wondering how she would take all this, but Therese was smiling and visiting with her people. The bottles began to circulate, with one or another taking a nip and handing it to someone else. Dirk could not follow the conversations, but he did translate scraps of the tongue, enough so he knew these people were talking about the death of the Sylvestres. The fiddlers slowed their tunes, until Dirk realized they were melancholy. The fiddlers were playing soft lamentations. This was not at all like a wake, nor was it like his wedding celebration. It was something else, a way of loosening up the soul to grieve.

He felt his usual aloneness. Once in a while Therese eyed him and nodded. But it all came to nothing. Reilly sat in a corner, red-faced, hogging a bottle of redeye, working hard at it, glaring at all the rest. He was as far removed from this event as Dirk was and looked ready to bolt.

Dirk didn't feel much like drinking. He thought maybe he'd go catch his buckskin and ride away, maybe up to Reilly's place. If this was mourning for the dead, he couldn't fathom it. Who were the Métis, anyway?

He rose, but Reilly bellowed at him. "Sit here, Skye. I can't understand a bloody word these savages are saying."

"I'm going to ride to your place," Dirk said.

"Quitting me, are you?"

"Yes."

"Well, I'm coming with you. Help me unload that coffin, and we'll get the hell out of here."

"They need you, Reilly."

"Hell they do. Trouffant's got a wagon and a dray."

The pair headed for the cabin door, unnoticed as the mournful fiddles wailed dirges and the Métis sipped brandy or redeye and sat sadly, saying less and less to one another.

The icy air outside felt good. The silence felt even better. The autumnal sun had plummeted below the southwestern horizon, leaving only an afterglow.

"I don't like them Métis one bit," Reilly said. "Help me unload these buggers, and we'll get out of here."

Dirk thought that was a good idea. The box rested darkly in Reilly's wagon bed. It would be heavy, and Reilly was not exactly sober, but somehow they'd lower the casket of Lorenz and Maude Sylvestre to the ground, and be on their way.

They hefted the box, found it lighter than expected, and started to lift it free.

"Please, Dirk, please no." It was Therese, silhouetted in the open door by the lamplight within.

"Trouffant can carry these."

"You are ill at ease, Dirk. You are trapped, *oui?*"

"Your ways aren't my ways, Therese."

She approached him, while Reilly stared meanly. "We will go now. Just you two and me, and we will bury our friends."

Reilly stared. Dirk stared. She slid inside, got a shawl, and then settled on the wagon seat.

"There are shovels over there," she said.

They drove quietly away, Reilly's ox lumbering through town and up the grade, the three of them sitting tightly on the bench. No one said anything. Not even Reilly, who was oddly quiet for a mouthy man.

The churchyard was dead silent. A rim of afterglow lined the western horizon as Reilly steered the ox toward the hallowed ground.

This was going to be hard work, especially if Reilly was half-loaded.

But it went oddly well. They lifted the box out and rested it beside the grave. Dirk got down and received the box as Reilly slid it half into the grave. Then Reilly joined him and they eased the coffin into the cold earth.

They climbed out, and Reilly turned his blue scarf into a stole once again, and committed the bodies of two beloved Métis to the earth and their souls to God, while Therese stood quietly in the cold air and made the sign of the cross.

Dirk and Reilly set to work with the shovels. It didn't go quickly or easily, and Reilly wasn't helping much. But through the quietness of dusk and darkness, they heaped the cold clay onto the casket, until in deep dark they piled the last of the good earth over the grave and smoothed the earth into an orderly mound.

It was full night. They stood, staring. Reilly had indignantly wrapped his scarf around his throat once again.

Therese caught his hands and thanked him. And then she turned to Dirk, clasped her arms about him, and kissed him.

thirty-three

That kiss was the sweetest that Dirk Skye had ever known. But he rejected it. He had no intention of reviving a liaison with a woman who had abandoned him. That was cold hard reality. She was fickle. But that brief hug, and the touch of her lips, lingered through all of him.

"You heading for your place? Want company?" Dirk asked Reilly.

"I'm sure not going back there where a man can't hear himself think," Reilly said. "Damned Métis."

"I'll catch up with you. I'll escort Miss Trouville home first."

Reilly laughed, and Dirk couldn't fathom why. But the man whipped the ox into action and the farm wagon creaked away. Dirk led his horse and walked beside Therese, through the thickening cold.

"Are you leaving now?" she asked.

"Bain told me I must. But no, I'm not. There's work to do."

"Work? Translate?"

He wondered if he should tell her what he had in mind, and then decided to go ahead. "There may be more of your people burned out, abandoned, dying of cold, by Bain's night riders. I'm going to go look for them."

"Why?"

That response surprised him.

"I don't like people suffering, starving, dying from the cold."

"Even if they are Métis?"

"What has that got to do with anything?"

"You were with the army."

"I was discharged in the field by a captain."

"For what?"

"For interfering with command. My office was to translate."

"And?"

"I got riled up, I guess."

She pondered that and reached over to him and took his hand. *"Merci,"* she said.

Her hand felt good, but he was damned if he'd let some small affection trump what had happened at their wedding.

She sensed it and withdrew her hand. They walked quietly through the saloon area of central Lewistown, and he was glad he was there to offer some safety for her. And then he escorted her into the Trouffants' wood yard. The place had turned quiet. It wasn't that people were sleeping, but that they sat about, mostly inside, lost in their own reveries.

"Thank you for taking me home," she said.

"Yes, this is your home," he replied. "Your people."

She smiled softly, caught in lamplight from the window. *"Oui,"* she said.

She stepped in, and he could see the crowded mass of humanity there, quiet and sad, but somehow content with the evening.

He closed the door behind her, collected his buckskin, and headed into the bleak night. He'd catch up with Reilly and his lumbering ox soon enough. The air eddying out of the north whispered of snow, and even as Dirk rode through the night, the air turned bitter. The stars vanished and he let the buckskin pick the trail because he couldn't see it. He pulled his coat tight and endured.

The sound of the wagon's wheels groaning on their axles greeted him out of the blackness.

"That you, Reilly?"

"Froze to death and it's all your doing. I should be tight in my cabin, storm coming, but you put all the Frenchies on me, and now I'm cold and stuck and needful."

"What do you need, Reilly?"

"I haven't any idea where I'm steering this ox, and I need a bottle to warm me."

"Well, we're both stuck."

"It's all your fault, Skye."

"Yes. Out in the night, burying people, and you don't have a drop with you."

"You're making fun of me, Skye, and I won't forgive it."

"This horse seems to know where he's going, because I sure don't. So we'll let him take us to your place."

"Or drop us in some ditch."

They proceeded through the blackness awhile, and then the overcast vanished and there was starlight again.

They were close to Reilly's place, with the black bulk of the Judith Mountains off to the right.

"There, luck of the Irish," Skye said.

"There's no such thing, Skye. We were born to misery and doomed to sadness."

"A bottle would fix you up fine."

"You're persecuting me, Skye. You haven't a Christian bone in you."

"I guess I don't, and neither do you."

"You go to hell, Skye."

The ox lumbered into Reilly's ranch yard.

"Go build a fire, Reilly. I'll put the ox out to pasture."

Reilly didn't argue. He had wrapped his scarf tight around his neck but still looked drawn with cold. Dirk unsaddled his buckskin, found some oats for it, and turned it loose in the pen. Then he parked the wagon, freed the ox, and hung up the harness.

Reilly had a fire going in the stove and hovered over it, his bony hands absorbing what small heat the infant fire threw up.

"You should have brought a bottle. That was the least you could do, after all I did for them Frenchies."

"I guess I should have, Reilly."

"Them people, there's more of them coming down from Canada, getting caught in the storms. They'll all croak. The ones around here, they're getting froze to death on purpose, Bain's night riders."

"Tomorrow, you and I are going to go save any we can, Reilly. Your horse'll be rested. We hitch up the wagon and go looking. We can bring some food and matches and whatever we can find. Flour sacks, gunny sacks. Anything."

"I knew you were going to say that, Skye. You just want to kill me off."

"I'll go alone, then."

"The devil you will!"

Dirk joined him at the stove, blotting up the heat, which finally was beginning to take the ice out of the cabin.

"Was that a wake at Trouffant's wood yard?" he asked.

"The Frenchies wouldn't know how to have a wake no matter how hard they tried. There's no such animal as a Frenchie wake."

"What did they have then?"

"Fiddle music and whiskey."

"Well, that's a wake."

"You get more and more insulting, Skye."

They hunted up stuff for the cold journey in the morning. There wasn't much. Reilly didn't live in luxury. But they managed a tin of hardtack, or ship's biscuit, Reilly kept for emergencies, and a bunch of burlap bags and a few flour sacks. Reilly added a couple of ancient shirts, but that was it. This wouldn't be much of a rescue. Still, Dirk had a feeling that some of the refugees were holed up and desperate for any kind of help.

"You got any riding animals? Mules, jackasses?"

"They can ride my hogs," Reilly replied.

Dirk napped restlessly, and at the first sign of gray morning, he was up, loading their miserable succor into Reilly's wagon, while Reilly made some tea.

"You're making me do this. I should stay here. It's about to snow. You're risking my life," he said.

"You stay, then."

"To the bottom layer of Hades with you."

They rolled out into a deep gray overcast and a north-west wind, and immediately the bite of cold chilled Dirk's face. Reilly simply hunkered low, wrapped in a blanket. Dirk had no idea where to go other than west, out upon lands controlled by Harley Bain, lands where the Métis wanted to settle. Dirk had no idea how many had filtered through that country. A dozen? A hundred?

The world was utterly silent. The north wind didn't blow hard enough to scrape the ears, just hard enough to burrow through anything Dirk wore. One good thing, Dirk thought. Bain's riders would be huddled around their stoves this day.

For two hours they spotted nothing. Then Dirk headed for a copse of naked trees, their bare limbs cobwebbing a bleak overcast. It was the first significant shelter they had come to, and Dirk intended to check any likely place where the desperate might harbor.

They rode in and found it empty, and Dirk steered the dray into the wind, north by northwest, toward another copse of naked trees at the base of a low bluff. The dray fought the lines, wanting to go downwind. This was a fool's mission. There were hundreds of square miles in the Judith country.

"You could have gotten me a quart of Jameson's before we started, Skye. You take me for granted, is what."

Dirk lacked any means of buying anything, least of all Irish whiskey.

They entered a sheltered area, brushy and protected from wind by cutbanks and juniper and slopes. There was something ahead.

"Jaysas," Reilly said.

There was a mountain of ash, the bare ruins of a Red

River cart, and little else except bodies. Barefoot, coatless, shirtless, bold, stiff, blue, naked against the bitterness. Six bodies, all deprived of footwear. Two children, three young adults, and one old man. They had survived a while, even barefoot, collecting anything burnable that could be dragged or carried to the dying embers of the Red River cart. But the time came when they could find no more deadwood, drag no more, walk no more on frozen ground with bare feet, and then they had perished in the cold. And now they were frozen hard, frozen to the ground, frosted into the earth. One had been mauled by a predator.

"A family," Dirk said.

"Jaysas," Reilly said.

The hog farmer knelt beside them, where they had huddled close to one another to fend off the icy breath of death. He muttered some sort of prayer, while Dirk stood, hatless, in the wind.

Dirk had never seen such a hopeless situation. No shelter, not enough clothing to fend off cold, no shoes or boots, no means.

"Let's go on," he said. "Maybe we will find the living."

"Who can we tell? Who can we shout at?" Reilly said.

"We will tell what we've seen if it's the last thing I do," Dirk said.

"Aye, and who'll listen? Frenchie half-breeds," Reilly said.

There was nothing they could do here. No way to bury them, no way to revive the dead, no way to identify them.

They clambered into Reilly's protesting wagon and continued, once again out upon the sweeping flats claimed by Bain. There was a hint of sleet in the air, needles borne on wind. The dray wanted to quit, struggled against the lines, but Dirk quieted him by turning southwest toward a group of low hills, cut sharply by one of the creeks running through the country.

And after a silent hour, they entered the hill country and followed the bed of the creek, which had a faint wagon track beside it.

And smelled smoke.

Dirk couldn't be sure. Smoke was elusive, a teasing hint on the wind, a faint notion that blossomed in the mind.

"You smelling it?" Reilly asked.

"I am."

"I'm ready to warm my bones. I'm so cold I'll join the Frenchies lest I got warmed up quick. Maybe it's the cowboys. Maybe I'm the hog farmer, but I'm planning on warming up real good, and maybe get me some redeye if it can be had."

The fickle winds were mostly blowing the smoke out of the creek bottoms, but once in a while Dirk caught wood smoke, heartening and plain, a sign of life ahead.

And when they rounded a bend in the creek, there was a goodly fire, and people lying about it.

"Hello," Dirk yelled. Only one of those at the fire raised his head. But then another did. And one struggled to sit up.

Dirk steered straight for them, even as others wrestled themselves up.

They were Métis, barefoot, half-naked, hollow-eyed, and alive beside the ruins of a farm wagon, its metal tires about all that remained.

thirty-four

*R*eilly didn't like it. "Now I'm stuck with more of them," he lamented. But he reached for the tin of hardtack, while Dirk grabbed what few flour sacks would have to suffice for warmth for these people.

One young man, dark and Indian, struggled to rise. He lifted a hand in supplication, a hand seeking food, any food.

There were six here, but one didn't move. She was ancient, thin and worn and blue, and without clothing save for a chemise and ancient skirt. Dirk knew he and Reilly were too late for her.

There were also two boys, a young woman, and a child, all sensate, staring at him.

Reilly was circulating among them, giving each a piece of hardtack.

But it was plain that the child and young woman were too weak to eat it. They could not shatter it with their teeth.

"Why does hardtack have to be hard?" Reilly asked. "Dumbest thing I ever heard of. It's British nonsense, is what it is."

The man and two boys nibbled bits of it, tiny pieces they broke away and chewed.

Dirk helped the woman and child. He crushed the biscuit into bits and handed the pieces to them. And then wrapped the two in flour sacks for want of anything else. He could see how this had gone. Night riders had burned them out, left them shoeless. But they were surrounded by deadwood, and the man and boys had managed to drag it in, day after day, keeping the sacred fire alive, the ruins of their wagon that still gave heat and protected life. And thus they had lived a while, starving more each day but alive because they had kept the fire going day and night. All the deadwood, mostly cottonwood, for fifty yards around had already been collected, and each day the survivors had to go farther out. They would not have lasted another day, Dirk thought.

"Merci, merci," the woman muttered. Even a little hardtack seemed to revive her faster than the others, who chewed slowly on the miserable biscuits that stored well and safely.

The child, a boy, was too far gone for tears, and couldn't eat. Dirk took hardtack to the spring and soaked it thoroughly, and then brought it back for the boy, who seemed five or six, and now the gummy baked flour was edible. Dirk returned to the spring with several more biscuits and soaked them all until they had softened, and handed them out.

Reilly unwrapped his blue scarf from his neck and hung it over his shoulders once again, and knelt beside the ancient dead woman. And there he prayed, muttering things Dirk couldn't hear or fathom, and then Reilly drew a cross upon the old woman's cold forehead, and slowly stood. The others stared and nibbled and clutched another piece of hardtack in their hands. The stuff would save lives no matter how miserable it was.

The fire was failing, and Dirk headed into the afternoon to collect more wood. These people had scavenged far, and he had to travel down the creek a bit before he found something he could drag to the fire. But he did return with several limbs and branches and tossed one into the faltering flame. It caught quickly. The lowering clouds were spitting snow now.

Reilly was wrapping the bare feet of the boys in feed sacks, which wouldn't help much. But the boys managed a smile or two.

Dirk settled beside the young man who apparently had kept this group alive for days.

"*Parlez-vous—?*"

"I can say the *Anglais,* English. Who are you?"

"I am Dirk Skye. My friend is Pap Reilly."

"Friend or not?"

Dirk was aware again that the Métis stayed together. "We've just fed you," he said. "And we'll take you to safety."

The man stared, as if not believing. "We are looking for friends, Sylvestre is their name. They have a place near here. They would shelter us."

Dirk stared at the fire, and finally said it plain: "The Sylvestres were burned out and are dead."

The man absorbed that slowly. "I am Gilbert Bonheur, sir. My wife, Lydie, my boys Pier and Alan, my child

Candide. And my mother, lost to us, Patrice. I'm sorry to be a burden upon you."

"We came looking for those in need. There's a group of ranchers here, wanting to drive you back to Canada—or let you perish."

"So we learned, Monsieur Skye. So we learned."

"What happened?"

"Night riders found us camped here, burned all our possessions, took away our shoes and moccasins and stockings, took away all our clothing save for this little bit. They killed my mother and almost the rest of us."

"I am sorry," Dirk said.

"I don't understand why we are driven into death by the Americans."

"You and I have two bloods, Mister Bonheur."

"Why would that change anything? Why is that against us?"

"I ask myself the same question."

Reilly joined in. "They're a tribe, same as I'm from another tribe, and it's all one tribe against other tribes. Say, Bonheur, where'd you learn the tongue?"

"Red River colony. It was governed jointly for a while by British and French-speaking Canadians. I was one of the governing council. I learned swiftly."

"What did the night riders say?" Dirk asked.

"They said we were Canadians, and it didn't matter if I spoke English. They were going to send us packing. Back to the border. Or die. Only they had no intention of taking us back to Canada. They took our shoes."

"They could again, sir. Reilly and I are not armed. Tonight, when we can move safely, we'll try to get you back to his place. If the snow doesn't get worse."

"Our feet—frostbitten, ruined. We can't."

"Reilly and I will walk."

"Who says I'll walk, eh?" Reilly snapped.

Dirk was calculating what the worn-out dray would be able to haul back. Two in the wagon bed, one on the driver's bench, another on Dirk's buckskin, maybe two. It would have to do.

"If you're strong enough, we'll leave in an hour. If not, we'll camp here until you're able to move. It's snowing. A blizzard could mean—"

Bonheur stood for the first time. He was stocky, powerful, and worn. "We will go as far as we can before the snow drowns us. And hide by day if we must. And go again." He turned to the others and spoke in that odd part-French tongue Dirk could barely grasp.

The heavens were opening up now, a barrage of snow falling everywhere. Dirk worried. He had matches, but no match would start a fire in a blizzard. It would be all the way to Reilly's—or probably perish.

He took a moment to whittle some kindling, curls of wood, splinters, fluff, dry bark, inner bark, anything to start a fire, and this debris he jammed into his pockets. He had the uneasy feeling that this was all for naught. It was run or die, and they would run.

Dirk helped the woman into the wagon bed, and the child beside her, and put the two weak boys on the wagon bench, and Bonheur on the buckskin, and then he and Reilly led the dray and the buckskin east, the driving snow on their backs, prickling his neck, lashing his cheeks.

The snow whipped them along, a giant breath from behind, hurrying the dray and the buckskin, even as the world whitened under leaden skies. Dirk had the impression of speed, not slowness. He walked swiftly, and old Reilly was grumbling right along. Those in the wagon huddled miserably. But even as the wheels cranked around, they all nibbled hardtack, as if it were some life-preserving elixir. They had been days without food, and now there was food in their cold hands.

They reached a sheltered area, thick with brush and out of the wind, and there Dirk and Reilly rested the horses for a while. The snow fell steadily, but the flakes were not heavy, and there wasn't much moisture in them. That was how snow fell in Montana Territory, light and dry and a cheat to the grass and trees.

They scarcely could find their way, but the northwesterly winds clued them, and there were landmarks, such as the Judith River, which they crossed easily on a gravelly shallows. They had long since lost sight of any trail or road. The afternoon passed, and they faced a decision: keep on or find shelter and build a fire? But then the decision was made for them: the storm passed, the skies opened, and Dirk could see a whitened landscape, including the Judith Mountains ahead. Even a dark night would not obscure those mountains.

They kept on. Luck of the Métis, he thought. Reilly grumbled and kept an eye on the refugees. When Bonheur became chilled, Reilly helped him off the buckskin and they walked side by side, until Bonheur's blood was running strong again. The temperature was dropping now; the snow had been a precursor of bitter air out of the north, a sort of line demarcating the end of fall and the beginning of winter.

It would not be long until Christmas, Dirk thought.

The whitened world gave them bearings, and the

steady wind at their back hastened them along. It was then that Dirk knew they would make it. The human cargo, shivering in the wagon, would not perish. But it took another hour before Reilly led his dray up a long two-rut lane and into the yard of his hog ranch. A lamp burned in the improvised bunkhouse; the Métis had returned from Trouffant's gathering. Dirk didn't know whether to call it a wake. But they were here, and even as the Bonheur family struggled out of the wagon, the others came running, and soon Reilly's cabin was aflame with warmth and the alien tongue of those people.

The chilled were swiftly fed and wrapped in robes or blankets.

"Don't know how I can afford to feed the whole lot," Reilly muttered. "I'm running out of hogs."

Dirk headed out into the sharp night, unhooked the faithful dray and led it and his buckskin into the pens. Snow caked the back of the dray. Dirk scraped away the snow, brushed both animals in the deep quiet, found some oats gotten from Fort Maginnis, and poured some into two mangers. The horses pushed their cold muzzles into the oats and tongued the grain into their mouths, noisy with pleasure. Dirk checked the runnel that watered the pen and found water running unfrozen. His task was completed. He had taken care of the horses that had saved a family of these people. Dirk paused, sensing this night was heading toward bitter cold. He felt lonely. He was glad for these people. He thought of Therese. She would be pleased, no overjoyed, at the news. But maybe saddened, for the grandmother had perished, and God knew how many other families of her people were now only frozen bodies, lying in obscure place in the Judith country.

Was there no justice or mercy?

He headed inside, where a wall of heat smacked him. Too much heat, stifling and odorous heat. But it was the heat of life, the heat of salvation. It was heat generated by the wood these guests had chopped for Reilly. Outside were mounds of firewood, enough for the winter, cut piece by piece by the axes and saws of these people.

"I can't understand a damned word! I'm going to go to town and bunk there," Reilly said.

One of the women seemed to understand. She reached over to him, drew him into her arms, and kissed him soundly. Reilly squirmed away, looking like a man fighting an octopus, and wiped away the assault on his lips.

"I'm getting out!" he snapped.

But even as he spoke, the women were herding all the Métis through the door to the bunkhouse, and in an amazing passage, the people-choked cabin was forlornly empty, save for Reilly and Skye.

"What'd they do that for?" Reilly demanded.

"Oh, maybe because they love you," Dirk said.

"Well I don't love them," Reilly said.

"You saved five lives."

"And lost one, damn me. Now I'll have to go back there and fetch her and bury her. I can't leave her to the wolves."

thirty-five

*D*irk headed straight for the churchyard. He would spend this day working on Therese's church. The air was still, and that's all that mattered. He could work in deep cold so long as the wind wasn't lacerating him. The sun dazzled off the snow, making him squint.

Much to his astonishment, he found the walls going up. In just a few days, the Métis had managed to restore the rock foundation and shape one long log after another, until there now was a rectangle of logs, and a dozen burly men, many with elaborate mustaches, sawing and chopping at the logs, or ganging together to hoist them into place. He could scarcely fathom it. Where did all these people come from? And how had they managed to draw so many logs out of the forest, peel them, notch them, and shave the tops and bottoms into a tight fit? Yes, there were a dozen men here, but they seemed like fifty.

He knew a few by sight, and of course the Trouffants were at hand. He found a place to picket his horse and loosen the saddle girth, and then set to work. He lacked the skills of these woodsmen, but there was plenty he could do. He began sawing rounds, which would be split into shakes for the roof, and as fast as he cut a round, a cheerful Métis woodsman made off with the round and began whacking long, thick shakes from it.

The cold was invigorating. The wan sun was not far above the eastern horizon, and yet these men had toiled for an hour or so, and would toil until sundown, and enjoy the long day as well as the rising walls that seemed to grow, log by log, even as Dirk watched.

He saw her coming through the morning, the low sun making a halo around her scarf, which she had tied under her chin. She bore a basket, and he knew it would be something warm to sustain these cheerful toilers.

She gazed at the rising walls, almost as if she couldn't fathom how this thing had happened, and she saw some gentleness fill her face and make it glow. She set down the basket and pulled off the cover, and offered its contents to her men. They discovered hot cross buns, still warm from her oven, and they paused to snatch them up, one apiece, and talk in their Métis way with the glowing woman.

Dirk held back; he hadn't earned a bun yet, and in any case they should go to her Métis people, but she spotted him sawing through a thick log, picked up a bun and carried it to him and paused before him, as he stopped his sawing.

"Eat, *oui?*" she said.

She was smiling, the bun in her cupped hands.

"I will," he said.

"Thank you for coming," she said.

"I want to be a part of this. I want to leave something of me in your church."

"Ah, *bien, cher Étoile du Nord,*" she said.

She watched him pluck up the bun and eat. How strange it was to be watched, her gaze following his hand, his bite, his swallowing.

He noticed how the cold bit her cheeks.

"Your cheeks, they are red from the cold," she said to him.

"I was thinking the same thing of you. I guess our thoughts crossed in midair."

She smiled. "We don't think alike."

That somehow amused him.

"I think woman and you think man," she said.

He couldn't argue with that even if he had no idea what she really was thinking.

She reached out and patted his cheek, which was more than a little unkempt after missing a few weeks of shaving. "You're getting hair like a Métis," she said.

"My father had a beard when he was older."

"I like beards. They tickle me," she said. "Let it grow, Dirk. Make it a big black beard, and I will like it."

"With big mustachios?"

"Great big droopy mustachios."

"They would scrape your cheeks."

"Ah! You are so insolent! I will abandon you now. Have another bun."

He took it gladly and chomped away as she fled.

He watched her head for another laborer in her vineyard, and watched her peek back at him as she did.

He returned to his sawing, the slow rip of the saw straining his muscles. It was hard work, shaping a whole church from logs in a forest. He watched as she surrendered the last of her hot cross buns and strode forcefully toward the Trouffants' wood yard across town. The way the wind caught her skirts against her legs, she was beautiful.

He sawed away again, but wearied after an hour. How was it that he wore out while these Métis didn't? Their number increased through the cold day, jet-haired stocky males shaping and debarking logs, notching the corners, sawing floor planks, building steps at the front from sawn wood, and enjoying themselves as they toiled. Did they never tire? And where had they come from? Here were Métis he had not seen, men who knew one another, men who had filtered out of the north and found refuge in the basin, somehow out of sight of the powerful ranchers.

That brought to mind the possibility that Harley Bain and his riders might show up at any time, and burn down everything that was rising on this lot that Bain so grandly proclaimed was his own land. It so disturbed Dirk that he began keeping an eye on distant horizons. But except for an occasional spectator out from Lewistown, no one troubled the toilers.

Dirk rested awhile, found himself chilled, and set to work once again. He was determined to keep up with these people even if he was the schoolteacher and they were woodsmen and farmers. But by midafternoon he knew he could contribute nothing more.

He felt embarrassed. He set aside his saw and waved at the Trouffant boys.

"*Mon ami,* you need rest," Beau said. "This is not your work, eh?"

"No, I'm a teacher mostly."

"You work with your head, we work with our arms, eh?"

"I hadn't thought of it like that."

"*Mon ami,* you have given yourself to us. You sawed much wood this day, eh? We are pleased."

Dirk was pleased too. He thought to head out to Reilly's hog ranch and spend a quiet evening. But even as he collected his buckskin and tightened the girth, he spotted a rider approaching and wondered about it. The rider wasn't attired the way the cowboys were, but wore a suit of clothes and a riding coat with a split back, and a bowler hat.

He looked official, and that troubled Dirk. He wouldn't know how to speak to the Métis. So Dirk headed his way and intercepted him as he approached the churchyard.

The man was solid gray; gray-eyed, gray-haired, gray-suited, and trim.

He eyed Dirk. "I think maybe you're the very man I'm looking for. Dirk Skye, might it be?"

"Yes, sir," Dirk said, certain now that this man held some sort of office, and it likely spelled trouble for these Métis men pouring their sweat and pain into the church.

"I understand this will be a church."

"Yes, sir, if the world permits these people to raise it up."

"The world will. I am Strothers, William Strothers, a United States marshal. I believe you sent for me."

"I did?"

"Governor Hauser sent me, on your request."

That was bad news. Bain had said the governor was a friend, among many in high places.

Dirk nodded warily.

"I've done a little riding and exploring on my way over here," Strothers said. "This seems to be prime ranching country."

That boded ill, and Dirk nodded curtly.

"Maybe you could steer me to some eatery in Lewistown."

"We'll go, sir. I'm saddled and ready."

They rode quietly away. Dirk knew the Métis were staring. They probably sensed trouble, and they would be dead right.

Dirk headed for Mrs. Mazzoni's Kitchen on Main, and led the officer into its warmth. The man eyed a corner table, well away from anyone else, and pointed. So this would be a very private discussion, whatever it might lead to.

Dirk realized he hadn't a dime. "I'll just sit here with you," he said.

"Suit yourself," Strothers said.

He ordered a bowl of chicken soup and some bread.

"Hard to find good bread in the territory. Not enough women," Strothers said.

Dirk waited for the pleasantries to pass. This would not go well. Strothers, with Hauser behind him, would order the Métis out of the area and out of the country.

"I'm a tea man myself, Skye. You're half British, so I'd like to treat you to a spot of it."

Dirk nodded, wondering whether he should let himself be beholden. But the hot tea would be a treat after the cold work.

"I tell you what, Skye. While I tackle this soup, you can tell me the whole deal. I mean, the Métis. Why they're here. How they got here. What Bain and his riders are doing. The governor wants to know."

"I'm sure he does. He's Bain's good friend."

Strothers stared coldly. "Perhaps you underestimate the governor, Mister Skye. He has friends, and he has preferences, and he has his own politics. But he's also a man devoted to the public weal, to doing what is right. To justice. He asked me to come here and find out exactly what's happening, and to act as I see fit if law or decency or justice are being violated in any manner." Strothers paused, waving a spoon at Dirk. "You tell the story. Tell me about these Canadians. Tell me about the manslaughter."

"Manslaughter?"

"Exactly. Freezing innocent people to death, a deliberate act, a heinous act if ever there was one."

Strothers was waiting patiently.

Dirk nodded. Strothers spooned some soup into himself, and then tackled the steaming bowl, and the soft, yeasty bread hot out of the oven.

Dirk found it hard to talk. This officer was a white man. In the end, he would ally himself with the white settlers, with the white men's laws on the territorial books, with the ranching interests. With Indian removal, including mixed-blood people, to reservations where they could starve to death out of sight.

But at least Strothers was listening, so Dirk started in with the army's sweep, the translating job he had, and how he was dismissed in the field, and what happened since then, and where his sympathies were. And then he backpedaled and talked about his afternoon-long marriage to Therese, and how she had jilted him, and how he discovered she had received a vision to build that church, and how they had rediscovered each other far from Miles City. And then, at last, he talked about the Canadians, the first or Red River bunch long settled here, and the newcomers from the Northwest Territories rebellion, who were still seeking refuge here. He talked about Bain and his night riders, torching the homes of produce farmers, driving them shoeless and coatless into the cold. He talked about the Sylvestres, newly buried. He talked about the Trouffants, incredibly hardworking people who supplied all of Lewistown with its firewood.

"This café, sir, is heated with the wood cut out of the surrounding lands by these people, and sold at reasonable prices to the merchants here."

"They work hard, that's for sure," Strothers said.

He ordered another entire bowl, even while lapping up the last of the soup with his bread.

"And now, Bain," Strothers said.

"Actually, a cautious man, Marshal. Very careful. He is perfectly happy to see the Métis burned out and frozen to death. He simply doesn't want it pinned on him."

"That's my impression also, Skye. There's not much linking him to the deaths of these Canadians."

"I was afraid you'd say that."

"So I guess it's up to me to nail it down and bring a grand jury, and maybe an indictment. I thought maybe to take some testimony from the Métis themselves, if you would be so kind as to translate."

"I would do that gladly."

"I haven't a shred of proof, Mister Skye. I need evidence, not rumor. Not speculation. Even if we both know he's behind this business, I'll need to prove it to the satisfaction of the law and the courts. How shall I do that?"

"I can testify that he asked me to join him."

"He asked you, did he?"

"To translate. My pay, he said, would be my life."

Strothers contemplated that a moment, and his grin wrought crinkles in his gray flesh. "Would you say you've been paid?"

"Not yet," Dirk said.

"Well, if we can't nail Bain, how about his night riders? Could any of these Canadians identify the riders?"

Dirk shook his head. "I doubt it. Night, bandannas over their faces, darkness, fear, shadows, fire, terror. You can ask, and I'll try to translate. The Métis speak several dialects and I have some trouble with that. But if you want, I can round up a few. But they distrust you, Mister Strothers. You're the government. And they'll probably clam up."

Strothers nodded, stared at his empty plate, and came to a conclusion. "I think I'll invite Bain into town for a few talks. He just might talk a whole lot if I get him going."

thirty-six

irk made his way through Lewistown to Kiskadden's Saloon, which was probably a cut or two above the others. Just the place for the United States Marshal for the Territory of Montana to set up shop. Parked in front was Bain's ebony carriage, the matched trotters yawning in their traces. Dirk had a hunch about this, and now it was proving true.

This would be the confrontation. Strothers had gotten Bain into town for a talk, and what better way than to bring in Dirk, and start the talk with Dirk's letter to Governor Hauser. This wouldn't be easy. Bain would challenge everything. And probably play the Indian card too. They were white men.

He resolved to keep his temper, keep his voice low, and to lay out what he knew and what his friends among the Métis had experienced. He swung the creaking door open, found the long saloon poorly lit, discovered the barkeep staring, ready to boot him out for having the wrong cheekbones, but the keep subsided, wiped his hands on his grimy apron, and let Dirk pass along a row of bar stools to the rear, where there were four tables, one of which had Bain and Strothers sitting at it sipping something gold.

They looked oddly alike. Both were graying at the temples and had recently seen a barber. Strothers wore a three-piece suit of gray twill; Bain a charcoal three-piece suit with a woven gold watch fob draped across his waistcoat. They could have been brothers. They would be drinking Old Orchard, the best whiskey to be found in Lewistown, using hands with trimmed fingernails. Dirk felt a little uneasy, but pushed to the table.

"Ah, Skye, you're here," the marshal said. "Good. I presume you know Harley Bain?"

"We've met."

"Have a seat, Skye. I can't offer you a drink; it's against territorial law, of course. But maybe a sarsaparilla?"

"I'm fine without, thank you."

Bain gazed blandly, revealing nothing, his thoughts apparently buried deep. Yet his gaze was unblinking, and it traced Dirk, and somehow intimidated him. Bain was a man with some sort of wild force barely contained within him, a force that could burst out anytime. But for the moment, he merely nodded and even smiled slightly.

"Harley, how about another?" Strothers asked.

"Mighty kind of you, Bill," Bain replied.

The marshal signaled the barkeep, who nodded and began his pour.

"Now, Harley, young Skye here's written us in Helena, and we'll just go over a few things in his letter. I take it you're familiar with it?"

"Oh, I'm familiar with Skye here. He got booted by

the army and joined up with these illegal immigrants flooding down from Canada."

"He wrote out some complaints, Harley."

"I can't imagine what. But that's how it goes, you know."

"Do you know what they are?"

"Oh, the usual, you know. Not really. I haven't seen the letter."

"Well, Harley, have you been mistreating some redskins?"

Bain laughed. "Bill, I always mistreat everyone, red, white, or blue."

"What do you think. Shall we send this pup back to his reservation?"

Dirk was swiftly realizing that his foreboding about this meeting was well founded.

"What is he? Shoshone, Bill?" Harley asked.

"When you mix Shoshone with English, what have you got? A mutt!" Strothers said.

"I don't think you need me here," Dirk said, rising.

"Oh, sit still, Skye. Beg a little," Strothers said, amused. "Say woof, woof!"

The barkeep arrived, laid the two tumblers of whiskey, served neat, on the battered table, and stared at Dirk.

"I will leave you to your joking," Dirk said, and rose.

And found himself facing the muzzle of a small black revolver that had magically emerged from Strother's breast pocket. The marshal was enjoying himself.

"Sit. Stretch out those paws, pup!"

Slowly Dirk held his arms before him. Strothers tossed some black manacles to Bain, who snapped them over Dirk's wrists.

"Now, then, Skye, we've got some entertainment ahead."

Skye had sensed it all along and now was trapped. The options looked bleak. They might ship him back to Wyoming. But he doubted they would bother.

"Splendid father you had, pup. Barnaby Skye's a legend in the West," Bain said. "Too bad you don't carry more'n a spoonful of his good English blood."

Dirk refused to acknowledge anything. The half-dozen patrons were staring. The barkeep was blandly enjoying this entertainment.

Dirk eyed Strothers, seeing a different man from the one he had met a couple of days earlier. That Strothers was too good to be true. This one was the real article. Dirk felt himself sliding into melancholy, which happened now and then when he confronted the wall that stood silently between white men and himself. He wondered where it would lead.

"Well, Harley, I thought you might like to see justice done," Strothers said.

"Why, Bill, you and the governor are fine fellows, looking after the territory and its good folks. I must say, being libeled is something that requires your attention."

"This fellow's daddy was a well-known rogue, you know."

"Deserted, I heard. Stuffed it to the Queen and quit her navy. Sorry about the whelp here. You'll ship him out?"

"Oh, we'll think of something," Strothers said. "Now, then, Harley, how many of these Canadian rascals have slipped across the border, and what's being done?"

Bain glanced briefly at Dirk. "I think the matter's taken care of itself. Army drove them north, but a few of these carpet beetles have been sneaking back. They hid up in the breaks, but shot away all the game, and now winter's doing the rest of the job."

"Winter, Harley?"

"Can't get through a Montana winter on prayers," Bain said. "Trouble is, they're a shifty lot, slipping through at night, linking up with others, like they've got some private telegraph telling 'em where to go. Which is mostly right here, where this sorceress has 'em all fevered up to build a church on my land."

"Who's that now?"

"Therese somebody. I hear rumors that she's Therese Skye, married to this gent sitting here. But so far, I've not confirmed it."

"Well, we'll have to do something about that," Strothers said. "She your wife, Skye?"

"I don't know," Skye said.

They laughed. "Now there's the best answer I've heard in years. Skye, you're a card."

"She might be," Dirk said.

"Well, that makes a difference. I was going to export her to Canada," Strothers said.

"He's not a citizen, Bill. It don't make a bit of difference."

"He was born here, Harley. He's got rights. And if they're married, she's got rights. I have to follow the law."

Bain sighed. "You pick nits, Bill."

"Law's law, Harley."

They sucked more amber fluid and smiled like a pair of adolescent burglars.

"Harley, old pal, how the hell did you do it?"

Bain smiled. "I didn't do it. Winter did it. I just told

the boys, don't stick it to me. Don't waste powder on 'em. Just burn them out, grab their boots, and leave them in their winding sheets, and what's going to happen will happen, once the thermometer drops."

"How many, would you say?"

Bain shrugged. "I tell the boys not to tell me. There's whole canyons and coulees between me and what happens out there on my range. I'm not privy to what goes on."

"Your range, Harley?"

"You know as well as I do that when it comes to grass, you got what you hold, you keep what you defend. And I don't pay taxes on any of it."

"Were these all newcomers, the Canadians? The ones been drifting in this year?"

"Oh, not all. There were some around here who came in during the seventies, after that dustup on the Red River. They were using up good pasture here, and welcoming the new ones, so I told the boys it was time for a bonfire or two."

"The Sylvestres," Dirk said. "In the churchyard."

Bain smiled blandly. "They can be moved, boy."

Strothers stared at Dirk, as if he had entirely forgotten he had a prisoner sitting at the saloon table.

"I did the arithmetic, Bill," Bain said. "Each breed family that moved into the basin, here, cut my pasture back by fifty head. I've pushed about ten families out now, and that means I've saved pasture for five hundred beeves I would've lost. That's a lot of meat, and a lot of profit."

"Ten, you say?" Strothers asked.

"Oh, about that. My boys don't tell me, and I don't want to know, but just between us, it's ten or eleven. They won't be found. Just ash and bones and a rag or two, once the wolves get done. We never burned powder. Not one bullet. That was my rule. Just let nature rip."

"How many to a family?" Strothers asked.

"Those breeds are breeders, Bill. Lots of kitties in their litters."

"Lots of children, right?"

"I imagine so. That keeps the population down and keeps the basin open for the right people," Bain said.

Dirk had never seen the man so talkative. There were moments when he was so absorbed he scarcely remembered the manacles around his wrists.

The keep came over with the Old Orchard and refilled the glasses, and stared long at Dirk's wrists, and the chain knotting his wrists together.

"I didn't have to tell my boys a thing," Bain said. "They got the whole idea without my saying much. Just the general idea. I just told them to keep me out of it. I had five in particular, great fellas, Shorty, Swede, Lucas, Nate, and Barney. When they were out, I knew the country was being cleaned up fine."

The gents at the bar were staring, especially a pair of skinny ones with high boot heels.

Bain was sipping again, but Bill Strothers had stopped, and was staring off into the gloom of the lamplit saloon. The other patrons stared ahead, pretending not to notice or hear, but in fact nothing escaped them. Dirk eyed the door, wondering whether he could break into the night and escape before Strothers, in his cups now, could pull a gun and shoot. But he knew better.

"Skye, lay your arms ahead of you on the table, palm up," Strothers said.

Dirk did as he was told, and then Strothers pulled a

small key from a vest pocket and unlocked each of the wrist manacles.

"There," he said.

Harley Bain smiled.

"Harley, lay your hands out on the table," Strothers said.

Bain thought that was pretty funny until Strothers snapped the manacles over the rancher's wrists and tucked the key back in its vest pocket niche.

"What's this, a joke?"

"Pretty funny, burning out people and leaving them to the wolves and the weather, I guess, Bain. Clever too, not leaving anything behind, no thread connecting any of it to you, even telling your men not to let you know what was happening out there in that dark. It was pretty dark out there, Bain. People dying of the cold, barefoot, couldn't walk a hundred yards. Not a shoe or a boot or a moccasin that might have given them life."

"I thought I was speaking in confidence, Bill. Between old friends."

"Long trip to Helena, Harley. Do you want me to rent a saddle horse, courtesy of the territory, or shall we ride in that fine hooded carriage out of the weather? It'll take three, four days, more if we run into weather."

"Talk to the governor, that it?" Bain said.

"No, Harley, talk to the territorial courts and the prosecutor."

Bain stared. "Well, damn. I guess I'm going to have to fight you."

Strothers turned to Dirk. "Thanks for bearing with me," he said.

"Am I free?"

"I said thanks, dammit."

Only then did it dawn on Dirk that he was not a prisoner.

"I may need you to testify. And I'll get the names of everyone in the saloon. No one in this joint missed a word." He eyed the staring crowd. "Don't leave here before I get your names and addresses."

But the two little ones with the high heeled boots slapped coin on the bar and walked into the evening.

"Your riders, Harley?" Strothers asked.

"I didn't notice," Bain said, sounding like a church bell.

"Probably the last you'll see of them," Strothers said. "I'll get some warrants sworn out and go for a visit. But first we'll see about you."

Dirk stared at his freed wrists, arms he could move hither and yon, lift and lower, arms that could rein a horse, lift him into his saddle, and lift into a prayer of thanksgiving.

"And, Skye, if you haven't married the lady, do so. She's as sweet as they come."

thirty-seven

*R*eilly was furious. "He treated ye badly, putting irons on like that, letting you suffer and lose hope, while the pair of them downed their whiskey. Dirk Skye, ye've been done wrong."

"It was Strothers's game. It opened Bain up. It got him to blabbering."

"I don't care what it led to. It was wrong of that marshal to clap you in steel like that. It's enough to make a radical out of me. Give me some powder and I'll ignite it."

Dirk held up his wrists. "See?"

"Bloody bad business, if ye ask me, which ye won't because nothing I say matters to you or anyone else."

Dirk nodded. "It's not over. There's not a white judge or jury in the territory that'd convict Bain, and he'll be back in a fortnight."

"And his henchmen are sitting on his place, waiting for him to come back, I'll wager."

"Strothers told me there was more in the works. He said he'd get warrants for Bain's riders. Let's let them deal with it. This thing was planned by the marshal, and planned well. And he's taking Bain south to the railroad, so Bain can't count on being rescued by his gang."

"A lot of killers going free, that's what I think. Them that burned people out of their wagons and left them near naked in the winter, they're killers every one."

Dirk didn't have an answer to that. Bain had named five of his men, and those five had put humble and helpless people to death. And now they perched out on the Bain headquarters ranch waiting for the boss.

The mild December day had invited work on the church, and all the Métis people in the area had somehow assembled, along with Dirk and Reilly. There were more of them than Dirk had ever seen there, men and women from heaven knows where who mysteriously got the word and were present to help. How did they know to come? It was as if they had a secret telegraph furiously shuttling messages into obscure coulees and forests. But here they were, peeling and scraping the ridgepole and then hoisting it into the walls that had been prepared to receive it. It seemed almost as if these forest-dwellers had been trained all their days to work wood into whatever was needed. And even as the ridgepole was being anchored, other cohorts were laying on the rafters, while still others were sawing roof planks.

And overseeing this amazing effort was Therese, wrapped in a blue shawl, her gaze and smile settling on one and another of her people. She said nothing, but somehow her very presence inspired them all. Often she watched Dirk, who was carefully splitting shakes from rounds, a skill he had mastered only at this task. He was good; an easy strike with the axe shot a new shake free.

These would soon shingle the whole roof and draw away the rain and snow. Yet another cohort of Métis was sawing out window apertures and framing the openings. Still others were fashioning massive doors, each one of carved pine, and hanging them at the front. Still others were hauling gravel that would form a walkway at the front.

How many? Dirk paused, catching his breath. Maybe fifty men and a dozen more women, and a few children too. Even the little ones found things to do, things to carry. If they continued at this pace, and it didn't snow for a few days, they might complete the shell of the church swiftly. But then there would be pews and an altar to build, and other interior fittings.

She drifted his way, and he wrestled with the welter of bitterness and love that welled up in him every time they came close. But this would be all right. She would thank him and go on to someone else, preferably one of her own people.

"You came to work," she said, "and that is a mystery."

He paused, leaning on his axe. "Some things need finishing," he said.

"By the Métis."

"By anyone who cares."

Her smile vanished, and she looked sad and even disconcerted. "Why would you?" she asked.

He grinned. "Beats me."

"You brought the marshal here."

"I wrote the governor and the marshal."

"That is what was whispered. And this man Bain, when will he return?"

"I think he'll be back and start in again. You're up against a lot of white people making common cause."

Her gaze fled him.

"We will find a way," she said. "For this I have prayed."

"Your prayers count a lot more than mine," he said, faintly amused.

"Will he burn this church?"

"I have no idea. I think it will cross his mind."

"I have written the diocese for a priest."

"A congregation they didn't know about?"

"We are the world's unseen," she said. "The invisible people. But we are also the church."

"That will be a great moment, that service."

She smiled uncertainly. "When this is done, what will you do?"

"Look for work. And you?"

"I don't know," she said. "I await those days. But . . . *oui*, I know. My people are half starved, and cold, and without homes in a strange land. Most cannot even be understood by white men. I must give myself to them. I must find food and warmth and shelter for them. I must cook for them and mend their clothing and fill their hearts and minds and stomachs."

She seemed so distant, her gaze upon distant shores, and for a moment he thought she wasn't even aware of him. She smiled. "We are blessed," she said.

And with that she hurried off. He wondered what she meant. Who was blessed, and by what?

He raised his axe and let it drop in its familiar arc, and another shake flew off the sawed off round. He could do that all day and not tire and feel rewarded. He chopped through the mild day, and then food came in wicker baskets borne by the Métis women. It was their stew, meat and potatoes and all the vegetables carefully put away in root cellars or spring houses, and now well seasoned and hot and fulfilling.

Dirk ladled some into an iron bowl, drank, and felt refreshed. He would cut hundreds of shakes this day and count it good.

The faint clop of hooves caught the winter air, and men turned from their work to see what might be coming. And what Dirk saw was a blue column, a large patrol from Fort Maginnis, wending its way through Lewistown and climbing the long grade toward the churchyard. The soldiers wore their thick woolen coats and the heavy forage caps which the army had adapted, and there were carbines nesting in saddle sheaths.

Dirk felt ice water pour through his veins. He didn't want this. He couldn't endure it. He'd rather be shot than see these people driven away from their church. But the blue column riding frosted horses wended serenely up the long trail, even as work stopped entirely. Métis men, straddling the ridgepole, stopped. Men with saws and axes stopped. The women serving a noon meal stopped. There now were, in all, close to a hundred of these Canadians there at the churchyard, and now not a one moved. None fled. Most would rather die right there than flee. Most would turn their churchyard red than flee.

Dirk knew he would be needed to translate, so he slowly set down his axe and made his way toward the road where the troops were coming to a halt. At least they weren't bulling into the churchyard, but reining their mounts on the rutted road. They looked cold, far colder than the hardworking Métis, whose lungs plumed the air with moisture.

Dirk approached, dread coursing his every fiber,

and discovered this column was commanded by Major Brevoort himself, rather than some subaltern, and that meant that this was an important event.

"You, is it, Skye?" Brevoort said.

"I will translate, sir."

"That would be welcome."

Therese approached now, slim and straight, with that light blue shawl wrapped tightly over her jet hair.

"*Oui?*" she asked.

"Nice church there, madam."

That required no translation.

"It is our church, and soon we will dedicate it to God."

She stood there so fiercely it raised the hairs on Dirk's neck.

Brevoort lifted his field cap from his head. "I'd be honored to be invited, miss."

Dirk could scarcely imagine words like these issuing from a commander who a few months earlier was sending out patrols whose purpose was to drive these very people out of the country.

The Métis, still sitting on the ridgepole or standing near the structure, watched, bitterly. They knew those blue uniforms all too well.

"Mister Skye, tell them we've been asked by Governor Hauser to keep the peace in the Judith country. Now, you know, the army can't get into law enforcement, except during an insurrection. There's laws and rules galore that say it's not going to happen. But once in a while, when a governor requests it, some wiggle is allowed in that straight line. He says the territory hasn't the manpower to deal with disorders out there, and after burning up wires with Washington, I received orders to assist Governor

Hauser. What we're looking for is some cowboys, up from Texas, who took to burning out people who were traveling under the protection of the flag of the United States, namely these people here. So we're going hunting. I got some warrants for the arrest of five John Does, and permission to take into custody these and any others we find out were leaving people to die in the cold."

Dirk started to turn all that into the peculiar cobbled-up tongue of the Métis, but Therese stayed him. "*Merci*, and I thank Governor Hauser, and I will tell my people here what you have told me."

Dirk could scarcely imagine this outcome.

"Well, you build that church, miss, and we'll go on."

She knelt deeply, a curtsy to the major, who looked embarrassed.

Brevoort lifted an arm, and the column rode smoothly along the road and soon topped the western skyline and vanished.

She stared at Dirk. "This too is your work."

"I didn't do anything."

"Yes, you did."

She walked toward the long walls of the church, even as her people clustered about her, and she told them what had been said, and even as she told it, she saw smiles break out. And he knew that somehow, some way, the fiddles would sing and the brandy would flow this eve— and that if a priest were on hand, there would be a Te Deum sung in that half-done building.

Instead, they set to work, for every hour counted. A blizzard could stop them; a long cold spell could shut them down for all season. And with that, the Métis plunged almost frantically into their labor, and Dirk watched the rafters slide upward and lock into place, and the roof planks rise from the walls and gradually shut out the sky, and by December dusk there was a plank roof over the church, ready for the shakes that Dirk had cut.

As darkness settled and work was no longer possible, the men reluctantly put aside their tools and stretched in the frosty dusk. The Métis were grinning, as if anticipating something. One of them elbowed Dirk.

"Hey, hey," he said. "La jig."

Step dance. A party. That sounded fine to Dirk.

The man was speaking in the Michif tongue.

They were drifting toward Trouffant's wood yard and cabin, and Dirk drifted along with them. Reilly had vanished. The coward had disappeared when the soldiers came. Well, too bad for him.

The chill settled swiftly, hurrying these people along, but soon enough they collected at the wood yard, where merry fires lit the eve, and the cabin door was wide open, its lamps throwing light into the night.

One of the fires glowed red and hot, mostly embers, and there was Pappy Reilly, overseeing a pig roast. So, the man had been busy after all. And Dirk spotted pint bottles of brandy handed swiftly from one Métis to another, and separate ones for the ladies, and Dirk traced all that back to Reilly also. Leave it to a renegade to put a party together.

Therese welcomed him with a brief smile, but she was busy in the cabin, preparing food for dozens of hungry people.

Dirk heard the squall of the fiddles and then the place began to hop, with the fiddlers stamping the rhythms even as they scraped their bows over the catgut. Those fiddles were remarkable, cunningly built out of whatever wood was at hand by people with a genius for shaping wood. Dirk saw a lot of smiles, white teeth in bronze faces, as the brandy sailed down gullets, warming the cabin and the whole wood yard.

The tongues these people spoke were almost beyond his comprehension: Canadian French, Michif French, Michif Cree, and everything in between, including some English. Some of them had Scots blood and Ojibway blood. But a man who knew French, as Dirk did, could fathom these people—mostly.

He saw Reilly swallow a slug from a flask and smile beatifically. Dirk enjoyed it all, and every passage of a flask to his lips added to his pleasure. The gorgeous Métis women kept improving as the night raced on, and the smoke rose into the ice-chip sky, and the smell of roasting ham filled the evening.

But no one ate. It was as if they were waiting for something, some moment that Dirk could not imagine. And then, at last, Trouffant waved, the fiddlers stopped, and an odd silence filled the merry night.

"Monsieur Skye," he said, and beckoned Dirk with his finger.

Dirk didn't know what this was about, but hoped it would end fast.

thirty-eight

he Métis crowded close, while Trouffant took center stage.

"Ah, Monsieur Skye, it is time to make you one of us," he said.

There were instant translations, those who understood English offering the thoughts to others.

Dirk liked that.

"We have this thing for you," Trouffant said.

Someone handed him a long Métis sash, intricately corded in several colors, including red, orange, blue, and white. It had tasseled ends. The one in Trouffant's hands was a beauty, richly woven in bright hues, so that it shone in the lamplight.

"See now, this sash is the emblem of our people. I will tell you about it. See all the colors, all the strands. They have meaning. They are the different peoples and bloods that make the Métis, *oui*? They are the colors of the French, the Cree, the Scots, the Ojibway, the Canadians, *oui*? They are bound together with the white thread of God, *oui*?

See how long the sash is. It goes round and round if we want it to. It is wool. We tie our pants with it. We wrap it around our waist to tie our coats tight. We sometimes use it as a scarf to warm our neck, eh? We use it to keep our pants up, and we give it to you to keep your pants up, but, monsieur, no man should have his pants up at all times, so there will be times when you undo this sash, and that is good. But meanwhile, it is made so your pants will not drop around your ankles when you don't want them to."

The translators were busy, and the people were smiling.

"So, *mon ami*, Dirk Skye, we make you one of us with this sash. The colors blue and white, they are the colors of the flag of our nation, *oui?* Wear the blue and white and you are one of us!"

He handed the handsome sash to Dirk, who swiftly wrapped it around his middle three times, and tied it so that the tassels hung to his knees, just as these people wore their sashes. The red and blue and white and orange somehow added to Dirk's austere wardrobe, making him as gaudy as these Métis men around him.

The Métis cheered, handed Dirk their flasks, and he was obliged to sip on every one. The women touched his cheek and smiled. Therese stared, unsmiling.

"I will wear it proudly. I'm Métis now, and glad of it," Dirk said hoarsely. "How can I thank you?"

But Trouffant wasn't done. "Monsieur Reilly!" he bellowed.

"Oh no, ye don't!" the hog farmer bawled, but he let himself be manhandled into the center of the ring.

"Ah, monsieur, rescuer of our people, feeder of our people, we have a Métis sash for you as well," Trouffant said, even as someone handed him a beautiful sash, this one more blue and white and black, with less red corded into it.

"I can't even speak your tongue, ye bloody fools," Reilly bawled.

A large Métis male with huge mustachios handed Reilly a flask, and Reilly obliged them with a sip.

"You who sheltered us, you who fed us, you who fought for us, you who gave your ranch to the hungry, the cold, the poor, the desperate, now we make you one of us," Trouffant said. "Wear this sash and be one of the people."

There was only quiet. Reilly took the long sash gently, kissed it, folded it, and draped it over his shoulders. It had become a stole.

These people caught their breath. It was as if this gift had become an ordination.

"Ye bloody people, ye have made me whole," Reilly said. His hands pursued the sash running over his neck, following it up and down, catching the woof and weave of the cords, memorizing its sacredness.

"Aw, I got to look after the roast," he said.

The Métis reached out simply to touch him. One by one, they pressed their hands upon his arms and shoulders, or touched his hands, or touched his hair. Then Reilly fled to his fire and roast, the long sash flapping around him, and the fiddlers began a jig, a step dance, with a great scrape of their fiddles.

The women returned to their cooking, swaying to the rhythm.

Some of the crowd was dancing now, mostly outside because the cabin was jammed.

Dirk saw Therese at the kettle, her back to him, slowly stirring a stew.

He approached quietly, and somehow she knew he was approaching.

"Would you dance?" he asked.

She handed her wooden spoon to another woman and nodded solemnly, and she followed him through the door and into the cold night, where the fiddle music made the fires dance and the crowd clapped and sang.

They faced each other, not touching, arms falling languidly to their sides, for this was a dance of the legs and feet. He wasn't sure what he was doing, but it didn't matter. It would be whatever his feet decided to do. There wasn't time to learn anyway. So he began, tapping, forward, back, and she followed intuitively, a slow smile building on her face. He wasn't sure what her smile meant. But then she stopped following him and struck a tap on her own, and her smile widened. He saw how it went and caught her movements and duplicated them. And then almost before he could fathom it, they were tapping out elaborate rhythms, and the fiddling reached into their bones, and they stamped and tapped and sidestepped and clicked, almost a tango for toes. It wasn't until a long while later that they realized the others had stopped their own step dancing to watch, and that he and Therese had been dancing all alone to the fury of the fiddles.

At last the fiddlers fell into softer strains, and she tossed her head, throwing her jet hair to one side, and they headed into the warmth of the cabin, now filled with savory aromas. She paused, touched his cheek, and headed toward the knot of women ladling pork stew into bowls.

She was carefully ignoring him, her back mostly turned toward him, but he sensed she was aware of his every step. He decided on some roast pork and headed into the night, where Reilly was slicing slabs of white pork from the roast, his sash still dangling from his neck and shoulders, floating about like the vestments of a priest.

"Ah, it took ye long enough. Don't like my meat, eh? Can't stand Reilly, eh? Well, take this and suffer, Skye."

Reilly forked two slabs of dripping, steaming meat onto a tin plate and handed it to Dirk.

"Have a knife and fork?" Dirk asked.

"What do you take me for? Find your own," Reilly said. "And stop your whinin'."

"I danced with Therese," Dirk said.

"And it was a mortal sin if ever I saw it," Reilly snarled.

"You wouldn't know a sin from a good sip of whiskey," Dirk said.

"Is that how you treat me? I put a man up in me cabin, and this is how I'm paid."

Dirk headed for the cabin, searching for anything that would let him eat politely, but there wasn't a piece of silverware in sight. And then, oddly, Therese showed up with a fork. She had been watching him.

"Eat," she said.

He took it gratefully. She whirled away again.

The party evaporated as swiftly and mysteriously as it had formed. People ate and vanished into the night. The fiddlers put away their instruments in cases they had fashioned along with their fiddles, and walked into darkness.

Dirk couldn't imagine where they went. There were

perhaps a hundred Métis in the vicinity, somehow sheltering themselves against the elements. A dozen were
here at Trouffant's wood yard. Another bunch were staying with Reilly. Still more at Blanc's grist mill. But there
were scores more.

"You set to go?" he asked Reilly.

"Always nagging are you?"

"Thought you might like company."

"Company's the last thing I need."

Reilly took his knives and forks into Trouffant's cabin
and climbed into the wagon seat and started his dray
north. Dirk tied the rein of his buckskin to the wagon and
sat beside the Irishman.

"Wanting a free ride, are you? I should charge."

They rolled over frosted ground that rattled the
wagon, and soon were far beyond town and its lights.

"Therese Trouville and I are married, I think, but I'm
not sure," Dirk said.

"Not sure you're married? What kind of blather is
that? You been sipping?"

"No, I'm not sure. Maybe you can help me. You're
some kind of clergyman."

"Laddie, you are off on the far side of the moon, and
that's the last I'll say."

"Nope, I'm going to talk. Therese and I were married
in Miles City."

"By what? Some heretic?"

"Priest."

"And now you want to get out of it, that it?"

"She fled. We were having a celebration in a saloon
there and she disappeared."

"Our little saint did?"

"Out the door."

"And you've not spent time with her since? I mean, spent time?"

"We've talked."

"Then you're not married, least that's how I see it."

"How would you know?"

"Are you being nosy or what?"

"Were you a clergyman in Ireland?"

"Get this straight, bloody Skye. I'm a hog farmer."

"Why do I think you're a clergyman?"

"You want to get off this wagon, right now?"

"No, I want to dig into your past and find out what sort of trouble you got into. That's not a sash you've got around your neck; it's a stole."

Reilly flailed his arm. "Off!"

"I'll drive the wagon and you can ride my horse."

"It amazes me, Skye, that you have survived as long as you have. I don't know how that happened. It must be blind luck. No one's shot you yet."

The wheels ground over frozen clay, but little by little they were approaching Reilly's ranch.

"She's written the bishop in Helena. She wants to consecrate the church and all. That means getting a priest here, which isn't easy in winter," Dirk said.

"That should be entertaining. Say, Skye, you got a nip?"

"Nope."

"Usually, when they have a new church they send a bishop. Fat chance eh?"

"Well, when you build a church, you want it started up right."

"We'll see," Reilly said. "Sometimes, they don't want help. They've got budgets and goals and plans. And they don't like surprises."

"How do you know?"

Reilly sighed. "I'm not going to talk to you anymore. I thought you were a friend. But you're the serpent in the Garden of Eden."

"I sort of like the idea," Dirk said. "How about boa constrictor? Or cobra? And what'll I say to Eve?"

But Reilly had clammed up.

When they reached the ranch yard, it was plain that the bunkhouse was empty. No smoke rose from its stovepipe. Reilly's guests were staying in town, no doubt to continue on the church while the weather lasted. Dirk wondered where all those people had collected.

Reilly was still angry, and he stomped into his cabin, leaving it to Dirk to unharness the dray and take care of the horses. When Dirk finally did get to the cabin, he found it cold. Reilly had climbed into his bedroll. Dirk lit the wick of a lamp, built a small fire in the stove to take the chill off, and was heading for bed when he saw Reilly's sash, carefully hung on a peg, its tassels just off the floor, hung with all the care of a vestment.

Dirk unwound his own sash, which wrapped his waist. It was odd; he wasn't the owner of a Métis sash; it was just the opposite. The sash owned him.

thirty-nine

$\mathscr{S}$ now wrapped the little church. It settled on the shake roof, plastered itself against the log walls, mounded around the foundation, and skidded past the stairs to the double front doors. But snow couldn't find its way inside, where the Métis people were finishing the last of the pews, setting a simple altar in place, and walling off a sacristy.

A stove and stovepipe, supplied by the mercantile in exchange for a season's firewood from the Trouffants, heated the building. The Métis had fitted wood together so skillfully that there were no drafts, even though the storm eddied into every seam and joint and juncture. There were things still to do, varnish to be applied, stained glass for the windows someday, and yet all that could wait. The church was ready, and it awaited a dedication even as the first storm of December hurled its might against its solid walls. It was larger than Dirk had supposed.

It was dark for a midafternoon, between the storm

clouds and the low sun, and now the Métis simply sat in pews, feeling the strength and grace in what they had built. Dirk, who was never comfortable in white men's edifices, felt serene there. Reilly sat beside him, scowling, looking ready to burst. Some of the Métis women entered, wrapped in shawls and coats. They genuflected even though there was nothing to genuflect to; not yet. One of these was Therese, who was returning from Lewistown's business district. She bore an envelope.

"Please read this to me," she said, handing it to Dirk. "I tried, and don't know enough."

The letter bore the return address of the Diocese of Helena.

Dirk studied the letter, which was from the vicar. "They're welcoming you and pleased to hear from you, and saying they knew nothing about your church, Therese. This is from the vicar, the deputy of the bishop. He says this is not the time of year to send anyone, but in the spring they will begin an inquiry. That's necessary according to the laws of the church to learn about the unknown congregation, and your church records. Baptism, confirmation, and all that."

"But we have none! They're in parish churches in Canada."

"Well, he goes on to say that if the need is found to catechize the people here, that would be the next step, and if the inquiry comes to a happy conclusion, the bishop himself would arrive here sometime in the next year to consecrate the church and make it a part of his diocese."

Reilly, who was listening closely, was cackling. "Do it as slow as possible," Reilly said.

Therese clouded over. She sat rigidly in the pew, lost

in sadness. "That is how they are, how they were, how they always will be," she said. "We are Métis."

"You mean they would do it some other way if a European congregation petitioned?" Dirk asked.

"They'd stick to all the forms no matter who's involved," Reilly said. "They have to; it never changes."

Therese stared out the window into the whirl of white outside. "I have done what was given me to do," she said.

Some of this must have caught the attention of the Métis men still finishing the interior because they stopped their work and stared.

She eyed them. "It's nothing. The bishop will come to us. It will take a little time."

"How much time?" asked one.

"I don't know," she whispered.

"Can't someone come and bless this church and send us a priest for now?" asked another.

Reilly stood. "Dirk, tell them there's no way to hurry the church. But you could organize prayers here while you wait."

"How do you know this?" Therese asked.

"Don't ask a man questions that aren't your blooming business."

It was odd, but the Métis set down their saws and chisels and hammers until all work ceased, and came to Therese in her pew and sat down close to her. The place had grown very quiet.

Trouffant stood. "Mademoiselle, we need to do other things, then. There are many of us here, barely sheltered, who don't know where their next meal will come from. And they have no good place to stay. Some can stay here. This is a good, warm building. It is a haven for the Métis. From here we can walk into Lewistown. Some of us can find work. Food and clothing and shelter, eh? We have made a house."

It seemed a good idea to Dirk. These people had been building their church even before they found food and shelter and jobs to support themselves and their children and grandparents and the injured and sick. Most of them were on the edge of grief.

But Therese sat silently, lost in her own reverie. Dirk knew what was afflicting her. It was as if her vision had been nothing but a foolish dream, and now reality had arrived.

Reilly stood again. "I'll do it, I'll do it."

He unwrapped his Métis sash from around his body, draped it over his neck as a stole, and walked to the bare altar.

"I'll serve ye," he said.

The silence thickened. Instead of staring at Reilly, people looked every which way, every direction except the bare altar with Reilly standing before it, his back to them, apparently talking to someone, the something that lay beyond.

Then he turned.

"Skye, you tell these Canadians what I'm saying. I'll go slow."

Dirk rose, stood before these people, and waited.

"Far across the sea," Reilly began, "I left behind me a broken woman, two daughters and a son, my own blood. I left behind me an unhappy bishop, yes, and a hundred others wearing the cloth. For I was one of them. Now I'm a hog farmer, but these are consecrated hands, and that never changes, and if ye want a priest, ye have one, and we'll proceed even if the bishop and all think it ought not to be, or it's irregular, or it's this or that or the other. So I'd be a rogue in a rogue church, if ye want it, but these hands, straying as they may be, are consecrated and could serve ye if ye wish."

Dirk struggled with words, not because he couldn't make Reilly's ideas plain, but because Reilly was talking in poetry and he didn't know how to turn Reilly's poetry into Métis poetry. Still, Reilly's body, his gestures, and the very tone of his voice were poetry also, and that might carry meaning even more than anything Dirk could manage.

They listened from their pews. The silence thickened. Dirk knew what these hardworking people were thinking: it was not their decision to make.

Therese sat quietly, and then suddenly stood, softly and gently, and walked forward toward the altar, where Reilly stood. She paused, stared into Reilly's face, and took both of his hands in her own, and kissed each hand.

Then she turned to her beloved people. "We are a rogue people," she said. "We will have our own rogue church."

Then she returned to her pew and placed her hands upon her face, and knelt.

"Skye, tell them to come at six this evening, all of them. Tell them to fill every pew. Tell them to gather here, every last bloody one," Reilly said.

Dirk told them. They collected their tools and plunged into the whirling snow, Therese among them.

There was only Dirk and Father Reilly.

"Leave me be, ye bloody Englishman," the father said.

"What can I do for you?" Dirk said.

"Ye can go to the hog ranch and ye can get a black bag that's behind me cot, and bring it quick. It has the things I'll be wanting."

The buckskin was miserable and glad to be scraped clean of snow and on the way. Dirk rode quickly. It wasn't cold and there was little wind, but the snow fell. He found the black satchel just where Reilly said it would be, grained the horse, and started the long ride back, arriving just after sundown on a bleak December eve.

He found Father Reilly sitting, all alone, in the front pew, staring at the altar.

"Tell them that's homeless and in need, my ranch's for them all, for any that's needy, and my hogs are for all, for them that's got no food in their bellies, and whatever else is needed, they have."

"Where will you stay?"

"I'll have a cot in the sacristy, and a little wood for the stove, and I'll get along."

"I will tell them."

"Now leave me be."

Dirk slipped into the darkness. The snow had stopped and the night was still. He walked to the wood yard, which had become, it seemed, the place of refuge for Therese's people. They welcomed him warmly, and he told them that Father Reilly had given them the use of his entire place, and that he would find a niche in the sacristy for now.

"He will come to the dance, eh?" Trouffant asked.

"Dance?"

"Of course the dance. What do you expect after the mass, eh?"

Close to six that eve, a knot of the Métis, and Dirk,

trudged through the shining snow to the church on the slope, where lamplight spilled through windows. The Métis were dressed as well as they could manage, mostly in tall lace-up boots, leather trousers, woolen Hudson's Bay Company shirts, sweeping skirts, and bright shawls. Gradually they filled all the pews, which seated far more than anyone had imagined.

When they arrived, they found many others there, including three fiddlers, their instruments out and tuned. There were vessels on the altar and a Latin text. Father Reilly was not evident, but there was light in the sacristy. The Métis continued to drift in, children, elders, the sick and the lame, and more women than Dirk had seen together, all somehow shining and gay. The scent of leather and smoke filled the nave. At a chosen moment, the three fiddlers began, their music tentative and hopeful, and after some unmeasured time, Father Reilly appeared in white vestments except for the Métis sash he wore this hour as his stole. People saw him and sighed. Was this not a miracle? He strode forward, gestured to Dirk to come translate below him, and thus began the first service, a mass and dedication, in Therese's church.

He saw her settle near the rear, but Trouffant firmly lifted her elbow and escorted her to the front pew, and then sat beside her. And so it went. First a blessing. The Word of God. The Peace. A Prayer. Was this the Pappy Reilly Dirk had come to know? No, it wasn't. This was some other man bearing that name.

There were things in English, and then Dirk wrestled with the French Métis tongue, and managed to convey most of what the priest was saying. There came the dedication of the church and its naming, Saint Therese, the patroness of the one whose vision brought this church to life, and then a prayer followed, while the fiddlers played its words to life.

Then came the mass, the penance, the sacrament of communion, and Dirk wondered where the host had come from. This was Latin, and for Therese's people, so Dirk retired to a pew and watched the priest prepare and receive the host, reciting the liturgy, his arms sometimes rising, his hands supplicating, his white-robed back to the people, who all faced their Lord.

It came time for a benediction, an ending, and there the priest paused and faced the Métis people, and with a gesture summoned Dirk once again.

"At this moment, I wish to add a special blessing," he said. "Madame, please come forward." He gestured to Therese.

Dirk translated.

The Métis whispered. What a good thing, blessing the woman who had received a mission and had dutifully fulfilled it.

But she came forward, reluctantly, and awaited the blessing, which would of course honor her for all that had happened here, for this church, for this gathering of her people in safety, far from their homeland. She buried her face in her shawl so no one could see it, and she could hide herself even before this congregation of her own people.

Father Reilly beckoned, so she came closer, and finally he placed her next to Dirk, who was increasingly puzzled.

"Now, my beloved people, you Métis who have gathered here to consecrate a church and yourselves. We will bless one other thing this evening. We will offer a blessing to these two, Dirk Skye and Therese Trouville Skye, and upon their marriage, and upon the fruit of their marriage, now and forever more."

It didn't require translation. The Métis could scarcely believe what they were witnessing.

The fiddlers played.

Father Reilly offered a benediction, and the fiddles sang.

epilogue

One sunny September Sunday, Father Reilly baptized the sleeping infant boy wrapped in a gray blanket who rested in the arms of his mother. And the boy was christened Barnaby Montclair Skye in that hour, and was named after his grandfathers. The child had the olive flesh and strong cheekbones of both of his parents. The young couple, he in a stiff black suit and starched white shirt, and she in a pleated gray dress, smiled tenderly, and the congregation beyond them shared their joy. But the bronzed young man's dress was not quite ordinary, for within his suit coat was a gaudy Métis sash, wrapped thrice about his waist and tied there, its tasseled ends dangling below the suit coat. He might have different bloods, but the Métis were his people.

And so it was done. The child carried the European bloods of England and France, the indigenous bloods of Shoshone and Cree, and perhaps a little Scots and Ojibway, but he was an American, wrought from the ideals and visions of many peoples. The baby eyed his parents and the priest, yawned, and returned to its sleep.

There had been a tussle with the diocese, but now St. Therese's Church was in the fold, the building and land owned by the diocese, the priest especially loved by the congregation, for they had all struggled together. The bishop had not yet visited, but someday soon he would greet his newest congregation.

Its congregation was mostly Métis, and most of them did not speak English, and thus the church stood apart from other congregations in the territory. But that was changing. A parish school had been started, and its young headmaster was the man whose son was being christened. And his mother was the one who had, against all odds, brought these things into existence.

The surrounding country was peaceful, and many of the Métis had homesteaded there, starting family farms or orchards. An all-white jury had refused to convict Harley Bain, but he had returned to his ranch subdued and had devoted himself to a peaceful ranch life. His night riders had fled the country ahead of Major Brevoort's winter dragnet and were never caught or punished. If the Métis were not widely accepted, at least they were allowed to live in peace and put down roots in their new country. And just being left alone was as much a blessing as anyone could ask.

Later that afternoon, the fiddlers once again tuned their instruments and began the jig, for once again there was life to celebrate. And that young couple, so much in love that everyone saw it, and so brimming with austere joy, danced the first dance with their newborn in their arms.